Boomerang

Jackie Coleman

Boomerang

ISBN 978-0-9834242-2-2

This novel is dedicated to
Tara, Jana, and Dave.

Acknowledgments

Special thanks to John, Bonnie,
Connie, Josh, Mike, and Patty.
Your advice and encouragement were invaluable.

Chapter One

April 1998

Dave Baldwin sat on a bench in Atlanta's Centennial Park, listening to the water cascade over the sculpted rocks in the Water Garden. It was an exceptionally warm day, and he was dressed too warmly for the weather. He could feel beads of perspiration rolling down his back, so he took off his jacket and laid it over the back of the bench. Most of his day had been spent in meetings with a wealthy developer and a team of lawyers negotiating the contract for a downtown renovation project. The meeting was extremely important to his firm, so he'd worn one of his power suits, custom tailored to perfectly fit his frame. He looked good, but Italian wool was better suited for the boardroom than the mid-day sun of Georgia.

Classically handsome, and sporting a tan from spring break in the Bahamas with his daughter Cathy a few weeks ago, Dave easily attracted the eye of women who walked by. Normally he welcomed the looks, and enjoyed playing a well-practiced game of making small talk as they walked by, seeing how many would pass before one sat down. Once they sat down, he was certain to get their phone number. Sometimes he called and sometimes he didn't. It was no reflection on them, but merely how lonely he was feeling.

Right now, he knew his heart was too fragile to enter into a romantic relationship with anyone. All he wanted was companionship; someone to spend time with and to stand by his side at the countless dinner parties he was forced to attend. Someone to make him feel alive, to make him feel anything besides the abject loneliness that permeated his life.

Today would be a good day to take the boat out — if I still had a boat, he thought wryly. He was trying not to let his mind wander to all he had lost in the past few years, but it was a battle he knew he would lose. It was a battle he always lost. The fact that Ginger had left him two years ago today made it impossible to think of anything else.

Everyone thought he was over her because he said he was, and because he pretended to be, but thinking of her still made him feel like he'd been punched in the stomach.

No one knew how badly he missed her. He loved her so much and would have done anything to make her happy. He had thought she was happy, but apparently she had been miserable. When she left, she stopped just short of saying she hated him. He felt like a failure, and no one could convince him otherwise. In his mind he was a failure because he failed at what mattered most. He had failed Ginger.

To those who knew him, Dave appeared to have everything. At thirty-seven, he was a partner in a prestigious Atlanta architectural firm. He had the luxury of working from his home in Savannah or his condo in Atlanta. In spite of a costly divorce, he had all the material trappings that showed the world how successful he was. He had memberships at all the right clubs. He was confident, charismatic, intelligent, and handsome enough to have an attractive woman on his arm nearly any time he desired. The only thing he didn't have was his wife.

It was still hard to believe she was gone. He should hate her for what she'd done, but he didn't. Despite hating what she had done, he didn't hate her. Quite the contrary — he hated himself, and blamed himself for everything.

He had never told anyone what she had done, and he doubted she had told anyone other than him. It was a secret he planned to carry to his grave. It was a secret he wished she'd carried to hers. He knew why she had told him, but knowing why she told him hurt almost as much as knowing what she had done.

Dave remembered every detail of the day she left. The complete silence in the house had immediately told him something was wrong. Ginger couldn't stand silence. It wasn't uncommon for every radio and television to be blaring, rarely on the same station. She had been sitting on the sofa, wearing white jeans and a red sun top, her dark hair pulled back into a loose ponytail. Even after ten years of marriage, Dave still thought she was the most beautiful woman in the world.

"Where's Cathy?" he asked nervously, slowly making his way into the room. "What's going on?"

"Cathy's spending the night with Rachel," she replied, her voice flat and emotionless.

She took a deep breath, and then added, "And I'm leaving,"

"What do you mean you're leaving? Why?" He collapsed into a chair opposite her, his mind reeling.

"I met someone."

Dave felt like the air had been sucked out of the room. One sentence changed his life.

Ginger sat watching, waiting with prepared answers for the questions she knew he would ask. Choking on his tears, the questions poured out.

The longer they talked, the more he realized no amount of crying and begging could convince her to stay. She wasn't interested in even trying to work things out. With sickening clarity, he realized she'd actually left a long time ago. Even before she'd met this guy, her body had been here, but not her heart.

When had she quit loving him? How had he not noticed she was so unhappy? How could she carry on an affair for six months without him seeing some sign of it? At that moment, nothing made sense. After all they had gone through with her accident, the drugs, and the rehab. He thought they were closer than ever. She'd been clean and sober for five years. To Dave, those five years had been the best years of his life, yet Ginger described them as dreadful.

Ginger wasn't interested in custody of Cathy. She told Dave she'd get in touch with him later and arrange for a visit with her, but she wasn't interested in any set visitation. "I don't want to see Cathy right now. She'll just remind me of a life I'm trying to forget."

As she left, she stopped in the doorway "I need to tell you one more thing — a little secret I've been hiding."

Dave froze. If she was about to tell him Cathy wasn't his, he didn't want to know.

Ginger saw the look of alarm on his face and knew what he was thinking. "Relax," she said. "It has nothing to do with Cathy."

And then, in the same tone one describes a mundane household task, Ginger told him her secret. Her confession left him speechless. A million questions ran through his mind, but he couldn't form the words to ask even one. How could she have kept a secret like that? Why had she told him now? If she had intended to hurt him, it had worked. He was devastated.

Dave sat in the darkened house, staring into space, wondering what to do. He started crying, which only made him feel worse. Men weren't supposed to cry. He wiped away the tears but it was a futile effort, as they were instantly replaced. What was he going to tell Cathy? How do you tell a child their mother wants to forget them?

The next morning, the sun was streaming through the windows. Dave opened his eyes slowly. For a moment, he didn't know where he was. He was still in his suit. He must have fallen asleep — then he remembered. Ginger was gone. A wave of nausea swept over him.

A few moments later, he heard a key turning in the front door. Ginger — she'd come back! Relief flooded over him. He looked up expectantly, his heart racing, as the footsteps drew nearer. Cathy bounded into the room. When she saw her disheveled father sitting on the sofa, she laughed. "You look like you slept in your clothes," then asked, "Where's Mom?"

———————————

Though Ginger had been gone two years, the pain was still fresh. His heart was still bleeding and raw. While he was over the humiliation of being left for another man, he couldn't get past the fact that he had failed at being a husband. How could he be so self-absorbed that he never even saw it coming? He was terrified of history repeating itself.

There had been a lot of women since Ginger left, but he never stayed with any of them long. He dated for companionship, and the sex if it was offered. To his pleasant surprise, it usually was. He would like to have someone special in his life, but after the way he failed Ginger, he couldn't allow himself that pleasure. He hoped he wouldn't make the same mistakes, but he could never be sure.

He had never been unfaithful to Ginger, but for many years he hadn't loved her and that had hurt her worse than any affair ever could. If there had been another woman, she could have identified and quantified the enemy. As it was, there was no one to direct her hatred towards. In the beginning, she directed it to herself. He wasn't sure when it happened, but at some point, she had directed the rage toward the person she perceived to be its rightful target — Dave.

He thought back to when he first met Ginger. They began dating his last year of college. She was one of several women he'd been seeing. As far as he was concerned, it was all in fun. She was tall, beautiful, and liked to party. He wasn't looking for a serious relationship. He had big plans for his life, and it didn't involve being tied down to one woman, not yet anyway.

Immediately after graduation, Dave was offered an internship with an architectural firm in Atlanta. He loved Savannah and had hoped to be able to stay there, but the job was too good to turn down. He didn't tell Ginger he was moving to Atlanta because it never occurred to him that she would care that he was leaving.

Ginger discovered she was pregnant a few weeks before graduation. She wondered how Dave would take the news. They'd only known each other a short time, and had been intimate only a few times. She was crazy about him, but was unsure of how he felt towards her, so she decided to wait until after the stress of finals and his graduation to tell him.

After graduation, she drove past his apartment nearly every day, but his car was never there. She left messages on his answering machine, but they were never returned. A few weeks later, as she was driving by, Ginger noticed lights on in the apartment. Kevin, Dave's roommate, looked embarrassed when she asked if he knew where Dave was. He told her Dave had moved and hadn't given him his new address or phone number yet, but he expected to hear from him soon. Ginger did her best to act nonchalant, but she was crushed, and her voice quivered as she thanked him.

From the window, Kevin could see her sitting in her car, crying. He picked up the phone and left a message on Dave's answering machine. "Dave, that tall chick, Ginger, stopped by to see you tonight. I told her you'd moved, but I didn't give her your number. You might want to call her. She seemed pretty upset. Later, Dude." He hung up the phone and looked out the window again. Ginger's car was gone.

At the end of that long ago summer, Kevin had invited Dave to spend Labor Day with him and his family at their beach house on Tybee Island, one of the barrier islands protecting Savannah and the Georgia coast. He was supposed to meet Kevin for a beer before they headed to the island. He was low on cash, so he crossed the street to the ATM, standing in line behind a rather large woman wearing a dress that looked like it had been made from the same draperies as a dress worn by Scarlett O'Hara in Gone with the Wind.

Ginger walked out of the bank and saw Dave standing in line for the ATM. Her first impulse was to flee, but she stopped herself.

"Dave?"

He looked up at the familiar voice. "Ginger," Dave exclaimed, trying to ignore her very swollen belly. "How've you been?"

"Fine," she said, nervously touching her stomach. "Actually, I've been better."

He could see tears welling up in her eyes. He really didn't want to listen to a hormonal pregnant woman rant and rave about the loser who had gotten her pregnant. He'd find an ATM later. "Hey, I've got to meet up with some friends, but it was great to see you." He gestured toward her protruding mid-section, "Oh, and congratulations."

Dave turned to walk away when she spoke, barely above a whisper. "It's yours. The baby is yours."

He spun around.

"It's yours. I got pregnant in April. I was waiting until after finals and graduation were behind you before I told you, but I couldn't find you. Why didn't you call me?" Tears were streaming down her cheek and people were beginning to stare.

"Come on, we need to talk."

They walked side by side, not talking until they reached Johnson Square, just a few blocks away. Johnson Square was the first of the now famous Savannah Squares laid out by General Oglethorpe when he founded this city on the bluff in the early 1700's. Dave and Ginger sat facing the fountain, watching the water dance down the tiers. The benches surrounding the fountain were nestled among a brilliant array of azaleas, and ancient live oak trees dripping with Spanish moss. Tourists were everywhere, but they were too busy admiring the beauty to notice the two of them.

Dave stared straight ahead, resting his elbows on his knees. "Are you sure it's mine?"

"Of course I'm sure. I'm positive. I don't sleep around."

"I didn't mean it like that. Look, I'm sorry." He wiped his face with his hand. "Why didn't you tell me sooner?"

"How? I didn't know where you were. I stopped by your apartment once, but Kevin didn't know how to get a hold of you. Why didn't you call me? Didn't I mean anything to you?"

Dave was caught, and he knew it. "Of course I cared about you, but everything happened so fast, and, you know, time just got away from me. I figured a beautiful woman like you wouldn't wait around for someone like me. I knew someone would scoop you up as soon as I was gone."

She wasn't crying as hard now. "You're quite the charmer. No wonder I fell so hard for you."

Dave knew this conversation deserved more than a few minutes. "Ginger, can we meet later?"

She exhaled loudly and rolled her eyes. She opened her mouth to say something, but Dave cut her off.

"No, I didn't mean it like that. I have plans with Kevin. I just need to go tell him something came up. Can you meet me back here in an hour?"

She looked at him and nodded, wondering if she'd ever see him again. "Sure. Wait for me if I'm a few minutes late." She knew she wouldn't be late. She had no where else to go. She'd be sitting on this bench the entire time, but he didn't need to know that.

Dave caught up with Kevin sitting at a sidewalk table at a bar on River Street, sipping a nearly empty beer. He motioned to the waitress to bring two more as Dave sat across from him.

"I just ran into Ginger."

"Yeah? I hope you invited her to Tybee. As I recall, she's pretty hot." He raised his eyebrows up and down for emphasis.

"She's pregnant."

Kevin's mouth fell open, but he said nothing.

"She says it's mine."

"Do you believe her?"

"I don't know what to believe right now. I'm supposed to meet up with her again in about a half hour. I need to talk to her and see what's going on. I'll catch up with you on the island."

The waitress brought the beers as Dave walked away. Noticing he was alone, she asked "You still want both of these?"

"More than ever, Darlin'."

Dave and Ginger were married a few weeks later. He walked through the door of his apartment with his very pregnant bride. An awkward silence hung between them. He barely knew her, and he didn't love her, but something told him the child growing within her was his. Marrying her, he told himself, was the honorable thing to do, but it sure didn't feel honorable. It felt confining.

He watched Ginger look around her new home. Even six months pregnant she was gorgeous. Tall and curvaceous, her long dark hair hung in soft curls down her back. He could do worse, he thought. They'd always had a good time together. Maybe, he told himself, things wouldn't be so bad.

So why did he feel like a condemned man listening to the cell door slam shut?

Chapter Two

Dave shook his head as if to clear the memories, forcing himself back to reality. It was barely April and it was almost ninety degrees — hot even by Atlanta standards, and he was roasting. If this was any indication of what lay ahead, it was going to be a long, hot summer. The Water Garden only reminded him of where he wanted to be — on the water somewhere with a beautiful woman in a too-small bikini and a bottle of wine. He could procure a boat and chilled wine, but at the moment, he couldn't think of a woman who would be open to the invitation without reading more into it, and he didn't want to lead anyone to believe he was ready for more than he was capable of giving.

He tipped his water bottle. The few drops that rolled onto his tongue did little to quench his thirst. He started walking towards the Fountainside Café in the center of the Park. The meandering paths were partially paved with bricks that had been sold to help finance the cost of building the infrastructure necessary to host the '96 Olympics. The bricks were engraved with personal messages, up to fifteen characters on each of two lines. It had been difficult to say something meaningful in thirty characters or less, and he'd been proud of himself for coming up with what he thought were very clever and heartfelt sentiments that fit those constraints. He'd even bought replicas, replacing two of the bricks on his patio with them.

Scanning the bricks as he walked, he easily picked out the brick he and Ginger had bought for Cathy. 'CATHY BALDWIN HUGS & KISSES'. He walked a little further and saw the brick he bought for Ginger. 'GINGER MY WIFE MY LOVE MY LIFE'. He stood looking at the brick, tracing it with his foot, aching for her. Those two silly bricks were among the very few tangible things that showed the world that Ginger had once been his.

He had been hurt at Ginger's reaction when he revealed the bricks on the patio. He expected her to get teary eyed at his romanticism. He'd led her outside by the hand, her eyes closed. She'd opened her eyes, looking around for her surprise. When he pointed to the ground, she said "They don't really match, do they? Couldn't you have given them two of our bricks so they wouldn't stand out so bad?" She walked back into the house without so much as a thank you.

He shook off the past, resuming his walk. He slowed his gait to fall into step behind two women walking ahead of him. The taller one reminded him of Ginger. They had the same body, tall, voluptuous, a few extra pounds without being overweight. She had on a tight-fitting skirt that hugged her figure. He could see a lacy camisole under her translucent blouse.

The other had the firm, slender body of a woman before she had children. She was wearing denim shorts that accentuated her shapely legs and bottom. The tight shirt emphasized her tiny waist. He loved her long, silky hair, blowing in the slight breeze. Though he was attracted to taller women, he had a weakness for long hair. His mind began racing, trying to figure out a way to meet them without looking like a stalker.

The taller one had a decidedly Georgian accent; the slow, soft, lilting voice of a very feminine southern belle. The other woman had a soft, sweet voice with only a slight accent. He was listening more to the sound of their voices than what they were saying when he heard them mention ice cream. He smiled to himself. He was going to meet these two beauties after all.

Dave walked around to the opposite end of the Café counter from the women. As the girl behind the counter began filling their order, Dave called her over and told her he would pay for the order she was filling.

A few moments later, the two women looked towards him, a confused look on their faces. They held their treats aloft and said "Thank you." Dave smiled and nodded in reply.

The two women sat at a nearby picnic table, keeping an eye on him. They tried, unsuccessfully, to look away and act disinterested as he walked up to their table. "Mind if I join you ladies?" he said, smiling his most charming smile.

Amy noticed his gaze fall briefly on her, and then stop on Jenny. Clearly, this man was interested in Jenny. Knowing the question was directed more to her friend than herself, Amy let Jenny answer.

Jenny smiled as she looked at the exquisitely dressed man. Tall, broad-shouldered, with a mischievous smile she couldn't resist. "Not at all," she replied. "Have a seat."

Dave sat down and extended his hand towards Jenny, the taller of the two. "Dave Baldwin."

"Jenny McIntosh," she said, taking his hand. "And this is my good friend, Amy Cooper."

"It's nice to meet you both." Dave was captivated by Jenny's smile. He was also happy to note the fact that there were no rings on her left hand. Amy, he noticed, had a very impressive diamond on her ring finger. "What brings you two here in the middle of the afternoon?" As before, he glanced briefly at Amy, and then let his eyes fall back on Jenny.

Jenny, a copy editor for CNN, had taken the afternoon

off and was just finishing a late lunch with Amy, her best friend since college. After that, she planned to go home and enjoy what was left of the afternoon. She didn't mention her children.

Amy, a flight attendant, was just back from a vacation in Hawaii, which would explain her tan and air of contentment.

"So, how 'bout you?" Jenny asked. "What brings you to the park on this fine spring day?"

He loved the sound of her voice. He explained about his meeting and stopping at the park on the way to his car. He found no reason at this point to mention his divorce or his daughter.

Amy watched her best friend flirt with this attractive stranger, offering a comment now and again when Jenny and Dave remembered they weren't the only two at the table. Amy secretly hoped this charming stranger would sweep Jenny off her feet. Even if they didn't live happily ever after, a decent man would restore her friend's faith that there were still kind, gallant men left in this world. After an abusive marriage and messy divorce, followed by a long string of losers, Amy hoped Jenny would meet a really nice guy.

"If you'll excuse me," Amy said, "My sister is here. We get to melt while Katy plays in the water." Amy waved to a very pregnant woman near the Fountain of Rings.

Dave smiled as he watched the young mother

attempting to take the shoes off a little girl who was literally wiggling with excitement.

Taught to stand when a woman did, Dave rose to his feet, extending his hand to her. "It was nice to meet you."

"It was nice to meet you, too." Amy shook Dave's hand, then started walking towards her sister. As she walked away, she turned to look at Jenny, holding her hand to her to resemble a phone, and mouthed '*Call me*'.

Dave found Jenny easy to talk to, and spent the rest of the afternoon with her. She had a really nice smile, great laugh and the bubbly kind of personality people were naturally drawn to. He tried not to make the comparison, but she reminded him of Ginger.

It was past five o'clock when they parted. He apologized for hogging her afternoon off. Jenny smiled sweetly and told him it was her pleasure. Dave headed home to Savannah with the phone number for the beautiful and enchanting Jenny safely tucked into his wallet, and a dinner date for the following evening. High on the potential of a new woman, he drove down the interstate with the convertible top down, the breeze countering the hot Georgia sun.

He hadn't intended to stay in Atlanta so long. He needed to spend time with Cathy. Having made plans to take Jenny to dinner for the following evening, he wouldn't be able to spend time with Cathy tomorrow night. Promising Cathy a day at the beach with her friends would go a long way towards appeasing his guilt.

Twenty minutes outside Macon, traffic was at a dead stop. Emergency vehicles passed him on the shoulder. A medical helicopter landed in the median a hundred or so yards ahead, while news helicopters circled above. He turned on the radio for a traffic report. The commentator gave few details other than a multi-car pile up with fatalities had all eastbound lanes of Interstate 16 at a complete standstill.

"Great," he grumbled. He called home to let them know he'd be late. There was no telling how long he'd be stuck here.

It was past dark when Dave pulled into the garage. Cathy was laying on the floor in the den, talking on the phone, the television blaring. How could she hear with the television so loud? She had surely inherited that from her mother. She waved at her father, then turned her attention back to the phone.

Agnes Singleton, his elderly neighbor and Cathy's surrogate grandmother, sat on the sofa reading a book, seemingly oblivious to the noise. Clarabelle, Cathy's cat, lay in her lap, feigning sleep.

"Mrs. Singleton, I apologize for being so late. I hope it wasn't too much of an inconvenience."

"Oh no, Dear, not at all." She gently shooed the lazy cat off her lap and stood. The cat rubbed against her old, but sturdy legs.

"Cathy's had supper, and I left you a plate warming in the oven." She crossed the room, reached up, and patted his cheek. "You work too hard. You need a wife. I won't be around forever you know."

He smiled and kissed her forehead. "Mrs. Singleton, you're healthier than I am."

"Well, I have a niece in Augusta. Pretty. Smart. Loves kids," she said, throwing another look in Cathy's direction.

"Mrs. Singleton," he said, in mock annoyance.

"I've got two more nieces in North Carolina, or is it South Carolina?"

They'd had this conversation before. "It's North Carolina, and I'm sure they have their hands full. If they inherited the allure of their bewitching Aunt Agnes," he teased, "they have more beaus than they know what to do with."

Mrs. Singleton laughed softly as she walked towards the door. She stopped in the doorway and blew a kiss to Cathy, who waved and mouthed *'I love you'*, before returning to her phone call. Dave walked Mrs. Singleton across the lawn and saw her safely inside. Having her next door had proven to be a godsend. Since Ginger left, Mrs. Singleton watched Cathy after school and on his frequent trips out of town. He didn't know what he'd do without her. With Ginger gone, and being somewhat estranged from his own mother, Agnes filled part of the void left by the women who had abandoned him.

Chapter Three

Amy wrapped her robe tighter, watching her fiancé, Pat, scribble on a yellow legal pad. She was silently fuming that he was ignoring her. Hoping for one more romantic night before returning to the working world, she had dressed in a sexy little teddy that he hadn't even noticed. They discussed what to order for dinner, then he buried his nose in his work.

Pat had turned the thermostat way down, and Amy was freezing. "I can see my breath," she said to him as she sank into a chair and burrowed under a quilt.

He glanced over at Amy, giving her a *'you're annoying me'* look, before returning to his work.

"I guess you don't want to hear about the penguins skating in the kitchen?"

"Amy."

"Okay, I'll be quiet. Besides, hypothermia is setting in. I'll be unconscious soon anyway."

"Good," he said, never taking his eyes off his work.

Chinese takeout was delivered from a neighborhood restaurant. She signed Pat's name to the credit slip with a generous tip. Amy had worked as a waitress during high school and college, so she knew how important tips were, and Pat didn't always tip well. He never tipped males more than the customary fifteen percent and looked for ways to cut this amount even further. Women fared much better. Their tips, to Amy's disdain, were directly proportionate to the size of their breasts or rear ends, regardless of the service.

She reached for the novel she had started reading on vacation, eating out of the carton with a fork in lieu of the chopsticks provided in an effort not to spill anything on the pages of the book. She tried to tell herself not to feel too neglected. Pat was a busy attorney coming back from vacation. For the most part, she'd had his full attention for the past week. She had forgotten how lonely she felt when he was working, which seemed like all the time. It bothered her that his work always came first. She knew his work was important, but letting it sit for an hour or two would go a long way towards soothing her wounded ego.

Pat was reading something, making notes in the margins, and correcting a word here and there. It was only eight o'clock, but Amy had an early flight in the morning and wouldn't be back for three days. She wanted to make love to him and fall asleep in his arms.

She moved to the sofa, kneeling beside him. "How much longer," she stopped to kiss his neck, "are you going to be?" She leaned in to kiss him on the mouth, which he returned with a grandmotherly peck.

"I'm sorry, Babe," he said, not taking his eyes from his work. "I've got a ton of stuff to do. I have clients coming in first thing in the morning for this." He held up the papers he'd been working on. "I should have finished it before we left for Hawaii. Go on to bed and I'll —"

The doorbell interrupted. Amy retied her robe and opened the door. Two policemen were standing on the porch.

"Is there an Amy Cooper here?"

"I'm Amy Cooper." Cold chills went up and down her spine. Two policemen came to her house when she was twelve years old. They brought news that her father had died rock climbing at the Garden of the Gods in southern Illinois with friends. Nine years later two policemen had come to her apartment in Athens, Georgia. Jenny, visiting with her new baby, had held Amy's hand as the policemen told her that her mother had died.

Two policemen at the door was never a good thing. She was almost paralyzed with fear. She couldn't bring herself to ask why they were at her door. She didn't have to ask to know she wasn't going to like the answer.

"My name is Officer Harris. This is Officer Doyle," he motioned to the policeman standing beside him, who nodded his greeting. "May we come in?"

"Yes, of course. I'm sorry. Yes, please come in." Obviously nervous, she stepped back and held the door open for them. They removed their hats as they entered, following her into the living room. Pat stood when he saw them walking towards him. *Why were the police here?*

Before he could speak, Officer Harris introduced himself and his partner. Pat shook their hands, muttering a polite but confused greeting. This didn't have a good feel to it.

"Please, have a seat," Officer Harris said.

Obediently, Amy sat. Pat continued to stand. "Do you have a sister named Susanna Hampton of Savannah, Georgia?"

The color drained from Amy's face and tears welled in her eyes. "She does," Pat answered for her. "May I ask what this is about?"

"I'm sorry to inform you that your sister has been involved in an automobile accident, just past Macon. She's alive, but critically injured. She was flown to Grady Memorial Hospital here in Atlanta. She's in surgery now. On the way over here, we received word that they delivered her baby by cesarean, a little boy, and he's doing fine. Her daughter is fine. She's at Grady being evaluated, but all the reports we have are that she just has some cuts and bruises."

He paused a moment before continuing. "We're sorry to inform you her husband, Gregory, died at the scene. We can drive you to the hospital if you like."

Amy couldn't speak. She nodded, tears streaming down her cheeks. "Um, yeah. Okay. I, uh, need to get dressed. Okay?" She walked toward her bedroom, her mind racing. Greg was dead? What would Susie do without Greg? Katy didn't have a Daddy anymore. She was only three. She wouldn't even remember him. And the new baby! The little boy they planned on calling Samuel Gregory — Sammy. Little Sammy would never know his father.

She threw on a pair of jeans and a t-shirt, and then grabbed a sweatshirt. It was warm outside, but hospitals were notoriously cold. She washed her face before returning to the living room. She could hear the men speaking softly.

She grabbed her purse. "Okay, I'm ready."

"We found an appointment card for her doctor in her purse," Officer Harris continued. "He gave us your name as her emergency contact. We'll need the name and address of your parents, and that of her husband's. We'll send cars to notify them."

Amy dug her address book from her purse, opening it to the page containing Greg's parents' address and phone number. She handed it to the policeman. "My parents are gone, and our brother lives in Oregon, so there's no one else to tell on our side of the family. Here's Greg's parents information, but they live in Tennessee. You're not going to tell them on the phone are you?" The last sentence was barely audible through her tears.

"No, ma'am, we'll call their local police, and they'll send someone over to tell them in person."

Amy was dreading the call to their brother, Andy, who was also Susie's twin. The three of them had always been exceptionally close, but like all twins, there was a supernatural connection between Susie and Andy.

They rode to the hospital in the police car, lights flashing. Other than the siren, the only sound to pierce the silence was Amy's fearful sobs. Susie never regained consciousness. Three days later, she succumbed to her injuries. She never knew her husband had died, and she never got to hold her newborn son.

Chapter Four

Dave had never been stood up before. He was surprised at how betrayed he felt. Fortunately, he was in a restaurant where he frequently dined alone, so the staff wouldn't think anything of tonight's solo sojourn. He was glad he'd never stood anyone up — he'd hate to think he'd make someone feel this way. Maybe, he told himself, she had a good excuse. He'd give her the benefit of the doubt.

Later that evening, he called Jenny. A child answered. "Hello?"

It was either a girl or an adolescent boy, it was hard to tell. "Hi. Is Jenny there?"

"Nope."

"Do you know when she'll return?"

"Nope."

This is informative. "Do you know where she is?"

"Somebody died."

Obviously, he wasn't going to get any real information. "Will you give her a message for me, please?"

"Yup."

Dave left his name and cell phone number. He didn't feel so bad now knowing Jenny hadn't just blown him off, and his ego re-inflated.

Jenny's son never gave her the message. When she didn't call, Dave assumed the death had been someone very close to her. Maybe it was best that she didn't call. A woman in mourning tended to be emotionally needy, and he didn't have the energy for an emotionally needy woman.

———————

Amy was exhausted. She hadn't had more than a few hours of uninterrupted sleep in almost a month and she missed Susie so bad she ached. The lack of sleep only fed her depression. If she didn't have the kids to take care of, she didn't know if she'd be able to force herself to get out of bed.

Sammy would probably be waking up in a few hours, but she needed to finish folding the laundry and pick up Katy's toys before going to bed. Pat was being less than tolerant when it came to accommodating a toddler in his space. They had never talked about living together, but Amy couldn't remember the last time Pat had stayed at his condo. Even though this was not officially his home, he bristled at sharing it. Amy hoped that if she had things more orderly, Pat wouldn't be so irritable.

With less than an hour until the baby awoke for another feeding, Amy checked to make sure Sammy was still breathing, and then crawled into bed. An hour or so wasn't going to be enough to refresh her, but if she didn't get off her feet for a few minutes, she was going to collapse.

Pat felt her get into bed and pulled her close, kissing her neck. As his hand slid over her stomach, he searched the opening of her gown.

"Honey, I'm so tired. The baby's going to be up soon. I really need to rest."

He let go of her and rolled onto his back.

"Don't be mad. I'm just so tired."

It was several minutes before Pat spoke. "How long is this going to go on?"

Amy was surprised at how angry he sounded. "The books all say he should be sleeping through the night around six weeks. That's just —"

"That's not what I'm talking about."

If that's not what he meant, she didn't have a clue as to what he was talking about. She was too tired to be having this conversation. She couldn't keep the frustration out of her voice. "Then what are you talking about?"

"When are you going to give these kids a real home?"

"Pat, I'm tired, and you're not making any sense. This is a real home. It's a little chaotic right now, but it'll get better."

"No, Amy, this isn't a real home. You don't know what you're doing. You said so yourself. What's going to happen when you go back to work? You're a flight attendant. You're gone for days at a time. If you think I'm going to stay home playing Mary Poppins, think again. Your brother said he'd take the kids. They've already got a kid so these things won't turn his life upside down."

Pat knew he'd made a poor choice of words, but he couldn't un-speak them.

"These *things*?" Amy sat up and turned the light on. She glanced at the kids to make sure they hadn't woken. Katy, terrified to be out of Amy's sight, was asleep on a camping cot at the foot of the bed. Sammy slept peacefully in his bassinet. She lowered her voice. "They aren't *things*, Pat, they're my sister's kids. She asked me to take care of her kids if something ever happened to her and Greg, and I gave her my word that I would. You know that. You drew up their will. That's how we met, remember? Why are you acting like this?"

"This is crazy. I know you love the kids and want to do the right thing, but the right thing is to give them to your brother. He offered to take them. You're being selfish."

"Selfish? How am I being selfish?"

"You just want them because they're Susie's kids. You don't even care what's best for them."

Amy turned away from him, crying. "They're all I have

left of my sister, and I gave her my word."

"I'm sorry you lost your sister, I really am, but I can't live like this."

Wiping her face with her hands, she turned around to face him, sitting cross-legged on the bed beside him. "It will get better. We'll figure this thing out. We'll be great parents."

"Baby, you're not listening to me. I don't want to be a parent."

"But you said you wanted kids."

"I do want kids, someday. My kids. Our kids. I don't want to raise someone else's kids. We're not even married yet. This is supposed to be our time." He paused a moment before adding, "You need to make a decision here."

"That sounds a lot like an ultimatum."

"I guess it is. It's either me or them." There, he'd said it.

She stared at him for a few moments, trying to process his words. "What? Are you serious? You're asking me to choose between the kids and you?"

He looked away, nodding. He knew he wasn't being fair.

"If you're willing to bolt at the first bump in the road, we don't stand a chance. Granted, it's a big bump, but it's not insurmountable. This is something we should be able to get past. I know raising my sister's kids wasn't in your plans. It wasn't in my plans either, and it damn sure wasn't in Susie's."

"A bump? Amy, *this* is not just a bump. A bump is if we can't agree on what kind of car to buy or what color to paint the kitchen. This," he threw his hands into the air in exasperation and shouted, "is a mountain!"

Sammy stirred in his bassinet, and then quieted. Katy didn't move. Amy spoke softly. "You're not willing to give it some time? See how things go?"

"Amy, Baby, I've given it all the time that I can."

"There's nothing that will make you change your mind?"

He shook his head, glancing at her, and then looked away, still shaking his head.

That was it — the gauntlet had been thrown down. "Just like that? It's over?"

"I'm sorry, Amy. I really am." He kept his head down. He couldn't bring himself to look at her.

Amy took off her engagement ring, and handed it to Pat. "You need to give me my key back." It came out sounding harsher than she had intended, but she was too tired to care.

"Right now? You're throwing me out in the middle of the night?"

She wanted to say yes, but she didn't. "Of course not," she said, "Just give it to me before you go to work in the morning." She turned out the light and collapsed back into the bed, as far away from Pat as she could get.

Pat reached over, trying to pull her closer to him. "Amy, come here."

She answered him by removing his hand from her hip.

Pat moved back to his condo the next day.

He was right about one thing — she couldn't continue working as a flight attendant. In the course of a month, Amy had lost her sister, her brother-in-law, her future husband, and her job.

Chapter Five

After much deliberation, Amy decided to move to Savannah. It was the only logical thing to do. She just hoped everything went as planned. She had a bachelor's degree in English and had her teacher's license, but she hadn't taken the certification tests. Not long before she graduated college, Amy had overheard someone talking of being accepted into flight attendant training. Listening to her classmate describe the job and all the places she'd see tugged at Amy's heart. She could teach later, after she married and had kids. Right now she wanted nothing more than to spread her wings, to travel and see the world.

Amy had been tied down with responsibility most of her life. She had helped her mother take care of her brother and sister after their father's death. After their mother's death, they had moved into her tiny apartment in Athens.

But now, with Susie and Andy graduating high school and starting college in the fall, she would be totally free. The Saturday she should have been taking the certification tests, she applied to become a flight attendant instead. By the time the twins had started college in the fall, Amy had finished training as a Flight Attendant was flying all over the country, enjoying a freedom she never knew existed.

Looking back now, she wished she had taken the tests and had gotten her certification right after graduation. But, as her mother used to say, there was no use crying over spilled milk. She would just have to study and take the exams in August. She could teach without the certification for a time, but at a lesser pay. The results would come back too late to be eligible for a full-time position, but she was assured they could keep her busy as a substitute teacher until a full-time opening became available. With only enough cash to last about six months, she needed to have a way to support the children.

Savannah was the only home Katy had ever known. It was a solid connection to her parents, to the home they had been renovating. The kids had lost everything that mattered most. Amy couldn't let them lose their home, too. Her townhouse in Atlanta was spacious enough, but the yard was virtually non-existent. Katy needed a real yard where she could run and play, as would Sammy before too long. Greg had built an elaborate wooden swing set, complete with a tree house. Amy laughed every time she thought about how Greg and Susie itched for days after removing the chigger-filled Spanish moss from the limbs surrounding the tree house.

There were other reasons Amy knew she have to leave Atlanta. Katy was terrified of sirens. Every time Katy heard an emergency vehicle, she would grow pale and shake uncontrollably. Amy never realized how many sirens there were in Atlanta. Watching the little girl tremble, Amy knew they had to leave Atlanta immediately. Savannah had sirens, too, but not like Atlanta.

Leaving Atlanta wasn't as hard as she thought it would be. Although it had been her home for almost a decade, she was gone more than she was there. Work kept her away half the time, and she would visit Susie and Greg several times a month. Atlanta, she realized, was home base, but it wasn't really home.

Shirley and Roger, Greg's parents, had stayed in Savannah after the funerals to help tie things up, allowing Amy to return to Atlanta with the children. Shirley had offered to come to Atlanta with her, but Amy knew Shirley's place was with Roger, so she politely declined. They would need each other as they sifted through the life that had once been their son. Shirley asked Amy if she minded if she and Roger took the animals, three dogs and two cats, that Greg had rescued. Amy readily agreed, relieved she didn't have to worry about taking care of them or finding them a good home. She hoped Katy wouldn't miss them too badly. Maybe someday they'd be able to have a dog or cat again, but right now, it was going to be all Amy could do to take care of the kids.

Amy sold her small sports car. It wasn't practical for her new life. Once she got to Savannah, she'd be driving Susie's minivan, but until then, she didn't have transportation. Jenny graciously offered to drive her to Savannah and stay a few days to help her get settled. Of all the things Amy was giving up, losing her beloved car was the most painful. She'd had a lot of laughs poking fun at her little sister for driving a minivan. All she needed was a *Baby on Board* caution sign to hang in the rear window, and the transformation would be complete. Now, it would be Amy driving a minivan.

The overcast skies mirrored Amy's gloomy mood. Her stomach was in knots as they turned onto the road leading to Susie and Greg's house. It was the first time she'd been to the house since right after the accident. The clapboard home had been built in the late 1800's. It had fallen into disrepair, almost to the point of condemnation, when Susie and Greg had rescued it from the wrecking ball.

Greg, a veterinarian, saw the potential of the antiquated house nestled among live oaks, magnolias, dogwoods and other assorted trees. Pecan and fruit trees lined the small creek that divided their property from their neighbor to the west. Wisteria draped itself through some of the trees, making it appear as though the clusters of purple flowers were part of the tree itself. The Spanish moss that gave Savannah its storybook-like charm dripped gracefully from the branches, swaying in the breeze. Even though the grounds were overgrown and the house dilapidated, Greg knew it would be the perfect place to raise a family.

Amy looked at the house now. It looked nothing like it had the first time she'd seen it. Greg had replaced the rotted clapboard siding, and painted the house a pale slate blue. Reproduction windows with hurricane safety glass and decorative hurricane shutters had been installed. The missing porch columns had been replaced, and the wide, wraparound porch rebuilt. The original porch had been brick, but due to time and money constraints, Greg had opted to use wood. He could brick the porch when their budget allowed. Flower pots and window boxes were filled with a brilliant assortment of flowers, vines draping lazily over their edges. The outside of the house looked amazing. Inside, the renovation was just beginning. Several rooms had only bare studs for walls. It was going to be up to Amy to somehow see that it was finished.

Jenny carried Sammy, while Katy held tightly to Amy's hand. The counselor at the hospital had warned Amy that Katy might be extremely clingy for a while. She was right. Terrified of someone else *going away*, Katy wouldn't let Amy out of her sight. Amy's heart broke every time she looked at the frightened, confused little girl.

"Are you okay?" Jenny asked.

Amy glanced at Jenny and nodded. Amy knew if she tried to speak, she'd start crying, and she didn't want to cry in front of Katy. Amy didn't know how much crying was normal, but she was sure she had surpassed that mark long ago. How was Katy going to get through this if she saw Amy couldn't? Somehow Amy needed to make Katy's life as normal as possible.

Jenny reached out with her free hand and squeezed Amy's shoulder. "Come on, it's starting to sprinkle. Let's get inside before we get soaked. We'll get our bags later. The truck won't be here until tomorrow, so we've got one day before the work begins. You take a nap and I'll take care of the kids. You'll feel better when you're rested."

Again, Amy nodded without speaking. *Sleep!* At this point in time, sleep seemed like the ultimate vacation.

Jenny stayed most of the week helping Amy take care of the kids and get settled into Susie's home. Amy got some much needed rest and was relieved to find out she did feel better. She was feeling more confident in her parenting skills, and Sammy had begun sleeping through the night. Soon she would have to begin the process of jumping through the required hoops to get her teaching certificate.

Jane Cavanaugh, who lived next door, worried about

Amy and the kids. Jane knew it was going to be a struggle for Amy to raise a newborn and an active preschooler. Raising kids, Jane knew, was difficult even under the best of circumstances. Amy's sudden responsibilities, combined with such overwhelming grief, were enough to drown even the strongest of souls. Amy never asked for help and often declined when it was offered, but Jane knew, for Amy's sanity, she needed a break now and then. Jane had a day with nothing planned, so she decided to give Amy a few hours away from Sammy. Amy would get a much needed break from the baby, Katy would get time alone with Amy, and Jane would get to cuddle Susie's sweet new baby.

Jane touched the worn edges of the handrail as she crossed the small bridge over the creek. Greg and Earl had built this bridge not long after Susie and Greg moved in. They had teased Susie and Jane that the bridge would save the two of them from having to go all the way to the road to gossip. Greg became the son Earl never had and the friend he never had time to make. Jane and Earl missed Susie and Greg as badly as if they truly had been family. Jane knew Amy must feel like the world had flipped on its axis and was spinning the other way.

Amy, feeding a ravenous Sammy, heard a knock at the back door. She looked up to see Jane on the back porch. "Hi, Jane. Come on in."

"Janie!" Katy exclaimed, running to hug the legs of her well-loved neighbor.

"Hi, Sweetie." She bent down to Katy's level and holding a sack in the air. "Guess what I brought."

"Did you bring your very special muffins that you only make for people you love very much?" Katy guessed, jumping up and down.

Amy laughed. Obviously, Jane had brought her very special muffins over more than once.

"Yes, I did. What a wonderful guesser you are." Jane hugged Katy and gave her the bag. To Amy she said, "I hope you like blueberry muffins. I brought coffee, too." Jane held a large thermos aloft. "Are you a coffee drinker?"

"Coffee sounds heavenly right now."

"Let me feed that little man for you so you can eat," Jane said, reaching for the hungry baby.

Amy handed Sammy to Jane. "Thank you. Can I get you anything?"

"No, I'm fine." She said, smiling at the baby in her arms.

In the few weeks Amy had lived in Susie's house, she had grown to love Jane and her family. They were friendly without being intrusive. Amy knew the meals and desserts Jane brought over weren't the leftovers Jane claimed them to be. Amy was grateful this generous woman cared so much. There were times Amy was so tired she could barely make herself walk. The thought of cooking dinner seemed Herculean, and then Jane would show up with a casserole or a plate of something Earl had grilled.

Jane suggested that Amy take Katy to Forsyth Park to play and have lunch downtown. "Girls Day," she said to Katy, "No boys allowed. Sammy has to stay here with mean old Janie."

"You're not mean, you're nice." Katy exclaimed.

Jane and Amy laughed. Both women noticed Katy didn't correct her about being old.

After exhausting themselves at the playground, they ate at a restaurant on historic River Street. On their way to the promised ice cream cone, Katy skipped beside Amy on the sidewalk, singing a little song she made as up she went. Katy looked so much like Susie had when she was little. The same long blonde hair, big blue eyes and a little pug nose. More than once, Amy caught herself just before she called the child 'Susie'. It made Amy's heart glad to see Katy happy. It was only recently that Katy had begun to giggle and smile again.

"Amy, can I have a really big ice cream cone?" Katy raised her hands as high as she could to show how tall her ice cream cone should be.

"Because you're such a Sweetie-pie, you can have a really big ice cream cone." Katy looked up at Amy, smiling, her tiny face full of innocent excitement. Amy's heart almost burst with love for her.

Inside the candy store, Katy ran immediately to the taffy

machine, watching it pull the taffy. A man removed the taffy from the puller and loaded it onto the machine that would package it. A wide-eyed Katy watched the machine pull the taffy, cut and wrap it, then send it along the conveyor belt that snaked across the ceiling. The still-warm candy traveled lazily over their heads until it was deposited into the proper bin.

Katy clapped her hands as she watched it fall from the overhead conveyor. "Can I have some?"

"Sure, Baby, what flavor?

"That kind," she said, pointing to the candy falling from the ceiling. Amy had to laugh. The little girl literally wiggled with excitement. Amy handed her a few pieces of the soft, warm taffy. "Ready for some ice cream?"

"Yeah," Katy yelled, clapping.

After getting their ice cream, Amy steered Katy outside. "Let's go sit over there," she said, pointing to a bench across the street, overlooking the river. "We can watch the big boats go by, okay?"

Katy, who was paying more attention to her ice cream than to the street, tripped and fell on the uneven cobblestones. Her ice cream cone landed upside down in front of her. Katy sat up and grabbed her knee, crying.

Amy helped her stand. It wasn't cut badly, just a scrape, but it needed to be washed out. Still crying, Katy started to reach for her ice cream. "No, Honey, you can't eat that now. It's all dirty. We'll get another one."

Katy continued to cry. Amy wasn't sure if her knee hurt, if she was upset about her ice cream, or maybe she just needed to cry. Amy needed to get Katy's knee cleaned, and she needed to clean up the spilled ice cream. Instead, she knelt in front of Katy and held her.

Chapter Six

From his vantage point across the street, Dave saw a pretty, young mother walk out of the candy store with her daughter. The little girl looked to be about three or four years old. To Dave, that's how old Cathy should be. It didn't seem possible that she was twelve years old — twelve and a *half*, according to Cathy. Dave and Cathy were closer than the typical father and daughter, but she was at the age where spending time with her friends was becoming more important than spending time with her dad. Dave missed being her whole world. He missed reading her stories and tucking her in at night. He missed her wanting her Daddy to rock her to sleep. It had been a long time since Cathy had been little enough to rock to sleep. He loved the young lady she was becoming, but he missed the little girl she used to be.

He smiled as he watched the young mother and her daughter laughing together. Dave glanced towards a huge container ship as it drifted by slowly. When he looked back toward the shops, the little girl was crying in her mother's arms as pink ice cream melted into the cobblestones nearby.

Dave rushed towards them. "Let me help," he said, using his newspaper to scoop up the ice cream. He deposited the mess into a nearby trash can, and then held out his hand to help Amy stand. He noticed she didn't have any rings on her left hand as he led them to the park bench he had just vacated. "I'll get something to clean her knee."

"Thank you," Amy said, sitting down on the bench with the sniffling child. She watched the man disappear into the candy shop, grateful for his assistance. He looked familiar, but she couldn't place the face. Most likely, he was someone on one of her flights. Working as a flight attendant for so many years, she saw a lot of faces she couldn't put a name to.

Dave emerged from the store carrying a wet paper towel, a band-aid and a pink ice cream cone.

Amy smiled as he approached. "Where's your suit of armor?"

He handed Katy her ice cream cone, then squatted in front of the little girl, gently dabbing Katy's knee. He looked at Amy. "We don't wear armor anymore. It tends to chafe."

Amy laughed, "Not to mention how noisy you'd be on

the cobblestones".

Dave laughed. "Look," he said to Katy, "a Big Bird band-aid."

"Yea," she said, giggling.

"There, all better." He stood up, looking down at Amy. She looked familiar. Where did he know her from?

"Thank you," she said, standing up. "It was very kind of you to help us. Let me pay you for the cone." She grabbed some bills from the pocket of her shorts, and then held them out to him.

"Think nothing of it, ma'am. It's all part of the job." He smiled, waving away her money. "The ice cream is my treat. Good day, ladies." He tipped an imaginary hat, bowed, and then turned to walk away. He turned around after only a few steps. "I know this is going to sound like a come-on, but you look terribly familiar."

"You do, too. Do you fly?"

He looked right, then left, as if to make sure no one was listening before he spoke. He leaned in towards her, lowering his voice conspiratorially. "We knights don't really fly. We have to rescue damsels in distress the old-fashioned way. It's our mutant cousins who get the super powers." He winked. "I may not be *the* Superman, but I've been told I'm pretty super."

"That was really bad," Amy said, laughing as she sat. "I meant do you fly on airplanes very often. I'm a flight attendant, or, well, I was until recently anyway. Perhaps that's where we've seen each other."

"That must be it. I don't fly as much now, but I used to have to travel quite a bit. Okay, so," Dave said, unable to think of anything else to prolong their talk, "Enjoy your afternoon."

"We will. And thank you again."

He started to turn away, but stopped abruptly. He turned back, pointing at her. "Centennial Park."

"Pardon?" *What was he talking about?*

"That's where we've met — Centennial Park. You were there with your friend. It was just after the park reopened in April."

"Oh, that's right. You and Jenny went out, didn't you?"

"Well, not exactly. We had a date, but she never showed up."

"Really? That doesn't sound like Jenny."

"I called her house and was told someone had died, so I guess she had a good excuse."

"Oh." Amy looked around for Katy, making sure she was out of ear shot. "My sister and her husband were in a really bad wreck that night on their way home to Savannah — to here. My brother-in-law died at the scene, and my sister died a few days later. Jenny took off work and stayed with me through it all. I hope you give her another chance. She's a great person." It was the first time she had talked about the wreck without breaking down. Her eyes began to mist, but she managed to keep her tears at bay.

"I'll keep that in mind. I'm really sorry about your sister and her husband."

For a moment, neither of them knew what to say. It was difficult to gracefully segue out of such a topic. Dave was uncomfortable and breathed a sigh of relief when Amy changed the subject.

"What brings you to Savannah?" She had to get thoughts of Susie and Greg, and that horrible night, out of her head. If she didn't, she'd start crying again.

"I live here. What about you? Do you live here? I guess I figured a flight attendant would live in Atlanta."

"I moved here from Atlanta a few weeks ago. I'm living in my sister's house. I'm the kids' guardian. And, I had to quit my job. It's hard to be a mom if you're not there, and if you're a flight attendant, you're not there a lot. I'm working on getting my teaching certification." Why was she telling him all this?

A look of surprise appeared on Dave's face. "Did it happen on I-16, just south of Macon?"

"What, the accident? Yes, it did. How did you know that?"

Dave sat down next to her. "I remember it. I was on my way home. I was," he stopped himself before saying stuck in traffic behind it. "I was on my way home. I saw it. Well, I didn't actually see the wreck," he corrected. "I was a little bit behind it."

Dave thought back to when he had met Amy in April.

Hadn't she just gotten back from her honeymoon? "What does your husband do? Does he work in the Atlanta area?"

"Oh, I'm not married," she said, wondering why Dave would think that. She wasn't wearing a wedding ring.

"Hadn't you just gotten back from your honeymoon that day I met you and your friend?"

"No. It wasn't a honeymoon, it was just a vacation. We were engaged, but he was less than thrilled about raising my sister's kids. He's still in Atlanta."

"If you don't mind my saying so, I think your fiancé could have had better timing."

"A lot of people are giving Pat a hard time about leaving, but I understand."

Dave didn't say anything, but he gave her a look that said he thought she was crazy.

"I know what you're thinking, and I thought the same thing. I was pretty upset at first, but now I know it was the right thing to do." Amy leaned back against the bench. She was used to the look she was getting from Dave. Everyone expected her to be angry at Pat, but she wasn't mad. More than anything she was just sad.

Again, Dave didn't say anything. He didn't know what to say.

"I know what you're thinking, but if Pat had loved me the way I thought he did, you know, like in the movies, that all-consuming, I'd-die-without-you, I-need-you-more-than-the-air-I-breathe kind of love? He wouldn't have left. If he had loved me like that, a couple of kids wouldn't have made any difference.

"And, I guess if I was totally honest with myself, I didn't love him like that, either. I think I thought I did, but I couldn't have, could I? If I had, I wouldn't have been so quick to let him walk away without a fight. Would I?"

It was a rhetorical question, so he didn't answer her. "Most people wouldn't be quite so forgiving."

"I know, and don't get me wrong — I was heartbroken, confused, scared, and pretty darn angry! But really, if you step back and look at it from his perspective, his life changed drastically — *overnight*. One night we're in Hawaii, and a few days later, we're raising two kids. I can't blame him for panicking. It really is a lot to ask of someone. At least he had the courage to tell me he couldn't handle it." She sighed, looking out across the river. "Besides, we can't have loved each other the way we should have. I thought I loved him, and I do — I *did*, but I guess it wasn't meant to be. And you know, I'd rather be alone, with these two kids, than spend the rest of my life with someone who resents us."

"Two kids?"

"Susie was eight months pregnant. They delivered her baby the night of the accident. A little boy named Sammy." Amy smiled for a moment when she spoke of the baby. "Anyway, about Pat, he's really not a bad guy. He's an attorney and he's handling the will, the probate, the guardianship, the adoption, and everything else for me. Free of charge."

"Adoption?" Dave asked.

"I'm adopting the kids. I don't want to be just their guardian. They deserve a mom. I'm not changing their last name though. I think it's important they keep Greg's name.

"Anyway, Pat may not have been my Prince Charming, but he's not a bad person. I appreciate that he was honest with me, and I know it wasn't easy to do. I respect him for having the courage to tell me, and I'm grateful he didn't screw up both of our lives by trying to live a lie."

He was amazed at her ability to forgive Pat so easily. It would be easy to verbally kick the guy around, like everyone else apparently was, but she was so gracious about it. "So, how do you like Savannah?"

"I love it. It's beautiful." She looked at him, smiling the sweetest, most genuine smile he had ever seen on an adult. "I've wanted to live here since the first time I saw it, but I needed to live close to the airport. Once Susie moved here, I hoped I'd be able to move here to be close to her when I started a family. What about you? You live in Savannah, but work in Atlanta? That's a heck of a commute."

"I'm an architect. Our corporate office is in Atlanta, but we have a branch here in Savannah."

"Do you have kids?"

"A daughter, Cathy, she's twelve now, almost a teenager. I don't know where the time's gone. She should still be her age." He nodded towards Katy.

They sat in silence, watching Katy sitting in the grass with her back to them, eating her ice cream. It was a pleasant kind of silence that neither of them felt the need to fill.

Dave knew she wasn't looking for a relationship, so he felt comfortable with her. He didn't have to impress her. He hadn't had a woman friend since college. To his amazement, he found himself excited at the prospect of being just friends with a woman. The fact that he found her extremely attractive might be difficult, but with everything going on in her life, he had a feeling she might be a little too high maintenance. She was very pretty and had a wonderful sense of humor. And she was so kind. Why had he preferred her friend instead of her? Then he remembered. Her friend, Jenny, had reminded him of Ginger.

"You know," Amy said laughing, "we've been sitting here talking all this time, and I have no idea what your name is. And just in case you've forgotten mine and are too polite to ask, I'm Amy Cooper, and she's Katy."

"Dave." He said, shaking her hand. "Dave Baldwin."

"It's nice to re-meet you, Dave."

Katy looked up and noticed Dave sitting next to Amy. She came scurrying up the hill towards them. She put her free hand on her hip and pointed her now empty ice cream cone towards Dave. "It's Girls Day. No boys allowed." She looked towards Amy, "Right?" Katy, ice cream on her face from ear to ear, was doing her best to look stern.

Dave looked at Amy, both suppressing smiles. "She's right. In fact, even Sammy couldn't come."

Dave turned to Katy, producing an exaggerated look of shock. "Miss Katy, I am so sorry. I didn't know it was Girls Day. Will you forgive me?"

"Well," Katy replied, contemplating his apology. "I guess its okay, 'cause you didn't know no better, but don't let it happen again."

"I give you my word. It will never happen again." Dave said to Katy. Turning to Amy, he asked, "So, how often do you have Girls Day?"

"I have no idea. My neighbor showed up with a bag of muffins, told us the rules, and then shooed us out the door."

"Would you mind if I called you sometime?"

"Well, I," she stammered. She didn't know what to say. As much as she enjoyed his company, and as tempted as she was, she knew she didn't have any business dating. Her life was in limbo right now. This was not the time to get involved with anyone.

"Oh, I didn't mean —" he paused a moment, a little embarrassed. "I meant, as a friend. Being new to town and all, I figured you could use a friend here, and I know I could."

Amy, too, was embarrassed. How foolish was it to think a man like Dave Baldwin would be interested in her romantically? "I'm sorry, and you're right. I could definitely use a friend. I don't know anyone here except my neighbors."

He took down her number and gave her his. Dave stood up, saying good-bye to Amy and Katy, and then walked away, looking back a few times until she was out of his sight. He admired her for raising her sister's kids. It had cost her everything. Not many people would be that altruistic. He liked her, and he looked forward to getting to know her better.

Amy watched Dave walk away. She saw him look back at her a few times, smiling. He was nice. Until today, she hadn't realized how much she missed talking to a man. Talking to Dave made her realize how lonely she was. She talked to Jenny every couple of days, and Jane popped over several times a week, but she still felt lonelier than she could ever remember.

She was used to working, meeting and talking to new people everyday. Staying home with two young children was proving to be more difficult than she had thought it would be. Whoever thought stay at home moms didn't work were crazy. And, she missed Susie more than words could express. It was all she could do to keep from being pulled into the depths of depression. The pain of losing Susie and Greg was overwhelming. If it weren't for the fact that she had to take care of the kids, she wasn't sure she would be able to find the strength to get out of bed.

She knew everyone thought she was doing this wonderful, selfless thing to raise Susie's kids, but she knew the truth — she wasn't saving those kids, they were saving her.

Chapter Seven

Dave rolled up the blueprints and put them in a tube. He had just enough time to make it to Atlanta for a meeting. The changes the client had requested weren't difficult to make, but they'd taken him all morning. Dave's mind had kept wandering. He couldn't quit thinking of Amy.

She continued to fill his thoughts all the way to Atlanta, throughout the meeting, and on the drive back home. She had gone through a lot in the last few months, and he thought it wise of her to avoid dating at this point. Getting involved with someone in her circumstances was a bad idea. Even so, he couldn't quit thinking about her.

She wasn't like the women he normally pursued, so why did he want her so badly? She was very pretty, but she wasn't drop-dead gorgeous. She wasn't tall. She was so — average. Was that it? Had he not seen her beauty because there was nothing about her that was extraordinary, at least not extraordinary *enough* for his taste?

He laughed at how ridiculous that was. He would be lucky if Amy settled for him. He was surprised at how shallow he was. He had never thought of himself as shallow, but he apparently was, and that bothered him.

So the question remained — if she was not what turned him on physically, what was it? She was certainly easy to talk to. Was it an emotional connection? Intellectual? Or was it the fact that she made it clear she didn't want him? Did he want her simply because he couldn't have her, because she made herself unavailable to him?

Yesterday he had been excited at the prospect of having a woman friend. He needed to quit trying to think of Amy as a dating prospect and accept the friendship she offered. In truth, he needed a friend, too. Besides, Amy was too emotionally vulnerable for anything more. By the time he returned to Savannah, he'd talked himself into believing all he wanted from Amy was her friendship.

———————

It was eight-thirty on a Friday night. Instead of getting ready to go out with friends, Amy was folding laundry. She looked around the family room. The wood floors had been stripped, but Greg hadn't stained or varnished them yet. Drywall had been hung, but it hadn't been taped or mudded. Amy wished she could ask Jane's husband, Earl, to show her how to finish some of the projects Greg had started, but she was afraid he'd finish them himself, out of pity. She needed his help, but she didn't want anyone to feel sorry for her. Amy planned to buy the house from the estate, and she wanted to keep the selling price as low as possible, so finishing the renovation now was not to her benefit.

When her father died, her mother was forced to work two jobs to keep them from losing their home. Unbeknownst to the children, her mother had taken out a large insurance policy on herself. Her will stipulated it was to be split equally among the children, and was to be used exclusively towards buying a home. Her mother didn't want Amy or the twins to have to work as hard as she did just to keep a roof over their heads. Susie had used her money to help buy this property. Amy's share, still held in trust, would be used for the same purpose. She'd buy Susie's home, and the profits of the sale would go into a trust for Katy and Sammy. It would be more than enough to send them to college and perhaps provide a nice down payment on a home of their own some day.

When Susie and Greg first showed Amy the house they had bought, Amy had started laughing, thinking it was a joke. "Well, one thing's for sure, it's not haunted."

Susie laughed with her sister. "It's not, huh? "

"No. No self-respecting ghost would live here."

"Very funny, Aim." Susie laughed, gently pushing her sister. She turned back towards the house, looking at it dreamily. "Won't she be beautiful?"

"You're serious?"

"Yes," Susie answered excitedly. "Just think of how beautiful she was when she was first built, how beautiful she can be again. She's got good bones. We'll start on the outside and then work our way through the house, room by room until she's done."

"She?"

"Yeah, she's a she. Greg even named her. He said every beautiful southern home deserves a name."

Maybe so, but this could hardly be called a beautiful Southern home. "I can't imagine what he named her. No, wait, let me guess. Casper's Castle?"

Susie's eyes never left the dilapidated old house. "Magnolia Manor."

The magnolia part was true enough. There were several overgrown magnolia trees attempting to swallow the house. But manor? The house was hardly a manor.

"Aptly named. It will cost a fortune to renovate. How are you guys going to swing it?"

"Greg's dad is a contractor. He can get us materials wholesale, and his brothers will help him do the work. We're not going to do it all at once, just a little at a time. One day, this house will be magnificent."

"Magnificent Magnolia Manor," Amy quipped.

As Susie talked, Amy got caught up in her excitement. Amy draped her arm around her sister's shoulders. "She does have good bones. It's going to be a great home, but she needs a lot of work." Amy paused a moment. "My visits are going to be spent working, aren't they?"

Susie laughed again. "How sweet of you to offer."

Once the exterior had been taken care of, Greg and his brothers gutted the interior down to the studs. They brought the wiring and plumbing up to code, and then started stripping woodwork and hanging drywall. Amy remembered Susie calling, saying she had exciting news — after two years of using sheets for privacy, she had real walls in her bathroom again. And, she was pregnant! Susie was so happy, and Amy was thrilled for her. Susie would be a great mom.

Girls Day had worn Katy out. Amy carried her to bed when she fell asleep on the sofa after dinner. Amy stood in the family room, looking around at all of Susie's things. She missed Susie. She needed Susie. Susie was the one who'd read all the parenting books. Amy had routinely taken care of Katy, but it was always a short term kind of thing. Amy had been the beloved aunt who spoiled her sweet little niece. Now she was the mom and found it a constant struggle. She'd never had to worry about nutritious snacks or three well-balanced meals every single day. Why was raising kids so much harder than it looked? Susie had made it all look so easy.

Amy's days became a blur of bottles, diapers, naked Barbie's, and mind-numbing educational television. With no job outside the home, the only thing that distinguished one day from the next was what she ate and what she wore. She had no real friends in Savannah. She had Jane, of course, but as kind as Jane was, she wasn't a friend of Jenny's caliber. She had never been so lonely in her life. She was fighting a depression that threatened to engulf her. Working herself to the point of exhaustion was the quickest way to get to sleep. She woke up just as tired, but at least sleep provided a few hours respite from the pain and grief and loneliness.

The phone rang, startling her. *Who would be calling at this hour?* Could it be Jenny, calling to apprise her of a surprise trip to Savannah? She grabbed the phone before looking at the caller ID.

"Hello?"

"Hi. I didn't wake you, did I?"

It took her a moment to place the voice. "Dave?"

"Yes. Expecting someone else?" he teased.

"No, just surprised, and you didn't wake me. I was awake. What are you up to?"

"Not much. I've got a house full of twelve year old girls. I'm just in need of some adult conversation."

"You're preaching to the choir, buddy. I'm so desperate that an eight-year-old would qualify as adult conversation." They laughed easily together as they recounted their day.

After their encounter on River Street, Dave had begun calling her every night, even when he was out of town. He looked forward to talking to Amy. He would like to talk to her in person, but he didn't trust himself to be alone with her.

Amy tried to have all her work done by ten o'clock each evening, when Dave would normally call. His calls were a wonderful diversion to what had become a mundane, monotonous existence. Amy found it comforting to have found a friend in Savannah, even if it was limited to the phone. Perhaps this was best, she told herself. It would be hard to be around Dave without it being obvious that she was falling for him.

Amy cradled the phone to her ear as she curled up in the wicker rocker in the screened-in porch. The moon was full and the clear sky was full of stars. Fireflies flew haphazardly around the yard.

"It sure is good to hear your voice." Dave said, sounding tired.

"Bad day?"

"You could say that," Dave said, his voice nearly drowned out by music blaring in the background. "Hold on a second, Amy." Dave covered the phone with his hand and yelled to Cathy to turn the volume down.

When Dave came back on the line, Amy asked, "Is

Cathy home? I thought she was going to Atlanta to see her mom this weekend."

"Ginger never came to pick her up. Cathy finally got a hold of her. Cathy thinks she woke her up, but I think she was on something."

"What? You mean, like drugs?"

"I think so. She was groggy and didn't really make much sense."

"Could she have been asleep?" Amy asked.

"I don't think so. It wasn't that kind of groggy."

"What makes you think it was drugs? Did she do drugs when you were married?"

"She was addicted to prescription pain pills for several years. It was a nightmare."

"How did she get addicted to those?"

Dave told her Ginger had run a stop sign and was hit broad side. She was wearing a seat belt, which probably saved her life, but even after two surgeries and a year of physical therapy, she had debilitating back pain. It was a stretch financially, but Dave hired a woman to cook, clean the house, and care for Cathy and Ginger.

One morning, about two years after the accident, Dave left the house for a meeting in Atlanta. He was an hour away when he realized he'd left the blueprints back at the house. When he arrived home, he heard the vacuum cleaner running in the family room. He poked his head into the room to say hello to Tina, the housekeeper, but it wasn't

Tina vacuuming — it was Ginger.

Dave retrieved the plans from his office, and then left quickly, without Ginger knowing he had been there. It had crossed his mind to confront her, but he had stopped himself. He needed time to think before approaching her. His hands were shaking as he backed out of the drive. *Why was Ginger lying about her injuries? How long had she been lying? What was she doing with all the money they were supposedly paying Tina?*

As soon as his appointment ended, Dave hired a private detective to find out what Ginger was up to. It didn't take long for him to report back. Ginger had visited three doctors in less than a week. Following each appointment, she stopped at a pharmacy and filled a prescription for either OxyContin or Percodan. In an effort to hide her addiction and lessen the paper trail, she bypassed insurance, paying cash. At least, Dave thought, he knew where the money was going.

He had photographs of her entering and leaving the offices of several doctors and area pharmacies. He also had photocopies of the prescriptions, and her signature for the controlled substance medications. Dave didn't ask the detective how he obtained his information. He wasn't sure if it was obtained legally or not, but it was irrefutable.

Initially Ginger denied the allegations, but confessed when confronted with the evidence. Ginger broke down crying, begging him to forgive her, promising to quit. He knew she was sincere in her desire to quit, but he knew a little about addictions, and he knew she needed help.

He forced her to enroll in an inpatient drug rehabilitation program. She didn't want it on her medical record that she'd had a substance abuse problem, so he promised not to use their insurance. He visited her as often as the program directors would allow, sparingly at first, then more often as the treatment progressed. She relapsed within days of being released. The pattern would repeat itself many times over.

Dave's feelings for Ginger, ambivalent up to this point, began to change. He realized how much he loved her, how much she meant to him. He would do whatever it took to cure her, to save her. He would rescue her, and he'd be her hero.

He missed so much work that first year he nearly lost his job. He reluctantly confided to his partners about Ginger's addiction. They were sympathetic, but warned him he'd have to get his personal life under control or take a leave of absence. Everyone, including Dave, recognized his work had been suffering for many months. The quality of his work had been acceptable, but the amount of work he was getting done was not.

Faced with mounting debt from multiple rehab programs, Dave had no choice but to use the insurance when Ginger entered rehab yet again. When Ginger found out her addiction would become a permanent part of her medical history, she flew into an explosive rage. Dave continued to visit, but Ginger refused to see him. She relented when she found out she would not be released until she took responsibility for her actions and her reason for being there in the first place.

It was nearly three years after the accident before Ginger was living clean and sober again. Dave wanted to celebrate her sobriety and his love for her with a new baby. She had been thrilled with the idea of having another baby, and for the first time in their marriage, Dave felt whole. He had a sweet little girl and a beautiful wife, whom he loved more than he had ever loved anyone before.

Within six months, Ginger was pregnant, but she had a miscarriage at seven weeks while Dave was out of town. He flew home on the next flight out. He held Ginger in his arms, trying to comfort her as she sobbed. She held her now empty abdomen and cried herself to sleep. Night after night, Dave would gaze at her face as she slept, finally at peace; her torment in remission until she awoke. Her pain only doubled his agony.

Ginger had been unable to conceive again. Dave knew Ginger was beating herself up, thinking her drug abuse had caused her to miscarry and possibly become sterile. He had the same thoughts, but he didn't blame her — he took it as a sign that they weren't meant to have any more children. After they had raised Cathy, he would spend the rest of his life spoiling Ginger.

Amy held the phone to her ear, aching for all of the pain Dave had gone through.

Chapter Eight

Dave settled into his favorite chair, holding the phone between his cheek and shoulder as he pulled the lever to recline. "So, where are you from? You lived in Atlanta and your sister lived in Savannah and your brother lives in Oregon? Where were you all born?"

"Indiana. Evansville, Indiana."

"Indiana," Dave said. "The Hoosier state."

"Yup."

"I've always wondered," Dave asked, "what exactly is a Hoosier."

"You'd be surprised how many times I've been asked that. I looked it up in the dictionary once. It says, and I quote, a Hoosier is a native or resident of Indiana. Helpful, isn't it?" Amy laughed.

"Well, glad we cleared that up." Dave laughed with her.

"Were Susie and Andy born in Indiana, too?"

"Yup, we were all born in Evansville."

"How did all you Yankees end up in Georgia?"

Amy said it was a long story.

"I've got all night, doll."

Amy told Dave to get comfortable, and started her story beginning with the third grade, when she'd first met Molly Montgomery. They quickly became best friends.

As high school graduation neared, Amy and Molly began to seriously look at their options. Both were good students and could get scholarships to most any school, but they both came from working families. Even with scholarships, many colleges were too expensive. When Molly's boyfriend, Scott, was accepted into the football program at the University of Georgia in Athens, Molly begged Amy to apply there with her. As the first one in her family to go to college, Amy had no allegiance to any particular college. The University of Georgia was an outstanding institution, and she couldn't imagine college without Molly by her side. They both applied to the University of Georgia, and were accepted.

Scott thought his athletic prowess would carry the same academic advantage in college as he'd enjoyed in high school. He spent more time drinking and partying than he did studying. Midterm grades landed him on academic probation. At the end of the first semester, he had flunked every single class and lost his scholarship. Blaming everyone but himself, he went home. Despite Amy's efforts to change Molly's mind, Molly dropped out of college and went back to Indiana with him. Amy was assigned a new roommate, Jenny McIntosh, and they had been friends ever since.

During their sophomore year, Amy and Jenny rented a small one bedroom apartment near campus. Jenny found out she was pregnant just after Christmas. She married her boyfriend at the Justice of the Peace and moved out. Amy had to work two part-time jobs to pay the rent. Despite the sacrifice, she liked living on her own. Rather than move back to Indiana for the summer, she stayed in Athens, working as many hours and saving as much money as she could, hoping if she saved enough during the summer, she wouldn't have to work so many hours once school started up again.

Just after Thanksgiving break, two policemen came to Amy's apartment in Athens. As gently as possible, they solemnly informed Amy that her mother had died. Amy was dumbfounded. Her mother was only forty years old. She was so healthy. How could it have happened?

Still numb with shock and grief, Amy drove home to Indiana. At her first opportunity, she sought out the doctor who had treated her mother, listening to him explain that her mother had died of a brain aneurism, using a lot of medical terms Amy didn't understand or have the presence of mind to question.

After the funeral, Susie and Andy moved into Amy's small apartment in Athens. Amy and Susie shared the bedroom, and Andy slept on the sofa. Amy continued to work and go to school, as did Susie and Andy. They were all used to working and helping each other just to survive. Amy remembered better times, but it was the only life the twins had ever known.

It was late by the time Amy hung up the phone. She fell asleep, grateful to have a friend to talk to. Meeting Dave was the only good thing to happen to her in months.

Dave looked forward to talking to Amy every day. They talked about their kids, the dreams they'd achieved and the ones they'd let go. They talked of new dreams they hoped to attain. They talked of their mistakes and regrets. They talked of their deepest fears and fiercest longings.

He found himself telling Amy things he'd never told another living soul. The only thing he didn't reveal was Ginger's secret. Was it the relative anonymity of being on the phone that gave him the courage to bare his soul to her? It had to be. The alternative was that he was falling for her, but that couldn't be. He was still too much in love with Ginger. He wasn't falling for her, he told himself. She was simply a friend he could trust with his secrets.

Amy anxiously awaited his nightly calls. To her dismay, she found herself disappointed when the phone didn't ring, and couldn't help but wonder if he was on a date. Her stomach would churn at the thought of him out with someone, holding her, kissing her, touching her — making love to her. She'd go to bed, aching for him, willing him to call, and he often did. She would lie in bed, listening to him talk, in a voice so sexy it made her skin tingle. Being woke up in the middle of the night and talking for hours left her exhausted in the morning, but it was worth it. Dave made her feel more alive than she'd felt in a long time.

What kind of woman was she that she could be falling in love with someone so soon after losing someone else? She couldn't help but wonder if perhaps she had stayed with Pat so long because he was the first man she'd made love to. She had dated some in high school, but she'd never had a steady boyfriend. When she moved to Athens to go to college, she was free for the first time in her life. After years of helping her mother with the house, working part-time after school, and watching over her brother and sister, she didn't have to take care of anyone but herself. Luxuriating in her newfound freedom, she didn't want a boyfriend. She didn't want to have to think or worry about anyone else. When Molly returned to Evansville just to please Scott, it only reaffirmed her vow to remain single and enjoy life on her own for a while.

She was still a virgin at twenty-six when she met Pat, a fact she had been a little embarrassed to admit to him. Amy hadn't necessarily been saving herself — Pat was simply her first serious boyfriend. It seemed incredulous to Pat that someone could be a virgin at her age.

She'd become a flight attendant right after graduating from college. Most guys her age wanted someone more accessible than her work allowed. She met a few guys she initially thought might have the potential to be Mr. Right, but they quickly grew tired of her extended stays out of town and found someone with a more accommodating schedule. Pat, on the other hand, didn't seem to find her absences an inconvenience. He had a busy law practice and saw her time away as a good chance to catch up on work. She never worried when she was away from Pat that she would come home to find another woman had taken her place. Was that why she had stayed? Because he had been safe?

She could never let Dave know she had feelings for him. He'd made it obvious he wanted nothing more than friendship from her. She hoped it was just loneliness that made her want him so much. She needed him so much, she told herself, because he was all she had. She kept telling herself that once she got back to work and had friends and a real life again, Dave wouldn't mean so much to her, and it wouldn't matter that she meant so little to him.

Chapter Nine

"What are you doing for the Fourth?" Dave asked. The Fourth of July fell on a Saturday. It would be a long holiday weekend, and he hoped to spend it with Amy.

"I thought about taking Katy to the fireworks at the river, but I can't put insect repellant on Sammy and I'm afraid he'd be eaten alive. I think this year we're going to stay home and play with sparklers in the backyard after the baby goes to bed. Sounds pretty exciting, huh?"

"I'm spending the weekend on Tybee with an old friend. His family has a house right on the beach. I was wondering if you'd like to come with me. I'd love for you to meet Cathy."

Amy didn't answer for a moment. "I don't know. I'm not sure that's such a good idea."

"Why do you say that?" He hoped she couldn't hear the

disappointment in his voice.

"Sammy's just three months old and Katy's only three. I don't think we'd be very good house guests right now. They're both pretty high maintenance."

"They'll be plenty of people to help you with the kids. It would do you good to have a few minutes without having to take care of someone else."

"What will Cathy think, what with me having a brand new baby and no husband? It doesn't look very good."

"Amy, loosen up. I'll talk to Cathy so that she knows you're not a woman of *loose morals*." Dave teased. "You'll have fun, and Cathy will adore the kids."

Amy didn't answer. She wanted to go, but she was afraid to be around him. Could she hide the fact that she was falling for him? Would her feelings for him ruin their friendship?

"No strings attached. You and the kids will have your own room, with a crib for the baby. We're going Thursday afternoon, coming back Sunday night. We could stop by and pick you up, or I could give you directions and you could come at your leisure." He paused. When Amy didn't answer, he continued. "Sammy could sleep safely inside, away from the mosquitoes, while we sit on the deck watching the fireworks. No fighting traffic to get home." Was he being too persistent? Could she tell he was practically begging her to go?

"Can I think about it, maybe let you know in a day or

two?" She twirled her hair tightly around her finger, let it unravel, and then twirled it again.

"Sure. I didn't mean to pressure you. I just figured you could use some adult company."

She loved the sound of his voice; very masculine, very sexy. She liked him, and it would be a refreshing change of pace to have a conversation with someone who could pronounce all their consonants. Why was she putting him off? "Actually, I could use some adult company. What time should I be ready Thursday?"

Dave was elated. They discussed the details of the trip, and then the conversation fell quiet. He could hear her breathing into the phone. In the silence, his mind began to wander. She was probably in bed, and he wondered what, if anything, she wore to bed. He closed his eyes and could see her long, silky hair spread across her pillow. His desire for her was growing. What was she thinking? What would she think if she knew what he was thinking?

"So," Amy said, breaking the lull, "you've told me about college and beyond — tell me about your childhood."

"It wasn't the Brady Bunch, I can assure you."

"Whose was?" she replied softly.

Dave told Amy he was the oldest of four children, born in fairly rapid succession. His parents divorced when he was six years old. His mother and father didn't love each other and had little in common. The only bond they shared was their children, which they both treated as more of a burden than blessing. They married after his mother became pregnant, having dated only a few months. Years later, the irony of his own marriage mirroring their failed union wasn't lost on him.

In the early 1960's, a teenage pregnancy was social suicide. Only sixteen years old, Dave's mother was forced to drop out of high school to become a reluctant, stay-at-home mom. Her dreams of college, prosperity, and in her eyes, happiness, were no longer attainable. She watched her friends go to dances and proms. She listened with a growing ache as they described their dresses, which cost more than her husband made in a week. By the time her friends went away to college, she'd had another child. By the time they'd finished college, she'd had two more.

Dave could remember lying in bed in the tiny room he shared with his three sisters, listening to his parents fight. Though they never became physically violent, Dave often feared they would. Living in a small, two-bedroom trailer, it was impossible for Dave to sleep through the fights. To his amazement, his two youngest sisters often did. He would hold Paula in the upper bunk they shared until they fell asleep out of sheer exhaustion, or until their parents tired of fighting. The word divorce was thrown around a lot in the last year.

Mainstream America had yet to embrace the concept of divorce, and few children of the suburbs had even heard of the word. But in the dingy trailer park the Baldwin family called home, divorce was a way of life. At least half the trailers parked in the treeless terrain were inhabited by divorced women and their children. Strangely, the idea of divorce didn't frighten Dave. An over-the-road truck driver, his father was gone a good deal of the time. His mother, sick of being a mom, was gone most of the time as well. It didn't worry him that his parents would split up. What worried Dave was how he would feed his sisters should their only source of income walk away. Even with his father working, they were desperately poor. How would they buy food if his father left? It wasn't long before he would find out.

Dave often wondered why his mother had children at all, much less so many. She obviously had no maternal instincts. She made sure they had the physical necessities, but little more. With her husband out of the picture, Dave's mother felt free to become the carefree, single woman she never had the chance to be. The sexual revolution was in full swing, and the advent of the birth control pill assured no more unwanted pregnancies.

She didn't allow the fact that she had four children, ranging in age from two to seven, to interfere with her lifestyle. His mother took a job as a waitress at a nearby bar. After work, she would frequently go home with the drunken patrons. She would often be gone for days at a time. Being the oldest, Dave had instructions to take the two younger girls, Wendy and Tammy, down the street to

Mrs. Gardner's before walking to school with Paula. After school, he and Paula would stop by Mrs. Gardener's to pick up their little sisters. If asked, he was to tell Mrs. Gardner his mother had to work early or had had to work late. His answer was to depend on when the question was asked.

Looking back, Dave realized Mrs. Gardner had to have known the children were alone most of the time, but in the early 1970's, people minded their own business when it came to what went on in other peoples' families. No one thought to question them to find out exactly how much their mother was gone, much less report her neglect to the authorities.

The children were clean and didn't seem hungry, nor did they appear abused. But Mrs. Gardner knew they were neglected, so she did what little she could. She'd tuck cookies or sandwiches in the diaper bag, telling little Dave she'd made too many at lunch. Sometimes she'd ask them to stay for supper or give them a pot of something to take home. It wasn't much, but it soothed her conscience somewhat.

Dave changed baby Tammy's diaper and ultimately potty trained her. He gave his sisters baths, washing their long hair and carefully brushing out the tangles until they were old enough to do it themselves. He made sure they ate, mostly cereal and sandwiches, until he was tall enough to reach the stove to heat up soup or some other canned delicacy.

With no adult supervision, they were free to do whatever they wanted. Dave, a daredevil, led the adventures. Looking back, with him at the helm, he realized it was a miracle any of them lived through their childhood.

From time to time, his mother would allow her latest boyfriend to move in with them. The liaisons never lasted very long, and the children soon lost count of how many men had passed through the revolving door of their mother's bedroom.

By the time Dave was in high school, he both loved and hated his mother. He was now old enough, and had seen enough, to understand the way he lived was not normal or even acceptable in other families. His mother either didn't know, or didn't care when, or even if, he came home. He stayed out later and later with no recriminations. He had always resented shouldering the responsibility for the other children, but now he relished the freedom her absence allowed him.

One night Dave came in around one o'clock in the morning, tipsy from a small bottle of whiskey they had swiped from his friend's father. He could hear his sister, Paula, arguing with someone in hushed tones. As he approached her room, he realized she was arguing with a guy. *She had a boy in there! How could she be so stupid? Was she going to follow the same miserable path as their mother?*

Furious, he threw open the bedroom door and turned on

the light. Instead of finding a hormonal teenager, he found his mother's current boyfriend, Ken, tearing at Paula's pajamas. When the light came on, a surprised Ken let go of Paula and stood up. Paula reached for a blanket to cover her exposed chest, grateful the ordeal was over. His other sisters, Wendy and Tammy, sat up, blinking the sleep from their eyes, half asleep and confused.

Dave raced to his bedroom to retrieve his baseball bat. He returned to find the stunned man still standing next to his sister's bed. Dave swung the bat wildly, screaming obscenities at the half naked man. Ken deflected the blow with his arm. The sickening crack filled the room. Ken fell back into the dresser. A lamp sitting on the dresser crashed to the floor and the mirror teetered precariously before righting itself. Ken grabbed his arm and stared at the wild eyed teenager standing before him. Dave stopped swinging the bat, but held it over his shoulder ready to strike again. Ken took advantage of the lull and burst towards Dave. Ken knocked Dave to the floor as he fled the room. A moment later, they heard the front door slam.

Dave let the bat fall to his side. He stood there a moment, breathing heavily as the rage and fear began to subside. He looked at his sisters, now huddled together in Paula's bed, their eyes wide with fear.

He was thankful he had come home when he did, and repulsed by what Ken had planned to do to Paula, and perhaps Wendy and Tammy, too. "Did he hurt you?" he asked, looking at all three of them.

They all shook their heads.

Nausea almost overtook him as a new question rose within him. He rushed over to his sisters, kneeling beside the bed. He touched their arms, their faces, their legs, looking for signs of abuse. "Has he done this before? Has anyone done this before?"

Again, they all shook their heads.

He threw his arms around them and held them as they cried. "I'll protect you. No one will ever hurt you. Okay?" The girls looked up at him, nodding their heads, smiling through their tears. "As long as I'm alive, no one will ever hurt you — ever." The girls could feel him tremble, but they knew that despite his fear, he would keep them safe.

The next day, Dave changed the locks on the house. He gave each of his sisters a key and made them vow not to give it to their mother. He put a new lock, deadbolt and chain on his sisters' bedroom door.

That night Dave was awakened by someone banging at the door.

"Kids, let me in."

Dave opened the door for his mother.

She staggered in, a man Dave had never seen before was close behind her. "My damn key wouldn't work."

"Something's wrong with the lock. Mine doesn't work either," Dave lied.

"Well, we need to do something about that, don't we?"

In a gesture of maternal love, she patted his cheek, rather roughly, before leading the stranger to her bedroom.

Dave knew she wouldn't do anything about the locks. Tomorrow morning, she'd be too hung over to do anything about it. More than likely, she'd never remember her key didn't work. He grabbed his sleeping bag and knocked softly on his sisters' room. "Paula, open up. Let me in."

He heard his sister fumbling with the new locks. She opened the door for her brother, locking the door again once he was inside.

"Mom's got another new guy here. I'm going to sleep by the door to make sure he doesn't get in here." Dave could see the fear in her eyes. He hugged her and whispered. "Don't worry. No one can get in here. Besides, I'm going to sleep on the floor in front of the door."

"You can't sleep on the floor," she protested.

"I have to. I can't let anyone hurt you."

Tears pooled in her eyes. She gave him another hug. "Thank you."

Dave turned out the light and settled into his bag. As soon as he was quiet, he heard Paula whisper. "Goodnight, Davy. I love you."

Amy fought back tears as she listened to Dave talk about the burdens his mother thrust upon him, aching for the young boy he used to be. Amy had shouldered a lot of responsibility growing up, too, but not at that age, and Amy's mother had loved being a mom. When her mother wasn't at work, she had been home, spending times with her kids.

————————

Amy grabbed the phone on the third ring, praying it didn't wake the kids. She glanced at the baby monitor. It remained silent. Good. She glanced at the caller ID. HAMPTON, ROGER. "Hello?"

"Amy? Hi, it's Shirley Hampton, Greg's mom."

"Hi, Shirley, how have you been?"

"We're doing okay. Some days are better than others, but I don't have to tell you that now do I?" Not waiting for an answer, she continued. "I know its short notice, so feel free to say no, but Roger and I were thinking of driving to Savannah to see the kids tomorrow. Now, I know it's a holiday weekend coming up and if you've already got plans, just tell us no, and we'll come another time. And don't worry, we wouldn't dream of imposing on you. We'll get a room somewhere."

Amy did her best to hide her disappointment. "I think that's a great idea. Katy will be thrilled to see you. You'll ncvcr gct a room anywhcrc ncar Savannah this close to the weekend, much less a holiday weekend. There's plenty of room here, if you don't mind your room being decorated with naked drywall." She saw her weekend with Dave vanishing as she spoke.

"Oh, Amy, we don't want to impose on you. We can

find a room somewhere."

Amy finally convinced Shirley that it wasn't an imposition. Amy loved Greg's parents, and had always looked forward to seeing them at family gatherings. If Amy had told Shirley she had plans, they would have graciously made the trip another weekend, but they were the only grandparents Katy and Sammy had, and they hadn't seen the kids in almost two months. Driving to Greg's home, knowing he would never be there, had been too painful, but the lure of the grandchildren was too strong to keep them away for long.

"Is Katy handy? I haven't talked to her in a 'coon's age."

"I'm sorry, Shirley, she's taking a nap."

"Oh, silly me. I didn't look at the clock before I called."

"They should be waking up soon. I'll call you when Katy wakes up."

"That would be nice, Amy. Thank you. And, we'll see you tomorrow afternoon."

"Sounds great." She stopped herself before adding 'drive safely'. "Goodbye."

Amy hung up the phone. Normally it would be good to see Shirley and Roger, but she had really been looking forward to spending the weekend with Dave, meeting his daughter and some of his friends. She had heard so much about them, and she had really been looking forward to finally meeting all of them.

Reluctantly, Amy dialed Dave, explaining the change of

plans.

"Don't give up yet. I'll call Kevin and see if there's room for them to come, too."

"No, that's okay. I don't even know him. I'm a guest. I hardly have the right to ask if I can bring guests myself."

"The house has five bedrooms, a family room with two sofa beds, and two more sofa beds in the living room. Depending on how many people he's already invited, there should be room for two more. It can't hurt to ask."

"Are you sure? He doesn't even know me, and I'm asking to bring the kids' grandparents. Don't you think it's, I don't know — pushy?"

"First, you're not asking him, I am, and second, I happen to know him extremely well. Don't worry about it. Kev's a great guy, and if there's room, he won't mind at all."

"Are you sure he won't think I'm trying to take advantage of his generosity?"

"Positive. I'll call you back after I talk to him."

Dave called back a few minutes later. "Kevin said the more the merrier. There's plenty of room. It's just going to be Kevin, his wife and kids, and whoever I bring. Do you still want to leave Thursday afternoon?"

"I'll have to get back with you on that. And, thank you, Dave. It's really sweet of you to include Greg's parents."

"Think nothing of it." Amy could hear the smile in his voice. "Besides, I'm looking forward to spending time with you, and I'm really anxious for you to meet Cathy. She's going to love you and the kids."

"I can't wait to meet her. She sounds like a great kid."

Katy walked into the kitchen rubbing her eyes, wearing only her underpants. Amy-reached down and picked her up.

"Dave, the kids are waking up, so I need to go. I'll call you after I talk to Shirley. And thanks again."

A short time later, Amy called Shirley, who thought a trip to Tybee Island sounded like 'just what the doctor ordered'. After they'd finalized their plans, Amy handed the phone to Katy.

Later, after the kids were asleep for the night, Amy curled up in her favorite wicker rocker on the screened-in porch listening to the sounds of the night. She had always envied Susie getting to live amongst the beauty of Savannah.

"Susie," she whispered, "I miss you so badly." Tears streamed down her face as she poured out her heart to the darkness. "I feel like I'm drowning. I need you. I don't know what I'm doing. I'm scared to death I'm going to screw your kids up. Oh, Susie, why did you have to die?"

Chapter Ten

Amy woke up to the sound of a phone ringing, disoriented. It was still dark. Where was she? It took a moment to realize she had fallen asleep on the screened-in porch. "Hello?"

"Hey, did I wake you?"

"Yes, but that's okay. I was hoping you'd call."

"Bad news."

"Bad news? What's wrong?" She sat up, pushing the hair from her face.

"Ginger wants Cathy for the weekend."

"Oh, no. I was really looking forward to meeting her." Amy remembered Dave's fear that Ginger was using drugs. "Did you talk to Ginger or did Cathy? How'd she sound?"

"We both did. She sounded sober, and Cathy really wants to go. I'm nervous about her being all the way up in

Atlanta. That's so far away if she needs me." Amy could hear the anguish in his voice. "I don't know what to do. You dated an attorney. Did anything like this ever come up in his practice? What do I need to do to get the courts to order drug testing?"

"Well, you know that dating an attorney doesn't make you a legal expert." She laughed. "Besides, Pat didn't really talk about his work, and he didn't practice family law. If you really think Cathy would be in danger, you can always refuse to let her go, but you'd be in contempt of court. I don't know how sympathetic a judge would be if your only evidence was that she sounded strange a few times. You'd need something concrete for a judge to stand behind your refusal to let Cathy see her mom, or to order drug testing."

"I know. I don't know what to do."

"If you honestly think Ginger is doing drugs, you need to tell Cathy. If she's going to be up there, alone, she needs to know she could be in danger and she needs to know what to look for. You'd have to ask her not to tell Ginger you suspect she's using drugs. Could she keep that kind of secret from her mother?"

"I think she could, if only to spare her mother's feelings."

"I read about something like this in the paper a few months ago that sounds eerily similar to your situation. The guy was married, but suspected his wife of using drugs. He bought a brush, brushed his wife's hair, then had the hair tested. There was a big deal about allowing the evidence into court because she hadn't consented to it or something. They didn't allow that evidence in, by the way, but they did order her to submit to new testing.

"So, anyway, my completely unprofessional advice, which I'm willing to dispense free of charge, would be to buy a brand new brush. Have Cathy tell her mom how pretty her hair is and that stuff and have Cathy ask to brush her mom's hair. Unless Ginger's all goofy about her hair, she'll let Cathy brush it. After Cathy brushes it, she needs to put it in a baggie. You can have her hair tested for drugs. You can decide what to do when you know what's going on."

"That's a good idea. I'm wondering how Cathy will feel about it, though."

"Tell her the truth. You're not doing it to hurt Ginger. You're doing it to make sure Cathy is safe. If Ginger is doing drugs, Cathy will want her to get help. Make sure Cathy knows this won't get her mom in trouble with the police."

"Thanks for the advice. It's nice to have someone to talk to like this."

"My pleasure," Amy said smiling.

––––––––––––––

Amy gave Dave her address, but he already knew where she lived. He'd driven by many times over the last month, debating on whether or not to stop. He never did. He was afraid to stop. He wasn't sure where this fear came from. He'd never been intimidated by a woman before.

Dave pulled into the driveway, behind an extended cab truck and a minivan. In front of the minivan were four chest-high stacks of brick. He looked at the front of the house. A typical Victorian, Second Empire. It was small for a Victorian, but considering the economy of the South at the time it was built, the owner would have been somewhat prosperous. It wasn't overly ornate, but the ornamental touches, such as brackets, spindles, and patterned shingles made the home look expensive. Amy's brother-in-law had done a masterful job with the restoration.

He heard voices coming from the back yard, so he walked around the house. Katy was swinging. An older couple sat on a love seat making over an infant. Amy was standing with her back towards him, her long hair pulled back into a pony tail. She had on shorts and a sun top, much like what she had been wearing that day in Centennial Park and again at the River. She had great legs, tan and strong. She had a fabulous body. She looked like a Barbie doll.

Katy saw him first. She leapt from the swing and run to him. "Are you Davy?"

Amy spun around, smiling when she saw him. "Hi. I didn't hear you drive up."

Introductions were made, followed by a few minutes of small talk. The men loaded the vehicles while the women double checked their lists and locked the house. After Amy strapped the kids into their car seats in Dave's truck, he backed out onto the road. "Did you give Roger directions, in case we lose them?"

"Yes, ma'am, and I told him to put his name in his underwear, too."

They laughed and talked easily during the short ride to the island, Roger and Shirley behind them the whole way. "Here we are." Dave pulled up in front of a huge, three story beach house. "We're the first ones here. That means," he said with a wink, "we get first pick of the rooms."

Amy gave herself a tour of the house. The décor was the typical nautical theme of beach houses everywhere. White wicker furniture with floral cushions and pictures of sea shells, lighthouses and pristine beaches hung on the pastel colored walls. The only thing unexpected was the white baby grand piano in the great room. She ran her hand along the smooth surface of its graceful curves. Does Kevin play? His sister? His mom or dad, perhaps? Someone loved to play, that much was obvious.

The phone rang while the men were unloading the vehicles. "Hello?" Amy said, feeling a bit like a trespasser.

"Hey, someone's finally there. This is Kevin. Is Dave there?"

"Yes, he's here. Hold on while I get him for you." She paused a moment. "Oh, this is Amy. Thank you for having us all this weekend. It's very kind of you to include my visitors."

"Glad to have you. Mi casa es su casa."

She took the phone outside to Dave. "Phone. It's Kevin."

Amy grabbed a few bags while Dave talked on the phone. After he hung up, he stuck the phone in his back pocket and gathered up as many suitcases and bags as he could. "Kevin said they're going to Galveston to spend the holiday with his wife's sister, so they're not coming. Looks like we have the place to ourselves."

After settling into their rooms, Amy found herself with Dave in the great room, dominated by the grand piano. "Does Kevin play?"

"Yes, they all play, but the piano belongs to his mom. She was a concert pianist. She was apparently pretty good. Kevin's dad saw her playing and was smitten. And the rest, as they say, is history."

"That's romantic."

"And sad."

Amy looked over at him questioningly. "Sad?"

"She gave up her dreams for him."

"Maybe she didn't give up her dreams," Amy said, "Maybe her dreams changed."

"Maybe. I never really thought of it that way."

Dave sat down on the bench and lifted the key guard and began to play.

"You play?" Amy said, obviously surprised. She sat

beside him and watched his hands gently caress the keys.

"Kevin's mom taught me. I'm not very good, but I enjoy it. Kevin and his sister are really good." He played a classical song Amy recognized, but couldn't name.

He finished the song and looked at Amy for approval.

Amy smiled. "That was really pretty. What was it?"

"Oh, just a little ditty I wrote as a child."

"Wow, you must be proud. It must be terribly fulfilling for you to have orchestras all over the world playing your song."

He looked at her, his face serious and speaking in a somber tone. "It's a humbling experience, to say the least." He laughed. "Okay, that was Beethoven's Moonlight Sonata, but here's one I really did write."

He started playing softly. The music was soothing, yet strangely haunting. The kind of music that makes you feel something deep inside. Amy watched his hands move effortlessly over the keys. She turned toward him as he started to sing, unable to look away.

I pass by so many paths
and wonder where they lead.
Which path is it that will take me
to what it is I need?

So many times I contemplate
what path I need to take.

Am I in charge of my destiny
or is it really all just fate?

Do I possess the courage
to venture into the unknown?
Will I just walk in circles
or will this path lead me home?

When he finished playing, Amy didn't know quite what to say. She hadn't expected him to be so good. "Wow. That was beautiful. Did you really write that? The music and the words?"

He nodded.

"It was," she paused, searching for the right word, "Incredible. Really. I'm impressed. I had no idea you were so talented."

He placed his hand on her leg, sending shock waves through her body. Her heart was beating so loudly she barely heard him reply, "Thank you."

He squeezed her leg playfully before closing the lid on the keys, breaking the spell. "So, now that I've wowed you with my musical ability, how about I astound you with my physical prowess. What do you say we all take a walk on the beach?"

They borrowed Katy from her grandparents and headed out the door. Dave grabbed a pail from a shelf in the mud room. Amy looked at him and smiled. "I like your pretty pink pail."

He shoved her playfully. "Your in-laws seem like nice people."

"They are, but they aren't my in-laws — they were my sister's in-laws." She laughed.

"I know, I just don't know what to call them."

"I know. I'm not sure anymore either. How about we call them Shirley and Roger?" she teased.

"Mommy," Katy called, "can I walk in the water?"

"Okay, but only right there, no closer." Amy had her walk at the furthest point the water washed ashore. The water would wash up on her feet, making her feel like she was walking in the water.

"Katy calls you Mommy now?"

"Sometimes Mommy, sometimes Amy. I don't correct her either way."

"Kids are so resilient."

"That they are."

Dave missed the days when Cathy was this young. Little kids were so easy to please. It took so little to make them happy. He hoped he had done the right thing by letting Cathy go to Atlanta with her mother. It made him feel somewhat better when she promised to call every night, but he'd worry until she was safely home again.

They walked for a while, then turned around and headed back. They held Katy's hand and ran through the surf, and helped her find seashells. By the time they returned, the pail was nearly full.

"See," Dave said playfully, "my pretty pink pail came in handy, didn't it?"

After dinner, everyone gathered on the third floor deck, sipping wine, making small talk, and listening to the wave's crash against the shore. Katy, still afraid to be alone, was sleeping in Roger's arms. Shirley held a sleeping Sammy. Dave was sitting on the porch swing, his arm casually draped across its back. Amy stole glances at him now and again, wishing she could cuddle up next to him. A few times, she caught him looking at her. She'd smile nervously, and then look away.

"Amy, I think it's time we headed to bed. Are you sure you don't mind the kids sleeping in our room?"

Do I mind? I'm thrilled. "No, I don't mind at all. I'm thankful for the break. That sounds terrible, doesn't it?"

"Honey," Shirley said standing, "Everyone here is a parent. We've all been thankful for every break we ever got."

Amy and Dave were alone on the deck, both lost in their own thoughts.

Dave knew he should go to bed, not because he was tired, because he wasn't, and not because it was late, although it was. He wanted Amy too badly to be safely alone with her. She'd taken her hair out of the ponytail she'd worn all day. She had the kind of hair one felt compelled to touch. Her sundress, though modest enough, was also revealing enough to drive him crazy with desire. She sat sideways to him, her legs curled underneath her. She knew he was staring at her and was purposely not looking in his direction.

If he sat looking at her much longer, he'd be ready to attack her. "Would you like to take a walk on the beach?"

She tucked her hair behind her ears. "That sounds nice."

They walked side by side, barefoot, along the beach. The sky was clear and the moon was almost full, illuminating the beach with just enough light to see everything clearly. They could hear music and laughter coming from many of the houses, but the beach itself was mostly deserted.

"I don't think I will ever get tired of walking on the beach. People who grow up on the ocean probably have no idea how wonderful it is. I was in college the first time I saw the ocean. The first time I stood on a beach staring out at all that water, I thought I'd burst with joy. I still get excited every time I see the ocean. I hope I never take it for granted. I hope the kids don't ever take it for granted."

"I can honestly say I do not take the beach for granted. I feel pretty lucky to live close enough to enjoy it."

"How about Savannah?" Amy asked, looking at his profile in the semi-darkness. "Do you have any idea how breathtakingly beautiful Savannah is? Do you know how lucky you are to live there? I feel, I don't know, almost honored, every time I drive through the city or even sit in my back yard. The Spanish moss makes everything look so beautiful — so romantic."

He stopped walking and looked down at her. "That's what I admire about you."

"That I think Spanish moss is romantic?" she joked nervously, aware of how close he stood to her.

"No," he laughed, "Although it is cute. I like that you can see the beauty in everything. Even after all that you've been through, you still see beauty. I'm not sure I could see so much good if I were in your shoes."

"Don't sell yourself short. Besides, it's easy to see the good side of things in Savannah. It's amazing here."

"I think you're amazing." Dave said, reaching out, taking her face gently in his hands. He leaned in to kiss her, slowly, waiting for her acceptance or rejection. She kissed him back tenderly, slipping her arms around him, leaning into him. She could feel his heart beating against her chest. He wrapped his arms around her, pulling her closer.

The kiss ended, leaving Amy breathless and feeling as though her legs could no longer hold her weight. Dave couldn't remember a kiss ever feeling so good. "Wow," he said, hugging her tightly. She laid her head against his chest, his heart pounded in her ear. Her own heart was beating so fiercely she was certain Dave could hear it as he towered above her.

Amy barely remembered the walk back to the house. Once inside, he kissed her as he scooped her into his arms and carried her up the stairs to his bedroom.

Dave laid her gently on his bed and stood looking down at her. She was so beautiful, so sexy.

Amy looked up at him. She could see the intensity of his desire in his eyes, and it merely fed her own. She took his hand and pulled him to her. Dave lay down beside her, alternately kissing her and unbuttoning her dress. He could feel her trembling. "Are you okay?"

She laughed nervously and whispered "I don't know."

He smoothed her hair from her face and kissed her forehead. "How about I just hold you?"

"Okay," she said, both disappointed and relieved.

She flinched when he resumed unbuttoning her dress. "I promise I'll just hold you. I just want to feel your skin against mine. Trust me?"

"I trust you," she whispered.

Dave wrapped his arms around her, pulling her close. Amy lay on her side facing him, her head resting in the crook of his shoulder, their legs intertwined. She knew she had to be careful not to fall asleep, but it felt so good to lie in his arms, she couldn't pull herself away to return to her room. She'd forgotten how good it felt to be held. For the first time since Susie had died, Amy fell asleep at peace.

It was still dark when Dave woke up. Moonlight filtered just enough light into the room to make out the details of

Amy's features. What little makeup she had worn the night before was completely gone. He liked her better without it. He pulled her closer, kissed the top of her head and stroked her hair. He'd been careful not to kiss her when he lay down with her. He desperately wanted to make love to her and kissing her would only fuel a fire already nearly out of control. His desire for her was obvious. He left it up to her to take things further or just lie in his arms. He knew she was afraid.

He had been with a lot of women, but he couldn't remember one filling him with as much satisfaction as Amy had. Obviously, it wasn't a sexual fulfillment, but an emotional one. He felt safe, and that was like balm on his fractured heart. Amy quenched a thirst Dave had been unable to satisfy since Ginger left. Dave pulled Amy closer, drinking in her scent. He fell asleep more content than he could remember being in a long, long time.

Chapter Eleven

"Mommy," a little, muffled voice called, "Are you in there? Mommy?"

Amy was exhausted. In a haze somewhere between wakefulness and sleep, all she could think of was that she wished that child's mother would find her so that she could go back to sleep. With a start, Amy snapped to reality. It was Katy outside the door — Dave's door, and she was in his bed, nearly naked.

"Dave, wake up." Amy whispered, gently shaking him. "I'll be right there Katy." They quickly threw on their clothes which had been thrown on the floor by the bed. Amy looked at Dave, wondering what he was thinking. He looked at her, smiled and winked, and her stomach did flips. She would give almost anything for another few hours alone with this man. Why had she said no? How had she said no?

Amy opened the door to a tiny waitress, delivering a donut and glass of milk. "For me?" Amy asked, taking the chocolate long john. "Mmmm, my favorite kind."

"Grandma was right," she giggled. "She said you'd like this kind best 'cause grown women need chocolate like daisies need sunshine."

"Grandma is a smart woman," she said. Amy kissed Katy. "Thank you, baby, this is very good."

"Amy," Katy said, looking confused, "What are you doing in Davy's room?"

Amy looked from Katy to Dave, completely at a loss for words. Dave came to the rescue. "I needed help making my bed, and your Mommy said she would help."

Satisfied with the answer, Katy smiled at Dave. "I'll get you a donut." Katy skipped out of the room, singing as she went. A moment later, she reappeared. "Davy, do grown up men need chocolate like daisies need sunshine?"

Dave laughed heartily. "Grown men just need donuts — any kind of donut."

Katy smiled and scampered out again.

"Amy," Dave said, taking her into his arms, kissing her passionately. "Thank you."

"For what?" she asked, nearly shaking with renewed desire.

"For last night." He kissed her again. He pulled her closer as she pressed herself against him. Neither of them heard Katy enter the room.

"Are you going to be my new Daddy?"

———————————

Amy was sitting sideways on the swing, hugging her legs with her chin resting on her knees. She had been feeling rather proud of her parenting skills until she watched the ease with which Shirley took care of the children. Knowing Shirley would come looking for her after she got the kids down for their naps, Amy forced herself to think of something other than her perceived shortcomings.

Shirley joined Amy on the terrace. "Where's Dave? I thought Dave was out here with you."

"He said he had some errands to run."

Shirley lowered herself into a rocker with a sigh. "He seems like a nice man. Sure seems crazy about you."

Amy didn't answer. She wasn't sure how Dave really felt about her.

"The kids are asleep," Shirley said as she rocked slowly. "The kitchen is clean and —". Shirley paused. Amy had laid her forehead on her knees. "Are you okay?"

Without looking up, Amy replied. "Do you think I'm being selfish?"

"Selfish? About what? I don't know what you mean."

Amy looked up and stared at the ocean. "I mean about the kids. Am I being selfish to keep them instead of letting

Andy, or you, or one of Greg's brothers raise them?"

"You're not being selfish. You're being responsible. This is what Greg and Susie wanted."

"They didn't want me to raise their kids. They wanted to raise them. I'm just what happens in a worst case scenario. They never really expected that I'd be the one to raise them."

"No one expects something like this, but you have to plan for it. What's wrong? Did something happen? Did I do something or say something to upset you?"

"No, no you didn't do anything." Amy pulled her legs closer as Shirley sat next to her on the swing. "I've just been watching you and the kids. You always know just what to do, just what to say. It all seems so easy for you. I have no idea what I'm doing."

Shirley laughed softly.

Amy stared at her, incredulous. She was in agony and Shirley was laughing at her?

Shirley looked at Amy and knew she didn't understand. "Amy, I had this exact conversation with Susie when Katy was about Sammy's age."

Amy continued to stare, still confused.

"Amy," Shirley said, "every new mother feels exactly what you're feeling. You didn't have the luxury of knowing this was coming for nine months. This was all thrust upon you instantly. It's okay to feel overwhelmed. You wouldn't be human if you didn't." Shirley's voice began to quiver. "I am so sorry for abandoning you. I'd been so caught up in my own grief, so afraid to come back to Greg and Susie's house, knowing they wouldn't be there — I didn't even think about what you were going through. I should have been there for you. Can you forgive me?"

"I didn't mean to imply," her voice trailed off as she closed her eyes. She felt terrible for making Shirley feel guilty about something that was not her fault. "You don't have anything to be sorry about. I'm sorry I made you feel that way. I just can't help but wonder if they'd want me to raise their kids if they knew I would be a single mom to them. I'm sure they thought I'd be married. I'm sure they thought a dad came with the package."

Amy relayed the story of Katy walking in on her and Dave kissing that morning. "That's not what this weekend was all about. I didn't come here with the intention of playing house with Dave. Besides, we didn't do anything. He just held me. Dave and I aren't", she stopped herself before she said *'even dating'*. "What kind of person am I? I was supposed to get married this fall, and here I am climbing out of bed with a man I met a few months ago? Even if we didn't do anything, it looks bad and it's confusing Katy." Amy ran her fingers through her hair. "It's confusing me. I have no idea what I'm doing."

"I'm not here to give you advice or to interfere. I'm just here to see my grandbabies, but you clearly need someone to throw you a lifeline." Shirley took Amy's hands into her own. "Amy, you've lost a lot lately. Dave makes you happy. I can see how much you care about him, and how much he cares about you. You need a friend right now, and he's offering his friendship. Accept it.

"As for these kids, well, Greg and Susie chose you to raise these kids. They talked it over with Roger and me, with Andy, with Greg's brothers, and with you. You were single when they chose you, and you're single now. They trusted you. You love these kids, and they love you. Katy is the same sweet little girl she's always been, and Sammy is a fat, happy baby. You're doing a good job.

"You look at me and think I'm doing so much better than you could, so let me tell you what I think. I think you're doing a great job. The kids are growing. They're healthy and happy. Every mother on earth has questioned herself, me included. If I thought for one second that these kids were in danger, or that you weren't capable of taking care of them, I'd step in. But I've seen you with these kids. I'm going to leave in a few days feeling confident these kids are in good hands. I have no doubt that you'd fight a grisly bear for those babies. You love them, and they love you. Will you make mistakes? Yes. Did I? Yes. Everyone does. It doesn't make you a bad parent, it makes you human. Okay?"

"Thank you." Amy reached over and hugged Shirley.

"Why don't you take a walk on the beach? It's a beautiful day. I'll be gone in a few days, and you'll be wishing you could take one more walk alone."

Amy put on her bathing suit and headed for the beach, smiling when she saw the little pink pail Dave had grabbed yesterday for Katy. Had that only been yesterday? It seemed so long ago. She thought of big, strong Dave carrying this tiny pink pail and smiled. It was so wonderful to spend time with him, but was she being fair to him? Her life was a mess. What did she have to offer a man like Dave?

Amy found walking on the beach cathartic. There was a healing quality in the wind as it blew in from the ocean, the salty smell of the sea, and the sound of the surf pounding against the shore. This weekend was a much needed respite from the stress of the last few months. It had been only three months since the accident, but Amy could hardly remember what it was like to walk alone, with her arms swinging by her sides, not carrying someone or something.

Chapter Twelve

Dave spotted Amy walking along the water's edge towards him, her head down as she looked for shells, unaware she was being watched. She had on a white bikini with big blue flowers, the exact same shade as her eyes. Her hair was tied in a ponytail, but some had escaped. He watched her tuck the long blonde strands behind her ears. She looked fabulous. He'd arranged for an afternoon of parasailing, but he wanted nothing more than to carry her back to the house and make love to her.

He jogged up to her without her noticing. She was bending over, her backside towards him, looking at a shell. "If you don't stand up soon, I'm going to ravage you right here on the beach."

Without standing, she looked around her legs at him. "Okay," she said, laughing as she turned back towards the small shells on the sand, purposely teasing him.

He patted her bottom as he walked around her, his hand lingering with the last pat. "I have a surprise."

She stood, smiling up at him. "Really? What?"

Without answering, he grabbed her hand and pulled her back towards the house.

"Where are we going?"

"You'll see."

Dave unlocked his truck and opened the door for her. "I need to tell Shirley and Roger I'm leaving." She looked down at her feet and laughed. "I need shoes. And clothes. I need clothes."

He pointed to her beach bag sitting on the floorboard. She didn't see the picnic basket Dave had placed behind her seat. "Shirley and Roger already know. And, I packed you everything you need." He handed her a pair of sandals. His eyes danced mischievously. "Trust me?"

"I trust you." She smiled as she climbed into the passenger seat. He helped her up, leaning in to kiss her tenderly before shutting the door.

They spent the afternoon parasailing, then Dave surprised her with a picnic on the beach. It was early evening when they returned home. Amy was exhausted, but exhilarated. She went to her room to shower and change for dinner. She opened her door and saw a huge vase of large, white daisies with bright yellow centers sitting on the table by the French doors that led to the deck. The water in the vase was filled with sliced lemons, their fresh scent filling the room. Amy smiled as she read the card "You're amazing." Suddenly, she wasn't so tired anymore.

After the kids were tucked in for the night, Dave turned to Amy. "Why don't you slip into that sexy little black sundress upstairs in your closet, and I'll take you out dancing?"

"You must be thinking of someone else. I don't have a sexy little black sundress upstairs in my closet."

"Sure you do," he said, a playful grin on his face. "Go check."

Thirty minutes later, with Amy wearing the dress Dave had bought and secretly hung in her closet, they pulled out of the drive.

"How did you know what size I wore?"

"I have sisters, remember?" He grabbed her hand and kissed it. "And, the clerk was about the same size as you. She might have helped a little."

Dave parked across the street from a nightclub near the pier and helped Amy out, breathing in her perfume. He closed the door and kissed her. The sound of a woman singing, slightly off key at times, filled the air. "Karaoke," they said in unison, laughing.

"Do you karaoke?" Amy asked Dave.

"I can karaoke all night. You?"

"Absolutely," she laughed. "When I was a flight attendant, it was one of the crews' favorite things to do on a layover. It's safe to assume that I have embarrassed myself in nearly every state."

A rush of cold air greeted them when they opened the door. The inside of the bar was crowded but there were a few tables unoccupied. Dave took Amy by the hand and led her to a table near the back. The waitress, a pretty bleach blonde of college age, wiped their table clean and took their drink order. As they waited for their drinks to arrive, they flipped through the karaoke songs in the binder on the table. Without letting Amy see what he chose, Dave wrote the required information on the song form and turned it in to the disc jockey. Amy chose a song and turned it in as well.

Dave stared across the table at Amy. Her hair was down tonight, silky blonde strands framing her face. Her big blue eyes sparkled in the dim, candle-lit bar. She had a sweet, innocent look. She looked at him, smiling, and he was instantly filled with desire for her. He didn't say anything; he just looked into her eyes. He was aware that his heart was racing, and his breath had quickened. He fantasized about clearing the table with one sweep of his hand, laying her on it, and having his way with her. He wouldn't, of course, but that didn't stop him from thinking about it.

Amy looked at Dave, staring at her with such an intensity she could barely breathe. He reached across the table, stroking her hand with his fingertips. She felt his touch not just on her hand, but on her entire body. It was such a simple, sensuous pleasure. Amy closed her eyes and exhaled deeply, silencing a moan. When she opened her eyes, Dave was still staring at her. The look in his eyes was unmistakable. She knew he wanted her, and it made her want him all the more.

The disc jockey called Dave's name, breaking the spell. He touched her cheek and winked before walking to the stage. He looked relaxed, obviously comfortable on a stage. Amy immediately recognized the song as it began to play — *You've Got a Friend* by James Taylor. He looked at Amy the entire time he sang. Amy rested her chin on her folded hands, smiling contentedly as Dave serenaded her. She was flattered, and she was proud to be his date.

It wasn't long before Amy's name was called. She flashed a nervous smile towards Dave, and then headed to the stage. She wondered if she should have chosen a different song. Too late now, she thought, taking the microphone off the stand. She took a deep breath and waited for the music to start.

Dave sat back in his chair watching Amy fidget nervously as the music started. She looked incredible. The innocent sexuality she exuded was more intoxicating than his drink. She had such a soft speaking voice, and he was surprised at the power in her voice as she sang an old love song by Roberta Flack, *The First Time Ever I Saw Your Face*. She was a pretty good singer, and he was impressed.

At the song's conclusion, the male population in the audience responded enthusiastically.

As Amy made her way back to the table, a man stopped her and said something, her long hair obscuring her face as she bent closer to hear him. She tucked her hair behind her ears as she stood up, laughing, shaking her head and gesturing towards Dave. The man watched to see who Amy was with, giving Dave the thumbs up signal as she sat down beside him. Several men, Dave noted with pride, watched Amy make her way back to him.

Together they sang *American Pie* before each singing another solo. Amy sang *The Rose* by Bette Midler, and was almost moved to tears by Dave's rendition of the Righteous Brothers' *Unchained Melody*.

On the way home, Dave held Amy's hand, lightly caressing hers with his thumb. Amy's entire body tingled at his touch. She closed her eyes and let the sensation wash over her.

Dave looked over at Amy. Her eyes were closed, her chest rising and falling in long, deep breaths. It had been a long time since simply holding someone's hand caused such intense desire. Not since Ginger. He didn't want to think of Ginger tonight. For the first time since Ginger had left, Dave was actually able to force thoughts of his ex-wife out of his head and focus entirely on the woman beside him.

———————

With Shirley and Roger taking care of the kids, Amy had the first carefree weekend since the accident. Amy took advantage of the much needed break, spending most of her time with Dave. Although they never made it to the beach early enough to watch the sunrise, they were out early, jogging on the beach before the crowds hit. Days were spent taking leisurely strolls and playing in the surf, and the evenings were filled with more walks on the beach looking for a perfect place to watch the sunset. They would sit close together on the warm sand, staring out over the water, watching the sky paint itself in rarely-seen colors. And each night, Amy fell asleep in Dave's arms, careful to slip back into her own bed before Katy rose and found them together. By the time the weekend was over, Amy was more rested than she'd been in months. She was also completely in love with Dave Baldwin.

Chapter Thirteen

Amy folded the last load of laundry, thinking about Dave, hoping he would call. She was anxious to hear how Cathy's long weekend with Ginger had gone. But that wasn't the only reason she wanted him to call. Just thinking about him made her yearn for him. She was surprised at how badly she missed him. It had only been two days since they had been together, but she ached to see him, to talk to him, to touch him.

The phone rang. Amy jumped to answer it, hoping it was Dave. MCINTOSH, J.

"Jenny. Hi."

"Hey, Aim. Have any plans for your birthday Friday?"

"No plans. Guess I'll be changing diapers when I turn thirty-one."

"What about Dave? Aren't you guys doing something

for your birthday?"

"I doubt it. He doesn't know it's my birthday."

"Oh, Honey, you're missing a prime gift opportunity here. You should have told him weeks ago."

"It's kind of hard to randomly work into a conversation." Amy laughed.

"Amateur," Jenny teased. "I can leave right after work Friday, and we can paint the town red. If you can't get a sitter, we can stay at home and paint the living room." Jenny laughed at her own joke.

"That sounds great. I've missed hanging out with you."

"If Dave calls and wants to take you out, I'll still come down. I'll watch the kids while you two go out. We can hang out the rest of the weekend."

The two friends talked a long time. Amy was smiling as she hung up the phone. She always felt better after talking to Jenny, and she was excited at the thought of seeing her friend again. Amy would be glad when she had friends in Savannah. The world was a lonely place without friends.

Amy picked up the laundry basket to put the towels in the linen closet when the phone rang again. Her heart leaped. Surely this was Dave. She held her breath as she looked at the caller ID. WALKER, PATRICK.

Exhaling in disappointment, she answered the phone. He'd received the life insurance checks for Greg and Susie. He had paid their funeral expenses, medical bills and Susie's van. There wasn't much left over. Unlike Amy's mother, Susie and Greg didn't have much insurance. Amy theorized it didn't seem a priority for a young couple in their twenties. Fortunately, Amy had never bought a house and still had the money in trust from her mother's insurance. Pat thought that would be enough to get the balance on the house down low enough for Amy to swing it on a teacher's salary.

Pat explained to Amy the adoption process, what to expect, and the time it took to process and finalize.

After business was taken care of, Pat's voice noticeably softened. "How are you doing, Aim, and I mean really. How are you really doing?"

She knew he was feeling guilty for what everyone perceived as his abandoning her in her time of need. "I'm doing fine, Pat, and if you're still beating yourself up over what happened, you need to stop."

"I don't have to beat myself up. Everyone else does it for me." She knew without seeing him that he was rubbing his forehead with his fingertips, the way he always did when he was feeling frustrated or overwhelmed.

"Pat, I'm not upset with you, and I agree with your decision. I don't blame you for anything, and I don't have any ill feelings about it. I have a great deal of respect for what you did. It's hard enough to make a marriage work, even in the best of circumstances. A lot of people wouldn't have had the courage to call it off. They'd have gone ahead, gotten married and been miserable, making everyone else miserable in the process. I think what you did was noble."

"Noble, huh? I appreciate that, Amy, but it wasn't noble. It was cowardly. You have no idea how badly I feel about —" he let the sentence hang. "I feel terrible about the way everything happened."

Amy couldn't share what was really in her heart, that his leaving her had actually been a blessing. She had loved Pat, but what she felt for Pat paled in comparison to what she now felt for Dave. She was amazed at the depth of love she had for Dave, having known him for such a short time. She had dated Pat for almost four years. In comparison to what she felt for Dave, what she had felt for Pat was merely — affection. If Pat hadn't left her, she might never have known what true love felt like.

"Pat," she said softly, "You did the right thing. We did the right thing. And ending things wasn't cowardly. What you did took a great deal of courage. The next time it comes up just tell them it was mutual, because it was. Nobody left anybody. We both decided to end it."

Pat didn't reply.

"Pat? Are you okay?"

Pat confessed an ulterior motive to the phone call. He was seeing someone. He didn't want anyone to tell her and have her blind-sided by the news. "Do you hate me?"

"No," she said in complete honesty, "I'm happy for you." She didn't mention Dave.

By the time Amy got off the phone and finished

straightening up the house, it was well past midnight. Dave hadn't called. Had something happened? Had there been a problem with Cathy and her mother? She thought this last weekend was the beginning of something special between them. Was Dave upset because they hadn't made love? She didn't think so, but his silence scared her. She had fallen completely in love with Dave. Amy was confused. And afraid. What if he never called? What if he never wanted to see her again?

Cathy had been quiet since her return from Atlanta. Dave hadn't wanted to interrogate her for news about Ginger, but his curiosity was overwhelming. When Dave finally asked her, Cathy said her mother didn't sleep much and acted strangely. "She'd wake me up in the middle of the night all excited about something." Cathy said Ginger would talk non-stop, but not make much sense, seeming to start a sentence in the middle of a thought. Most times, Cathy had no idea what Ginger was trying to say. "She's lost a lot of weight, too, Dad. She's way too skinny now."

Dave had mailed the hairbrush full of Ginger's hair to a lab for testing. It had been shipped with guaranteed overnight delivery. They had received it that morning — Dave had called the lab to make sure. They said they'd mail him a formal, detailed report, but that he could call Friday to get a verbal synopsis of the results. From what Cathy had told him, he already knew what the result would be. Ginger was using drugs again. He just didn't know what her drug of choice was this time around.

It was almost midnight. He thought about calling Amy, but changed his mind. She was probably asleep, but that wasn't the reason he didn't call. He didn't call precisely because he did miss her so badly. In many ways, he was closer to Amy than he'd ever been to Ginger, and that terrified him. It also angered him. He didn't want to be that close to anyone else. He knew it didn't make sense, but he still wanted Ginger.

Amy was complicating things. She was distracting him. He knew she was probably hurt that he hadn't called her, but it couldn't be helped. Ginger was using drugs again. She was going to face rehab and she was going to need him. A tiny flicker of hope began to burn.

When Amy awoke Wednesday morning, her first thoughts were of Dave. He hadn't called. She kept going over their weekend, trying to figure out if she'd done something wrong, said something that would push him away, anything that would explain his current lack of interest. She kept coming back to the sex thing. Was he that shallow? She didn't think so, but what else could it be? They'd gotten along fabulously. A sadness she couldn't shake hung over her. If she was right, she had severely misjudged Dave's character.

She kept telling herself she was jumping to conclusions. It had only been a few days, but it didn't feel like she was jumping to conclusions. It felt like Dave was no longer interested — and she had no idea why. Until now, Dave had called her everyday, sometimes several times a day. She could see his face in her mind. She could see the fervency in the way he looked at her. It might not have been love, but it was more than just lust. Wasn't it?

After putting the kids down for their afternoon nap, Amy took the baby monitor and the phone onto the patio with her. She stared at the phone, rubbing her thumb across the keypad, trying to work up the courage to dial the phone, hoping he wouldn't confirm her worst fears. Her heart was pounding in her chest as she dialed his number slowly, hesitating momentarily before entering the last digit.

Dave picked up on the third ring. "Hello?"

"Hi. Am I calling at a bad time?" Amy paced nervously as she talked.

He closed his eyes and exhaled slowly. Even though she was trying to hide it, he could hear the anxiety in her normally carefree voice. He was ashamed of himself for ignoring this woman. She was the one ray of hope in his life. She wasn't asking anything from him, just his friendship — and he needed her friendship. He needed her companionship. He didn't need her, he told himself, he simply needed a friend. Her voice warmed him and the wall he'd built up began to dissolve. "Hi, Doll."

"I hadn't heard from you. I was afraid something might have happened with Cathy or Ginger. Is everything okay?"

Dave explained that he was waiting on the results from the lab. "It doesn't look good. From what Cathy said, I'm sure Ginger is using again. The only question is what and how much."

Amy listened to Dave talk, about Cathy, about Ginger, about drugs and rehab. It was all so foreign to her, and it saddened her that it was so much a part of his world. Eventually the conversation rolled around to the long weekend they had just spent together. Dave remembered how much fun she had been, how easily she laughed, how natural it felt to be with her.

"Have you had lunch yet?" she asked nervously.

"No. I was going to finish these plans then I figured I'd grab a bite to eat somewhere."

"You're welcome to come over here for lunch, nothing fancy, just a sandwich and potato salad or something. My neighbor brought over one of her homemade peach pies and its blue ribbon material."

Hearing her voice, so sweet and unassuming, he was ashamed of himself for ignoring her. "That sounds great. Give me twenty minutes."

Amy hung up the phone, breathing a huge sigh of relief. She dashed into the bathroom to touch up her make up and comb her hair, hoping it didn't look like she had gone to any trouble. Dave liked her hair down, so she removed the pony tail that she wore to keep it out of the way when taking care of the kids. After freshening up she curled up in a rocker on the front porch, reading a book while she waited.

Amy watched Dave pull in and park next to the pile of bricks in the driveway. He walked to the bricks, inspecting them. They were used bricks, and old, but in great condition. Where had they been salvaged from? What were they for? If Amy had no use for them, he would gladly take them off her hands. "These are great. Want to get rid of them?"

Amy joined Dave in the driveway by the bricks, running her hand over their rough surface. "I bought them for Susie and Greg for Christmas last year. The house originally had a brick porch. They rebuilt it with wood to save money, but Greg really wanted to restore it to its original brick, so" she said, waving her hand like Vanna White revealing the letters to a puzzle, "I bought them old bricks to match the walkway and drive. Greg's brother helped me find them."

Dave looked down at the brick drive and sidewalk. They weren't a perfect match, but they were amazingly close. "If you ever want to get rid of them, I'll gladly take them off your hands."

The wind picked up, blowing Amy's hair across her face. Dave brushed her hair back. She glanced up at him and smiled, then looked off into the distance. It was a look he had come to know that meant she was thinking about her sister. He couldn't imagine losing one of his sisters, even if they weren't as close as they had once been. She was under tremendous pressure, and he was in awe of her strength.

Dave lifted her face towards him and kissed her gently. He pulled her close as she leaned into him. He didn't want a sandwich for lunch. He wanted Amy. The wind blew harder and thunder crackled in the distance. The first raindrops fell as they made their way to the house.

He followed her through the house to the kitchen. It was a large, airy room with sunny yellow walls. Dark stained floors stood in stark contrast to the creamy white cabinets. Granite tiles formed the backsplash and countertops. The center island was spacious enough to easily accommodate the four bar stools tucked under its ledge. A small, round dinette occupied the bay window. Crown molding framed the room.

"This is a great room. Are the moldings original?"

Amy looked up at the moldings. "Yes. They had been painted over the years, many times. Greg took them all down and had the paint stripped off. I helped him stain it since Susie was pregnant and couldn't be around the fumes. Of course, I only came down here three or four times a month, but I helped when I could." The sunny kitchen was in the rear of the house. An abundance of windows gave a panoramic view of the backyard. A computer sat on the work area near the mud room.

"I didn't know you have a computer," Dave said, clearly

excited.

"And we've got indoor plumbing, too." she teased.

"Do you ever use instant messaging?"

"All the time, that's how I keep in touch with my brother and friends in Atlanta."

"What's your name?"

"LadyBird67. What's yours?"

"MrVandelay." He said, a mischievous smile playing at his lips.

"Mr. Vandelay?"

"Do you ever watch Seinfeld?"

"Sometimes." She laughed when it dawned on her. "Oh, I get it. George's alter ego — the architect."

"Believe it or not, Art Vandelay was already taken."

Dave inspected the architectural details of the kitchen while Amy prepared sandwiches. This was a great house.

"Your feast, Sir Baldwin," she said, setting the plate on the counter. "What would you like to drink? I have soda, milk, juice, water, beer, wine or iron fortified formula."

———————————

After lunch, Dave lay down on the sofa in the screened porch off the kitchen and family room, patting the cushion in front of him, beckoning Amy to join him. Amy slipped into his arms facing him, her head resting in the crook of his shoulder. He wrapped his arms around her, burying his face in her hair, enjoying the light, clean fragrance of her shampoo. He loved the way a woman smelled. They lay together, not talking, listening to the rain. Amy closed her eyes. It wasn't long before her breathing was deep and steady, and Dave knew she was asleep. Dave watched her chest rise and fall slowly, resisting the urge to allow his hand to travel to her breasts. He fell asleep trying not to think about what it would feel like to make love to her.

Chapter Fourteen

It was the phone call that Dave was dreading. The lab confirmed his worst fears. The results showed long term methamphetamine exposure. A variety of prescription and street drugs showed up, but meth was the most prevalent. He hung up the phone, feeling every ounce of energy leave his body. He didn't know a lot about meth abuse, but he knew the rate of relapse was higher than with any other drug. He buried his head in his hands, thinking about the long fight ahead. Would she admit her problem and go into rehab voluntarily? He might not be her husband anymore, but as the father of her child, did he have any legal recourse to force her into therapy?

The phone rang, jolting him back to reality. He glanced at the caller ID display. It was a number he didn't recognize.

"Hello?"

"Dave, it's Jenny," she paused, waiting for an acknowledgement of recognition that didn't come. "Jenny McIntosh? Amy's friend?"

Why was Jenny calling? "Oh, sure. What's up?" Dave sat up suddenly. "Is something wrong?"

"Today is Amy's birthday, and I have an idea."

At first, Dave was reluctant to go along with Jenny's plans. He wanted to wallow in self pity. After a few minutes, however, Jenny's enthusiasm became contagious. He found himself thankful for something to concentrate on besides Ginger and her problems.

Jane's daughters, Tara and Jana, came over to watch the kids while Amy and Jenny went out. Tara was painting Katy's fingernails while the little girl talked incessantly. Jana was on the floor with Sammy, playing peek-a-boo. The girls were good with the kids, and Katy adored them.

From the bathroom, Amy could hear Katy's giggles. Hearing Katy laugh always made Amy smile. Jenny said to dress up, so she'd chosen a pale blue cocktail dress with a beaded bodice. High heeled sandals showed off her legs. She wore her hair pulled back in a loose half pony tail. A few wisps were already falling, framing her face. She looked at herself in the full length mirror. She still had a flat stomach and nothing was sagging yet. It was a good dress, complimenting her complexion and her figure. Not bad for thirty-one, she thought.

Amy checked the time. It was ten minutes after eight. Jenny should have been here by now. She couldn't help but worry when someone was late. Thoughts of an accident on the interstate threatened to send her mascara cascading down here cheeks when the phone rang.

"Amy," Tara said, handing Amy the phone. "It's Jenny."

"Hey, Jen," Amy said, relieved Jenny was okay.

"I'm running a bit behind Birthday Girl, but it's worth it. I rented a limo, and we'll be pulling up out front in a few minutes. Are you ready?"

"Yeah, pretty much. I did the best I could with what I had to work with."

Jenny laughed. "You dressed up, right?"

"Yes, mother, I followed your vague directions to the letter," Amy teased.

A few minutes later a well-dressed man rang the bell, ready to escort Amy to the limousine. Amy kissed the kids goodbye and gave last minute instructions to the girls. The chauffeur opened the door, and Amy slid inside.

Jenny was smiling like the cat that swallowed the canary. "Happy birthday, Aim. Hungry?"

"Famished."

"Then let's go."

"Where are we going?"

"Elizabeth on 37th."

"Elizabeth's? That's a little expensive, isn't it?"

"Tonight," Jenny said with theatric flare, "Money is no object."

The two women talked, reminiscing on past birthdays as they made their way to the restaurant. Amy had never eaten at Elizabeth on 37th, but its cuisine was legendary — and expensive. How could Jenny afford this extravagance?

"A limousine and Elizabeth's? Did you come into some money?" Amy joked.

Jenny answered with a wink, handing Amy a glass of champagne. They toasted Amy's birthday and their friendship. The ride was short, but Amy could already feel the champagne working on her when they pulled up in front of Elizabeth's.

The ambiance of the restaurant was in keeping with its reputation. Amy and Jenny were seated at a cozy, quiet table on the side. The women enjoyed another cocktail while they waited for their dinners. Jenny ordered chicken. Amy ordered seafood. They ate their salads, talking about what they should do the rest of the weekend.

"I need to visit the ladies room," Jenny said as she stood. "I'll be right back."

The waiter removed their empty salad plates, and promptly returned with their dinners. Amy's mouth watered as the food was laid before her. "Shrimp for the lady, and steak for the gentleman."

"There must be some mistake," Amy told him. "My friend ordered chicken. And I'm here with a woman. There is no gentleman."

Confused, Amy waited for a response. The waiter's smile never wavered. He stood beside the table, hands behind his back, as if he hadn't heard her.

"I may not be a gentleman," Dave said from behind her, "but I am certainly not a woman."

Simply hearing his voice made her prickle with excitement. Amy looked behind her. "Dave," she said, completely surprised. He gave her a quick peck on the cheek before taking a seat across from her. She looked at him, smiling at the playful grin that covered his face. Dressed in a suit, Amy thought he looked very handsome.

The look of surprise and happiness on Amy's face was tonic to his downcast spirit. She looked stunning. The plunging neckline, however, made it hard to concentrate on eating or talking. He reached across the table, taking her hand. "You look ravishing."

"This old thing? Why, I only wear it when I don't care how I look," Amy said in an exaggerated southern drawl, mimicking the line from It's a Wonderful Life.

Amy declined dessert, but Dave insisted. "It's homemade French vanilla ice cream with a touch of Kaluha, served in a praline bowl. I've heard," he leaned towards her and whispered, "that it's almost better than sex."

———————————

"Dinner was exquisite. Thank you." Amy said, as Dave led her from the restaurant. It was a typical Savannah summer night; hot, humid and sultry. Amy, dressed as she was, was fine. Dave, who began melting almost immediately, removed his jacket and loosened his tie.

"Where's your car?" Amy said, surveying the area.

"Right there," Dave said, pointing to a horse drawn carriage just down the block.

"Really?" Amy said, smiling with innocent delight.

Dave laughed at her enthusiasm. "Yes, really. Come on."

Amy leaned against Dave, his arm draped across her shoulder, his fingertips tracing imaginary circles on her arm. Now it was Amy's turn to have a hard time concentrating. Dave's voice was soft and knowledgeable as he pointed out historic homes, describing their architectural style, and telling the stories of those who lived and died long ago.

"See that house right there?" Dave asked, pointing to the grand, three-story mansion they were approaching.

Amy followed his gaze to the beautiful home on the corner.

"That's the birthplace of Juliet Gordon Low, founder of the Girl Scouts. Her parents were Willie and Nelly Gordon, and theirs is one of the most celebrated loves stories of Savannah. They were married for forty-five years when Willie died in 1912, and Nelly was heartbroken. Five years later, Nelly died.

"Legend has it that as Nelly laid on her deathbed, she suddenly sat up, a radiant smile on her face, then she lay back down and died, a look of peace and contentment upon her face. Without knowing about the other, their daughter-in-law said she saw General Gordon upstairs, just prior to Nelly's passing, and the butler reported that soon after Nelly died, he saw General Gordon descend the stairs, and walk out the front door, looking as handsome, and as happy as he'd ever seen him. The butler said *'The General himself came to fetch Nelly'*".

Amy looked at the house, a tender ache in her heart. "That's so sweet. I don't really believe in that kind of stuff, but still, I kind of hope it's true."

"I know what you mean," Dave laughed, "but most folks around here accept it as *fact.*"

They lingered in front of the house a moment before turning the corner, slowly making their way through the quiet streets as Dave continued to point out places of interest and regale her with the intriguing tales of Savannah folklore.

After a while, Dave fell silent. Amy leaned her head against Dave's shoulder and closed her eyes. The only sound she heard was the clip-clopping of the horses' hooves moving along the resplendent streets of what Amy considered the most beautiful city in the world.

"You're not falling asleep are you?"

"No, just enjoying the moment." She opened her eyes and looked up at him. "Thank you so much for everything. When did you and Jenny plan all this?"

"She called me this morning."

"You did this all in one day? I'm very impressed."

"Well, it's not over yet." He reached into his pocket and handed her a small box. "Happy birthday."

Amy's heart almost skipped a beat. It looked like a ring box, but why would Dave buy her a ring? There was no way Dave would have bought her a ring, but what else could be in a box that tiny? She sat staring at it, wondering what was in it. She looked up at him with a confused look on her face.

Dave laughed at her uncertainty. "It's okay. You'll like it. Open it."

She opened the tiny box slowly. Tears came to her eyes as she removed the dainty Mother's ring. It was the Mother's ring Greg had bought for Susie on the first Valentine's Day after Katy had been born. Next to the garnet for Katy, a diamond had been added for Sammy. While pregnant with Sammy, Susie had had to have the ring cut off when her fingers swelled. They had left the ring at the jeweler's to add a birthstone for Sammy after he was born. Amy had forgotten all about the ring.

Amy's eyes misted over, and she slipped the ring onto her finger. "It's Susie's ring. How did you know? I love it," she said, throwing her arms around him. "Thank you. This has been a perfect evening."

"You're welcome." He kissed the top of her head. "Shirley told me about the ring when we were on Tybee. She gave me the claim ticket to give to you, but I forgot. So, this present isn't really from me, it's from Shirley and Roger. I'm just delivering it. But," he added, "your birthday's not over yet."

"There's more?" Amy looked up at him, smiling. "What more could you possibly do?"

"I was thinking about taking a walk on the beach. You game?"

Amy nodded. "That sounds perfect."

"And, I have a key to Kevin's beach house. Jenny packed you a bag and said she'd stay with the kids. We can stay at the beach house, or I can take you home after our walk. It's your birthday, so you get to decide."

Driving to Tybee, Amy couldn't take her eyes off of Dave. He was so handsome, so romantic, so smart and sexy and intelligent. She felt like the luckiest woman alive. She reached over, stroking his temple with her thumb. He looked at her, winked, then looked back to the road as he reached for her other hand.

Dave and Amy walked silently down the nearly deserted beach, hand in hand. Dave was gently caressing Amy's hand with his thumb. The sensation set her on fire.

She turned to him, pulling him close. "Let's go back to the house."

He didn't think he could take another night of lying beside her and not making love to her. "You know," he said, taking a deep breath, "you and that dress have been driving me crazy all night. If we go back, I can't promise to be a gentleman."

Amy stood on her tip toes to kiss his neck, then whispered, "Well, if you can't promise to be a gentleman," she teased, "then I'm afraid I can't promise to be a lady."

Dave held Amy, oblivious to everything but the feel of her lips on his neck.

"If we don't get inside soon," Dave finally said, "we're going to get arrested and be banned from the beach."

Dave led Amy into the bedroom he had used the previous weekend. He opened the door to the balcony, filling the room with the roar of the surf. Amy pulled Dave to her by his belt, kissed him, then gently pushed him into a nearby chair. She straddled his lap, removed his tie and began unbuttoning his shirt. Dave reached behind Amy, unzipping her dress.

Amy stood up in front of Dave, removed the straps from her shoulders, letting her dress fall to the floor. She stood before Dave completely naked.

Dave groaned. "Do you mean to tell me that all night you haven't had anything on underneath that dress?"

Amy smiled, a little embarrassed, "I didn't want any panty lines."

Dave pulled her close and began dancing slowing,

humming a tune Amy didn't recognize. His hands felt like fire on her skin and she moaned softly. As they explored each other's body, their kisses grew more urgent. They made love, falling asleep as the first hint of light began to peek over the horizon.

Sunlight streamed into the room when Amy and Dave awoke, still wrapped in each other's arms. Dave looked over to check the time. "We still have a few hours to kill." He said, taking Amy into his arms. "Any ideas?"

After a leisurely morning in bed, they finally rose to get dressed. Amy opened the suitcase Jenny had packed and started laughing.

Dave peered in to find nothing but lingeric and an assortment of oils and lotions. He raised an approving eyebrow. "The next time we go anywhere," he said, "Jenny packs for you."

Chapter Fifteen

As July rolled into August, the teaching certification test Amy had scheduled for the middle of the month was looming large. She had to pass the test. Without it, she could still be a substitute teacher, but only for a limited time, and at a lesser pay. She'd been studying the practice tests in whatever spare time she could carve out. Many nights it was nearly midnight before she opened her books to study.

She settled down at the desk in the kitchen when the familiar ding of an incoming instant message pulled her from study. She smiled when she saw who it was. Ever since Dave found out she had an internet connection, they frequently used instant messages and email as a form of communication. Amy signed onto the internet to check her email several times a day. It always thrilled her to hear from

Dave.

MrVandelay: Hi, doll, what are you doing up so late?

LadyBird67: just studying — what are you up to

MrVandelay: sitting on the deck missing you

LadyBird67: that's sweet:)

MrVandelay: that's me in a nutshell

LadyBird67: lol

LadyBird67: I miss you tonight

MrVandelay: miss you too

LadyBird67: have a lot of work to do?

MrVandelay: just thinking

LadyBird67: have a lot of thinking to do?

MrVandelay: yeah

LadyBird67: Ginger?

MrVandelay: yeah

LadyBird67: what's going on?

MrVandelay: she called earlier in the week

MrVandelay: she wants Cathy the last couple of weeks of summer vacation

MrVandelay: I told her no

MrVandelay: got papers in the mail today from her lawyer

MrVandelay: she's taking me to court

LadyBird67: what for

MrVandelay: papers say contempt of court

LadyBird67: can she do that?

MrVandelay: and custody

LadyBird67: custody? She can't get custody can she?

MrVandelay: guess anything is possible

LadyBird67: what are you going to do?

MrVandelay: I'll talk to my lawyer tomorrow

LadyBird67: call me

MrVandelay: ok

It was past two o'clock in the morning when Amy finally crawled into bed. She lay there thinking about Dave and Ginger and Cathy. Dave couldn't introduce the hair follicle testing results because the hair had been obtained without her consent. With no concrete evidence, Dave would have to convince a judge to order a drug test for Ginger. Dave was going to ask for Ginger to have supervised visitation with Cathy, but that would be up to the judge. Judges, Amy knew, usually ruled with caution when the safety of a child was involved, but unless there was evidence that Ginger was using again, it was anyone's guess as to which way this would go.

Dave's worst nightmare was to involve Cathy, forcing her to testify about her mother's bizarre behavior. In order to prevent that kind of trauma to Cathy, he was going to have to hire a private investigator and pray he came up with something to convince the judge to order a drug test and limit Ginger's access to Cathy.

Amy ached for Dave and Cathy, but what was causing

the most pain, and what was stealing her sleep had little to do with Dave's current crisis. What haunted Amy was how Dave inadvertently referred to Ginger as his wife. Amy corrected him once or twice before giving up. With sickening clarity, Amy realized that Dave had not yet let go of the ghost of Ginger. It didn't matter that his divorce was final years ago. In his heart, Ginger was still his wife. Amy wondered, with his heart so full of Ginger — was there any room left for her?

August eleventh dawned sunny and clear. This was the day Amy had been both anticipating and dreading. Tara and Jana came over bright and early to watch the kids while she prepared to leave for testing in Atlanta. She was as excited as she was nervous.

Katy had been thrilled to see the teenagers and began jabbering to them immediately. She quickly finished her breakfast, then grabbed Tara's hand. "Let's go play," she squealed. Tara helped Katy put on her sandals and followed the little girl to the swing set in the backyard. Jana followed with Sammy, content with his own full belly.

Amy emerged from the back door, telling the girls she was leaving. Katy was in the tree house. "Watch what I can do Mommy."

The smile fell from Amy's face as Katy pulled herself up on the railing. "Baby, get down from there."

Tara ran for the ladder, climbing as quickly as she could. Katy lost her balance just before Tara could reach her. Katy hit the ground with a sickening thud and lay motionless. Everyone screamed and ran towards the unmoving child.

Amy yelled to the girls to dial 911 as she inspected Katy for any visible wounds, careful not to move her. Amy almost threw up when she saw the bone protruding from the skin on her left arm. Terrified, she felt for a pulse and found one.

"Thank God," she said, trying her best not to cry. If Katy woke up, Amy didn't want to scare her by crying. Amy smoothed the hair from Katy's face, talking tenderly to the unconscious child. After what seemed an eternity, but was in reality was less than a minute, Katy opened her eyes and started crying. She didn't speak or try to move and Amy wondered in horror if she could move.

Amy heard the distant siren just as Jana called from the house. "The ambulance is on the way."

"You'll be okay, Baby," Amy told Katy. "Just lay still."

As the sirens grew louder, the look on Katy's face changed from confusion and pain to absolute terror. She quit crying and began shaking with fear. Amy had nearly forgotten how terrified Katy was at the sound of sirens. Amy tried to calm Katy down, smoothing her hair and talking softly. "Its okay, Baby. I'm here. I won't leave you, I promise. I'll stay right here with you." Katy's fear-filled eyes never left Amy's face.

The paramedics arrived, asking everyone to step back so they could work on stabilizing Katy. Amy felt Katy's little body stiffen. Amy looked toward the paramedics. "Please let me stay with her." She looked towards Tara. "Tell him why I have to stay with her."

Tara whispered about the accident that had claimed the child's parents. They agreed to let Amy stay close to Katy. Amy tried to stay out of their way as they examined her for injuries, breathing a sigh of relief to see Katy move her good arm and both legs in response to the paramedic's requests. They started an IV, gave the child a pain killer, and prepared her arm for transport. The drugs calmed Katy and she stopped shaking. Soon, Katy's breathing relaxed. All trace of fear was gone. Her eyes drooped, then closed.

Jane, who had come running over when she heard the screams, stood off to the side, trying to console her distraught daughters. As they placed Katy on the gurney to take her to the hospital, Jane offered to go so that Amy could go to Atlanta to take the test.

"I can't go to Atlanta," Amy said. "I told Katy I would stay with her."

"Amy," Jane implored, "if you don't take the test today, you won't get another chance until December. You won't be able to teach until next year."

"I know. I'll just have to find something else for a while. I'll figure something out." No matter how much Jane pleaded, she could not convince Amy to go to Atlanta.

Amy rode in the ambulance with Katy. Jane followed behind in Amy's van with Tara, Jana and Sammy. A guilt-stricken Tara cried into her hands as Jana rubbed her back, trying to soothe her.

Surgery was needed to set the bone, but because Katy had eaten just before the accident, the operation had to be postponed until early evening. They admitted Katy to the hospital and assured Amy that Katy would be kept sedated and comfortable in the interim.

Aside from the broken arm, Amy was relieved that there were no other injuries requiring medical treatment. Knowing Katy was going to be alright, Amy let her mind wander to her other problems. Her savings were nearly depleted. The kids were receiving social security from Greg and Susie, but they had both died so young, it wasn't much.

Amy had really been counting on teaching this semester, but having missed the test, that wasn't an option. With a degree in education, her career alternatives were limited. She had begun training to be a flight attendant immediately following graduation. Other than a flight attendant, the only thing she was qualified to do was wait tables. While her typing skills were good, she had never been employed as a secretary. Securing a decent clerical job would be extremely difficult.

Katy was temporarily settled and asleep. Tara and Jana sat beside Katy on the bed. Jane left to get Amy some coffee. Amy knew she could have gone with Jane, but she didn't want to risk Katy waking and finding her gone.

Amy excused herself and went to the bathroom, splashing water on her face. Once alone, she let fear and depression envelope her. She'd have to do the only other thing she'd ever done — wait tables. It was such hard work. People could be rude and condescending. Men could be lewd and physically aggressive. People could be the same way on a plane, but Amy had authority there and unruly passengers were not tolerated.

She would apply to some of the more upscale restaurants first, hoping her experience as a flight attendant would give her the upper hand over other applicants. Wiping the tears from her face, she went back to Katy's bedside.

Jane and her daughters left soon after Jane returned with coffee and a snack for Amy, promising to come back before Katy's surgery.

Alone at last, Amy dialed Dave's number. She needed to hear his voice. She knew Katy was going to be okay, but it was scary.

Dave answered on the fourth ring. "Hi, Amy. Can I call you back?"

"Sure, let me give you the number." Trying, unsuccessfully, not to feel slighted, she gave him the number for the phone in the room.

Dave didn't recognize the number. "Where are you?"

Amy explained where she was and why. "I didn't mean to interrupt your work. Call me when you've got a few minutes."

"Okay. I'm researching rehab centers. I need to find something right away."

"Ginger agreed to rehab?"

"Not yet, but I'm hoping to convince her to go, and I want to have options to offer her."

"Oh, okay," Amy stammered, trying to hide the betrayal she felt. "Listen, I'll let you go. Call me when you have a chance."

She hung up and hugged her legs to her chest. She rested her forehead on her knees and let the tears flow. *Would anything ever matter more than Ginger?*

Two days later, Dave had not called back. Amy, hurt and angry, decided to call him.

"Hello?"

"She's fine."

"What?"

"Katy's fine. I know you must be worried sick about her, so I thought I'd let you know you can quit worrying. She's fine."

"Oh, Amy, I forgot. I've been completely obsessed with finding a treatment center for Ginger, and I think I found one." Excitement crept into his voice. "It's in the mountains, not too far —"

"That sounds great," Amy interrupted. "Hope it all

works out."

"What's the matter with you?" Dave didn't sound concerned, he sounded annoyed.

"I can't believe you just asked me that."

"I have no idea what you're talking about."

"That, my friend, is what's the matter."

"Amy, I have no idea what you just said. Just tell me why you're mad." Dave would never understand women. Why didn't they just tell you what they were mad at? Why did they always make you guess?

"I call to tell you Katy broke her arm and has to have surgery, but you can't talk to me, let alone visit or offer moral support because you're too busy finding a rehab center for your ex-wife, who, by the way, denies she has a problem and doesn't even want therapy. What makes you think she'd even consider going to a center you picked out?" She knew she was being hateful, but she couldn't help it.

"That was uncalled for. She needs me."

"I don't know if Ginger needs you or not, but it doesn't appear she wants your help. If she agrees to rehab, where she goes will probably be her and her boyfriend's decision, not yours."

"I've got a stake in this, too. She is Cathy's mother."

"I know she is, but whether or not you have a stake in the outcome isn't the issue. The issue is that you still think Ginger needs you. You still want Ginger to need you, but it doesn't sound like Ginger wants you to fix her life for her.

She probably thinks her and her boyfriend — what's his name? Dale? Anyway, they are both adults. They can most likely take care of things without your help."

"I'm concerned about her. I have a right to be concerned, don't I?" Anger was creeping into his voice.

"I know you're concerned about her." She took a deep breath before continuing. "It sounds like more than concern. It sounds like you're still in love with her."

"Part of me will always love her. We were married for over ten years. She's the mother of my child."

Amy's voice softened. "You love her with more than just a part of your heart. I don't think you've ever reconciled your heart to the fact that she's really gone."

Dave sighed heavily. "You don't understand."

"No, I don't suppose I do."

"You're making too much out of this. Can we talk about something else?"

"Actually, I need to get off of here. I just called to let you know Katy was okay."

No, you called to pick a fight. "I'll call you later, Amy."

"Okay." She hung up without saying or waiting for a good-bye. She realized she might have gone too far, but Amy knew until Dave left Ginger in the past, she had no future with him. Tears stung her eyes as she placed the receiver back into the cradle.

———————————

Dave hung up the phone, furious with Amy. Maybe he had been insensitive to Katy's injury, but it was only a broken arm. He knew she would be okay. Ginger, on the other hand, was an entirely different matter. Ginger was going to need an immense amount of help and support over the next several months, perhaps even years. Dale, Ginger's boyfriend, had no idea what lay ahead.

Dale. Just thinking his name left a bad taste in Dave's mouth. Ginger was going to see how worthless this guy was. Dave, on the other hand, was a seasoned pro at the rehab circus. Ginger would see who she could count on. She would see who really loved her. Ginger would see who the real man was.

Dave lay back on the bed and stared at the ceiling. He wasn't really upset with Amy, he was angry that she had figured out the truth. For over two years he had been hiding his love for Ginger. No one had known how he ached to hold her again. Until now, no one knew he was still in love with her.

Amy didn't understand. She was a woman, she couldn't understand. Dave knew a lot of men who cheated on their wives and girlfriends. Most of the men he knew cheated because the opportunity presented itself. They didn't want anything more than sex with someone different. Women, on the other hand, tended to cheat because they were unfulfilled, or because they felt unappreciated. They cheated because they were unhappy, to fill an emotional void. Men cheat for sex, Dave thought, women cheat for love.

It was a man's job to make his wife happy. It was a man's job to make her feel loved and appreciated and needed and desired. And he'd failed. To Dave, he had failed at what it meant to be a man — and it ate at him. How many nights had he lain awake, staring at this same ceiling, trying to figure out what he could have done differently? Even now it frightened him, because he still couldn't see where he'd gone wrong. He hadn't been a perfect husband, but he'd tried as hard as anyone ever could. His best hadn't been good enough. He just wanted another chance to show Ginger he could be enough for her.

Amy's anger was legitimate. If the shoe had been on the other foot, he would have been outraged as well. He would apologize, everything would be back to normal, and they would be friends again. He knew Amy was scratching her head at him, wondering why he would want a woman who had dismissed him so callously. Amy had to think he was terribly foolish for wanting Ginger back in his life. Amy would really think he was crazy if she knew everything.

Chapter Sixteen

List in hand, Amy headed out the door. The first stop was dropping the kids off at daycare, which she called school for Katy. Katy sang and chattered non-stop on the drive to Precious Cargo Daycare. If Katy was anxious about going, she sure didn't show it. Amy, on the other hand, was on the verge of tears at the thought of leaving them, despite the glowing reviews she had heard of this place.

Precious Cargo had been the brainchild of several local single mothers who worked odd shifts and found it difficult to find reliable child care. They opened a daycare that was open twenty-four hours a day, seven days a week. It was more expensive than conventional daycares, but for those who didn't work typical workday hours, it was a godsend.

Amy dropped Sammy off in the infant room, then took Katy to her classroom. Katy didn't let the fact that her arm was in a cast slow her down one bit. She kissed Amy goodbye, then quickly disappeared into the room of busy preschoolers. Katy's teacher, Miss Stacy, was obviously a pro at dealing with distraught parents, assuring Amy that Katy would be fine. Blinking back tears, Amy barely spoke.

With the children in daycare, Amy went to restaurant after restaurant, seeking employment. This hadn't been the plan. She had planned on working as a substitute teacher until a permanent position opened up, but she'd missed the test when Katy broke her arm. They had been living on her savings, and the money she'd received from selling her car. There wasn't much left. She had to get a job, anywhere, and soon.

None of the restaurants on her list were hiring. She lost count of how many applications she filled out. Out of desperation, she began stopping at every eatery with a wait staff. While filling out yet another application, she looked out the window. Across the street was a somewhat neglected building, draped in old fish nets, shells and assorted nautical items. A small sign was propped in the window 'Now Hiring - Servers Wanted'. Amy hurriedly finished the application she was working on and rushed across the street to The Seafood Station.

It was late afternoon, in between what would be considered the lunch and dinner crowds. Even so, the dining room was half full. The bar, to the right of the entry way was about half full as well, with people eating a late lunch or watching sports on the television while nursing a drink. The tables were old, thick and sturdy, worn and scratched from decades of careless dining. Though the rooms had a tired look, Amy found them charming.

"How many in your party?" The young woman at the hostess station said. Shannon, according to her nametag, was looking at her, smiling warmly. She had the southern accent of a Georgia native.

"I'm inquiring about a server position. Are you still looking for someone?"

"Oh, my goodness, yes," she gushed. "Let me go get Patsy. Come in here and have a seat. I'll be right back."

Amy sat at a table just inside the dining room, her back to the wall. A moment later, Shannon came back with an older, heavyset woman in an apron. Like Shannon, she had a warm, genuine smile that put people at ease. Amy stood as they approached.

The older woman wiped her hands on her apron, then extended one to Amy. "I'm Patsy Stone. My husband Ted and I own this place. Welcome. Please, sit down."

"Amy Cooper. It's nice to meet you." Amy shook her hand and sat down. Shannon brought Amy and Patsy sweet tea before resuming her place at the hostess station.

Patsy told Amy the history of the restaurant with obvious pride. Patsy laughed easily, and Amy found it impossible not to like her. A half hour later, Amy was sitting in the van holding her schedule for the next two weeks. Four polo shirts in bright, tropical colors emblazoned with The Seafood Station logo lay on the passenger seat.

Despite the fact that she had thought waiting tables was in her past, relief flooded over her. Working at a restaurant was hard work. Amy wasn't opposed to hard work, she had just always thought that by this point in her life, she'd be settled in a career. She didn't even mind the odd hours. What she wasn't looking forward to was prying men's hands off of her again. In today's age of enlightenment, did men still grope servers? Aside from the much-needed paycheck, Amy was anxious to meet new people and find some friends her own age. She had been desperately lonely since moving to Savannah. Work, if nothing else, would give her something besides tragedy and loss to monopolize her thoughts.

Dave hadn't called for several days. Amy wasn't sure if she would hear from him again. She hadn't been very nice when she last talked to him. She fought the urge to call him. He apparently didn't miss her. He still loved Ginger, and his time was spent trying to fix Ginger and win her back.

Thoughts of Dave caused her chest to feel as though it had been put in a vice. She felt foolish. She loved Dave and had thought he loved her, too. Had she just been a distraction to him? Something to take his mind off of Ginger while he waited for her to run back to his open arms? He had seemed so genuine. Was she seeing what she wanted to see rather than the truth? She played and replayed their times together, their long conversations on the phone, the instant messages, the emails. She concluded she wasn't imagining things. Dave did treat her like he loved her. He had likely never stopped to analyze how she would perceive his romantic gestures. It was possible he was just toying with her, but it made her feel better to think that he didn't realize it.

———————————

Needing both the money and a diversion from her pain, Amy worked as many hours as she could. Unwilling to record over Susie's voice and unable to hear it every time she didn't get to the phone in time, Amy had simply disconnected the answering machine. Aside from Jenny and Andy, no one else ever called.

Dave listened to the phone ring over and over. Where was she? Was she purposely ignoring him? She had to be. He'd called at all hours of the day and night, and Amy never answered. He knew he'd hurt Amy's feelings, but he didn't think what he had done had warranted severing their friendship. After a few more days of trying to reach Amy, he quit calling.

Perhaps this was for the best. He could now concentrate on Ginger. He convinced himself that the emptiness he felt was due to Ginger's absence, not Amy's.

Chapter Seventeen

Dave took another bite of Seafood Alfredo, mopping up some sauce with a freshly baked yeast roll. It had been a while since he'd eaten here. Ginger, preferring the new contemporary chain restaurants, hated this place and had refused to eat in *'that dump',* despite the fact they had some of the best seafood in the South.

The dining room and bar were usually filled with locals, although the occasional tourist would wander in. The Seafood Station was one of those fabulous restaurants that the travel magazines somehow missed on their journey through Savannah. He supposed it was because the exterior wasn't as inviting as some, but the building was solid and strong. It would be here long after the newer buildings fell victim to the elements.

A football game was on the big screen television in the

bar. Dave could see only a portion of the screen from his vantage point in the dining room. He didn't know who was playing, but judging from the crowd and the noise emanating from the bar area, it was a big game.

"Amy," a voice called from the bar, "Where are you? We need you, Amy."

Amy? The name piqued Dave's curiosity.

"If you boys don't learn to wait your turn, I'm going to sit you in time out," a feminine voice teased.

Dave immediately leaned back in his chair and glimpsed into the bar. It was Amy. What was she doing working here? Hadn't she said she was going to teach?

Dave watched Amy walk up to a large round table full of men. He couldn't hear their conversation, but he could tell Amy was speaking. The men erupted in laughter. One of them said something in return, and he could see Amy laughing with them while she cleared the dishes from the table. He was still watching when she returned a few moments later with several pitchers of beer.

As Amy leaned over the table, Dave noticed several men eying her backside approvingly. He was surprised at the intensity of his feelings, as jealousy surged through him.

Dave paid his bill, leaving a generous tip. Breathing deeply to calm himself, Dave walked into the entryway, as if to leave. Amy was leaning against the bar, propped on one elbow, her back towards the entry, waiting for the bartender to fill an order. Dave waited by the door, pretending to look in his wallet until Amy turned around and saw him. He looked up, feigning surprise. "Amy." He forced a confident smile, putting his wallet in his jacket pocket. "Hi."

A nervous smile appeared on Amy's face. She wanted to run into his arms and tell him how much she'd missed him, that she still loved him and thought about him every day. Instead, she simply answered, "Hi."

God, she's pretty, Dave thought. Amy stayed rooted to her spot, so Dave approached her and gave her a quick hug. "You look great."

"Thanks," she said, "You do, too."

"You work here?"

Amy nodded. "I started in August."

"I thought you were going to teach."

"I missed the certification test. I was getting ready to leave to take it when Katy fell and broke her arm."

Ouch! He hadn't wanted to touch that subject quite yet. "Look, Aim, I owe you an apology about that. I was insensitive and —"

Amy waved her hand, cutting him off. "No, you don't. I was out of line with you. I said some things I had no business saying. I was rude and —"

"Amy, here's your drinks." the bartender interrupted, "Your food order's up, too."

Amy looked at Dave apologetically. "I have to get back to work."

"Oh, sure. It was good to see you again."

"You, too." Her heart was pounding in her chest.

"Amy." The cry came from the table of men so friendly with Amy.

Amy rolled her eyes. "My fans beckon."

"Friends of yours?" Dave asked, walking with her.

"No, just regulars. Not sure which they like more; sports, beer, or crab legs." She smiled and walked away. Dave watched as she expertly held the tray with one hand and removed the drinks with the other.

She turned around just as the door shut behind Dave. Amy felt the familiar tightness in her chest returning. Seeing him hurt worse than she had expected. It felt like someone tore off the scab covering the wound Dave left in her heart, ripping the sore open all over again. She somehow forced a smile and managed to finish her shift without falling apart.

———————

Dave couldn't get the image of Amy out of his head. Nor could he erase the image of the men leering at her. He didn't mind men giving her an appreciative look, but he didn't like the way they looked at her. Seeing her rekindled the desire he had for her. She always had that effect on him, even when he tried to be just friends it had been all he could do to keep his hands off of her.

He supposed he shouldn't have given up on her so

easily. He tried calling her only a handful of times before deciding she was ignoring him. He realized now that she was probably working and had no idea he'd tried to contact her. She probably thought he'd been ignoring her. But why hadn't she called him? Or emailed him? On the other hand, why hadn't he emailed her? Question after question flooded his mind as he drove home; first and foremost being was it too late? Had he lost her for good?

———————

The old wooden floors creaked under her weight as Amy tip-toed to the doorway of Katy's room. It never ceased to amaze her that they could sleep through being taken from bed in the middle of the night, bundled up and transported across town, then continue to sleep as the process was repeated in reverse. Moonlight filtered through the curtains, casting lacey shadows on the walls. Katy lay on her side, one arm under her pillow, the other wrapped around her favorite doll and a small teddy bear. The doll used to be named Clementine, but a few months after the accident, Katy started calling her Susie. She called the bear Daddy Bear.

Leaning against the door frame, Amy watched Katy sleeping. How much would she remember of her parents? How much better would her life be if Susie and Greg hadn't died? "Please," she prayed silently, closing her eyes, "please let me do a good job raising these kids." Amy pulled the door closed and walked to her room, pulling off her shirt as she went. She threw her clothes on the chair, put on pajamas and climbed into bed.

Even though it was well past midnight and she was exhausted, she couldn't sleep. Why did Dave have to show up now, just when she'd met someone else? She'd been going out with Jason a few weeks now. He was a single father sharing custody of his kids. They had met dropping their kids off at daycare. He had been asking her out since August, but she couldn't get Dave out of her head, so she declined his offers. But his persistence paid off and she had finally agreed to go out to dinner with him a few weeks ago. He was surprisingly funny, and she enjoyed his company. He worked as a civilian Aeronautics Engineer at Hunter Air Force Base. Though she tried not to, she often found herself comparing Jason to Dave. Jason was a great guy — but he wasn't Dave.

She enjoyed being around Jason and was just beginning to feel like she might be able to open up her heart to him, and then she saw Dave. She knew she was still in love with Dave, but she hadn't expected the feelings to be so intense still. She hadn't been prepared for how hard it would be to see him or to talk to him again, much less try to hide the fact that it felt like her heart was being ripped from her chest the entire time.

Like every other night, Amy's last thoughts before sleep took over were of Dave.

———————————

Dave woke early. The sun wouldn't be up for hours. He'd be back in plenty of time to get Cathy up and ready for school. He shaved, showered and headed out the door.

He turned off his headlights as he pulled into Amy's driveway. He shut off the engine and sat in the dark, wondering how receptive Amy would be to him. He took out his phone and dialed. One ring. Two. Three. Four. Five. He was just about ready to hang up when she answered.

"Hello?" her voice was groggy.

"Hi, Doll"

Dave? Dave was calling her? Hearing his voice sent her heart racing. "Hey, Stranger." He could hear the smile in her voice.

"What time do the kids wake up?"

"Around seven. Sometimes they sleep clean up to seven-thirty."

"Can I come in?"

"Where are you?"

"Out front."

"Of my house?"

"Yes, can I come in?"

Amy looked over at the clock. It wasn't even four o'clock yet. "Okay, sure."

"Open the door, then go back to bed," he instructed.

She laughed nervously. "What exactly do you have in

mind?"

Dave laughed. "Nothing, I promise. I just need to hold you. Trust me, okay?" His voice was soft and soothing. And sexy.

"Okay," she whispered, "I trust you."

Amy unlocked the door then climbed back into bed as directed. She lay on her side, waiting for Dave's silhouette to appear in the darkened doorway. A few minutes passed before she heard his footsteps in the hall. Anticipation welled within her. Was he back for good? Dare she hope to believe her prayers had been answered?

He came into the room and lay on the bed next to her, pulling her close. He kissed her on the forehead.

"I've missed you."

"I missed you, too." she whispered, burrowing deeply into his embrace.

"Close your eyes and go back to sleep" Dave whispered. "And don't worry, I'll make sure to be gone before Katy wakes up."

For once Amy just enjoyed the moment without trying to analyze it. She fell back to sleep content, relaxed, and happy. Dave was back, and Jason became a thing of the past.

Chapter Eighteen

"What are you doing for Thanksgiving? Do you get together with your family?" Amy asked Dave as she snuggled against him on the sofa a few weeks later.

"We get together with my mom at a restaurant on Thanksgiving. My dad invited all of us this year, but none of us have seen him in years. He's in Ohio now. I think Paula and Wendy are driving up that Friday. Tammy isn't going. I haven't decided if I want to go or not. It would be really awkward to sit around with him pretending to be a family again."

Dave's father, an over the road truck driver, saw his children only a handful of times after the divorce. He was a stranger to them. He didn't call or send a card for their birthdays, and there was never a present under the tree from him. Dave knew this for a fact. He searched under the tree year after year, hoping his father had sent something for them. He couldn't remember how old he was when he came to the conclusion that when his father walked out the door, he divorced not only his wife, but his children as well.

"Maybe he's sorry. Maybe he's trying to make it up to you guys." Amy suggested optimistically.

"Maybe." Even if his father wanted to make atonement, Dave didn't know if he'd ever be able to forgive his father for all the years of neglect.

Amy put a pillow on Dave's lap and laid her head on it. He instinctively played with her hair.

"Would you like to go to a party with me?" Dave asked.

"When is it?"

"Friday at seven o'clock. It's for work. It's really just a long, boring, holiday cocktail party."

"Gee, how could I say no to an offer like that," she teased.

"Sorry," he laughed. "They're not too bad really. It gives the women a reason to wear a fancy evening gown and hang around in a room full of men in penguin suits."

"I love men in penguin suits," Amy said smiling. "Count me in."

"Do you have a dress to wear, or do we need to go shopping?"

"I have something. I can even give you a fashion show and you can decide which one you like best."

"Hmm," Dave smiled, "I like the sound of that. Can you

do me a favor?"

"Sure, if I can."

"Wear your hair down, in curls."

"Curls, huh?" She looked up at him.

"I have a weakness for curly hair."

"I suppose I can do curls for you."

"So, what about you?" Dave asked, "What are you doing for Thanksgiving?"

"Andy and Cindy are flying in with little Mikey. I'm really looking forward to seeing all of them again. And Cindy's pregnant again! I sure wish they'd move closer."

"Too bad you have plans. You could have joined my family for our blessed gathering."

"Gee, that does sound tempting." Her voice was muffled in the pillow. "If you keep playing with my hair," Amy said, "I'm going to fall asleep on you."

Dave spanked her bottom. "Well, then, I'll stop. I have other plans." He rolled her over and kissed her before carrying her to her bed. "Do I get my fashion show before or after?"

"You're incorrigible."

The cocktail party that Friday was the first of several Amy attended with Dave. Despite having been forewarned that these functions were somewhat boring, Amy found them to be quite the opposite. She enjoyed being around

Dave and getting to know the people he spent his days with. The fact that Dave was incredibly handsome in a tux didn't hurt, either.

Tonight's party was being held at the estate of Mr. Anderson, the senior partner at Dave's architectural firm. He had built an antebellum style home in the countryside of Chatham County. The ornate mansion rivaled anything the wealthy plantation owners of pre-civil war America had ever dreamed of building. It stood to showcase both his wealth and his firm's exceptional talent. It did both exceedingly well.

Amy had labored over what to wear, laying dresses out on her bed, grateful for her flight attendant days spent bargain shopping all over the country. With little else to do on layovers other than sleep or work out, Amy and her co-workers would hit outlet malls and thrift stores. Everyone, it seemed, knew of an out of the way shop that sold expensive clothing for a pittance of their original cost. Amy had been able to find extraordinary deals. Designer dresses with rips, tears or stains, originally selling for thousands of dollars, would sell for the price of a discount store skirt. It took the talents of a skilled tailor to repair some of the dresses, but Amy had been able to fix most of them on her own. The result was an impressive array of cocktail dresses and evening gowns she bought wondering if she would ever have an opportunity to wear them. To her pleasant surprise, they had come in handy when she dated Pat, and they were once again proving their worth with Dave.

After trying on all the gowns and carefully scrutinizing herself from all angles in the mirror, she decided on a non-pedigreed evening gown of burgundy silk. To Amy, it was the epitome of understated elegance; a halter-style dress with the tiniest of straps that crisscrossed over the open back. She slipped on stiletto sandals, surveying how the dress lay against her curves. A cashmere wrap to ward off the November chill and the ensemble was complete. It was tasteful and appropriately sexy.

Dave looked across the room at Amy, talking animatedly with a group of people. She wore her hair pulled away from her face, loose curls trailed down her back. He could hardly take his eyes off of her. She looked stunning in that dress. At one point or another, every man in the room had glanced longingly at her. She was elegant, gracious, charming, and funny. A great conversationalist, she could fit in at any party. Everyone seemed to love her. He was proud to walk into the room with her on his arm. He knew he was lucky to have Amy in his life, and yet he couldn't stop wishing she were Ginger.

In anticipation of the drive home, he had switched from whiskey to water. He made his way down a darkened hall to the restroom off the study. As he was returning to the party, he overheard two women talking. He recognized one of the voices. It was Missy, the receptionist at the firm. The other voice sounded familiar, but he couldn't place it. They were talking about Amy. He stopped in the hallway, around the corner from the women, eavesdropping

"Did you see that Dave brought Amy again?" Missy said.

"Yes." The other replied, in obvious amazement. "What's that make now? Three?"

"Four, I think."

"Well, this is a record for him. I can't remember seeing the same girl twice before Amy."

"Me either. Did you ever talk to any of his other dates?"

"I always tried to spend as little time as possible with Dave's dates." They both laughed. "Amy sure is sweet, though, isn't she?"

"Yes, she is. His taste is definitely improving, but anything is an improvement over those anorexic amazons he used to bring. And you know, you can tell he really cares about Amy. I can see it when he looks at her. He never looked like that at those bimbos he used to bring."

"I noticed that, too. I think he's really serious about this one."

"I wouldn't be surprised if we were invited to a spring wedding."

"But you know, even those airhead bimbos were better than Ginger."

"Tell me about it. She sure didn't like any of us, did she?"

"I'm not even sure she liked Dave." They continued

talking, their voices growing faint as they walked away laughing.

Their words cut through him. They hadn't liked Ginger? Why? He was dumbfounded. He thought everyone had loved Ginger. And just because he'd brought Amy to a few business parties, they thought he was serious about her? He hoped they hadn't picked out a dress to wear to his wedding because he wasn't marrying Amy in the spring. He wasn't bringing her to any more parties, either. And, he quickly decided, he also wasn't going to introduce Amy to his family. He didn't want them getting any ideas about the way he looked at her. He knew it was irrational, but he was suddenly furious with Amy.

Dave took a moment to compose himself, then walked into the room, intent on finding Amy and leaving. Before he could locate her, a couple of women approached him. "Dave, where's your girlfriend?"

He pretended to be confused. "My girlfriend?"

"Yes. Where's Amy?"

"Amy's not my girlfriend. We're just friends." No sooner had the words left his lips than he saw Amy walking up behind the women. She was looking right at Dave. He saw the look of pain in her eyes, but only for a moment. She quickly recovered her equanimity as she walked around the women, linking her arm through Dave's.

"Dave and I aren't dating. We're just friends." She leaned towards the women. "I have a little better taste than this." She motioned with her eyes and head in Dave's direction. Everyone laughed.

Amy was smiling and laughing, making small talk with his coworkers. She appeared happy and carefree, but Dave knew better. She could hide her feelings from everyone else, but he knew her well enough to see through her façade of gaiety. He had really hurt her. He was dreading the drive home.

Amy chatted with another couple as they walked to Dave's car. Once inside, she sat quietly. Her head turned slightly away from him, she simply stared out the side window into the blackness. Dave had been prepared for her to lay into him, but she didn't. Her arms were crossed, holding the wrap tightly around her.

They drove in silence until they reached town. This was almost worse than getting yelled at, Dave thought. He contemplated what to say. Nothing was adequate. He simply said. "Amy, I'm sorry."

She waited a few moments before answering. "I know," she replied, not turning to look at him.

He looked at her, wishing he could say something to make things right, but what could he possibly say?

In her peripheral vision she saw the light change. Dave made no attempt to move.

"The light's green," Amy said. Her voice sounded sweet. And fragile. And full of pain. He'd expected her to be full of rage, but she didn't sound mad. She sounded tired.

And betrayed.

He pulled to the side of the road and put the car in park. He reached over and rubbed her cheek with the back of his fingers. "Amy, I—"

"I know you're sorry," she interrupted him. Still looking out the window, she continued. "I just don't know what you're sorry for. Are you sorry about what you said or that I heard it? Are you sorry for humiliating me or just that it was done it public? Are you sorry that what you said hurt me or sorry that it's true? Are you sorry for leading me on or sorry that your cover's blown? I know you're sorry, Dave, I just don't know exactly what you are sorry for."

"Everything," he said softly. "I'm sorry for everything." He wasn't angry at her anymore. He was angry at himself.

Amy looked down at her fidgeting hands. She took a deep breath and spoke from her heart. "Do you know I thought you loved me?"

Dave remained silent. Yes, he knew that — now. Unspoken, but implied, was that she was in love with him. He had been very selfish when it came to Amy. He loved being generous. He loved being romantic. It made him feel good to see her eyes light up when he did nothing more than bring her a pack of her favorite gum. The only problem was he never stopped to consider that Amy didn't know the things he did were as much for him as they were for her, and for that matter, neither had he — until now. He had felt so dead inside since Ginger left. It made him feel alive, if only momentarily, to make a woman happy.

She turned to face him. "Will you make me a promise?"

"What?"

"Don't treat me like I'm your girlfriend if I'm not. Don't touch me like you love me if you don't." Her voice was barely above a whisper.

"I give you my word." Dave put the car in drive and pulled away from the curb.

"I'm cold. Can you turn on the heat please?"

Dave immediately turned the heater on high.

The rest of the drive was quiet — and hot — but he wasn't about to complain about the heat after what he'd done to her. Dave pulled into her driveway, thankful for a reason to get out of the car turned sauna. Amy was out the door before he could turn off the engine, let alone walk around to open her door. He got out, intercepting her in front of the car.

She stopped, looked at him briefly before looking toward the house and the safety it offered. "Thank you for tonight," she said, her voice shaking. "Mr. Anderson and his wife were very gracious hosts."

"Can I come in?"

She shivered. It was colder than she had anticipated and the thin wrap was insufficient protection against the weather. "I don't think that's a good idea." She didn't want to be alone with Dave right now. She was feeling vulnerable, and it would be easy for him to take advantage of her. "It's late and I have to get up early in the morning."

"I wish you'd let me come in."

"I'm really tired. I just need to get some sleep." And sleep until the pain goes away, she thought. She glanced again towards the house. She needed to get inside before she lost control and started crying. "Besides, I don't think I'd be very good company." Why would he want to come in, she wondered? Surely he wasn't expecting her to make love to him after what he'd said.

"Amy, you're my best friend. I need you. I need your friendship. Can we still be friends?"

She didn't want to be just his friend. She didn't know if she could be just friends. But, unless she was ready to let him slip from her life completely, she didn't have much choice but to agree.

"Sure, we can be friends." She felt the fissures in her heart beginning to give way. She searched in her purse for her keys, desperate to get inside. Relief flooded through her when she found them. Now she could go inside and fall apart in private. "Goodni—"

Dave cut her off. "I go to court again tomorrow. They announce the results of the drug testing and decide about visitation."

"I know. I've been praying things go well for you."

Dave fell into step beside her as she walked briskly towards the door. "I appreciate that. I'll call you tomorrow." He barely got the words out before she slipped inside, leaving him on the porch alone. He rubbed his face with his hand. He closed his eyes, shaking his head. "Damn." He'd really screwed up this time.

Amy changed out of her dress and sat in the sunroom, illuminated only by the light of the moon. She had always heard people did strange things during a full moon. Could she blame Dave's callous comments on the moon, even if it wasn't quite full? It would be nice if she could, but she knew the moon had nothing to do with Dave's actions. The pain of the evening, coupled with the pain of the last half year suddenly seemed too much to bear. Great sobs wracked her body, and she softly cried out for answers. A lonely silence answered her gut-wrenching pleas. If the night held any answers, it kept them hidden well. Amy sat in the dark wondering when the pain would end, wondering when the crying would end.

She had heard a story once of a couple who caught a mouse in their kitchen. Not knowing what to do with it, they threw it in a bucket of water to drown. Not having the stomach to watch it suffer, they decided to take a walk, knowing it would be dead when they got back. Upon their return, they looked in the bucket. To their surprise — and horror — it was still alive. It was standing against the side on its hind legs, with only its nose sticking above the water.

That's how the last few months had felt; like she was standing on her tip toes, with only her nose sticking out of the water. She couldn't relax, or she'd drown. There was no family or friends to turn to anymore. She'd left all of those behind. It was just her, praying for the strength to make it through another day.

Dave had inspired her. He had given her the strength to stay on her toes one more day. He had given her hope that she wouldn't be struggling alone forever. With Dave, she had tasted love. True love. The kind of love everyone dreamt of. The kind of love that caused a little old man to die within hours or days of losing his beloved wife. The kind of love most people thought was only a myth. Maybe the myth was that both people would feel that way.

With Dave, she was *Amy*, not mommy, or the cook, or the housekeeper, or the nurse, or one of the other dozen hats she had to wear. She was just Amy. A woman. It felt so safe to be wrapped in Dave's strong, capable arms. Snuggling into Dave felt like coming home.

Now here she was again, her heart broken, willing herself to breathe in and out. Willing herself to believe that life wouldn't always be so hard and lonely. Willing herself to believe that she would love once again — and that it would be returned.

But tonight, it was hard to believe in anything besides the pain. This time, her heart didn't just break, it exploded, and she wasn't sure if it was possible to ever be whole again.

She was pulled back to reality by the sound of Katy's frightened whisper.

"Mommy, are you okay?"

Wiping the tears from her face, Amy reached out, beckoning Katy into her outstretched arms. "Sure, Baby, come here," Amy said. Katy flew onto her lap. "Mommy's okay. I'm just a little sad right now."

Katy's face contorted with fear and concern. When she spoke, her little voice quivered. "Why? Did somebody else have to go live with Jesus like my Mommy and Daddy?"

"Oh no, Baby, nothing like that." Amy saw relief flood over the little child's face. Amy pulled her close. "It's kind of like, well," Amy paused, searching for the right words. "It's kind of like when you skin your knee. You know how it hurts really, really bad when you first do it?"

Katy looked up at her, nodding.

"And then it feels better the next day? And even better the day after that? Then pretty soon, the boo-boo's all gone and you feel all better?"

Katy nodded again.

"That's kind of how Mommy feels right now. I'll be really sad today, but I'll feel a little better tomorrow and a little better the day after that. And pretty soon, I'll feel all better again. Okay?"

Katy sat up, turning to look at Amy's knees, searching for the tell-tale scab or bandage. "Did you fall down?"

"No, Sweetie, it's a different kind of boo-boo. It's one you can't see."

Katy reached up, gently wiping the tears on Amy's

cheek. "Mama, if you show me where it hurts, I'll kiss it and make it all better."

"You've already made me feel better. Just holding you makes me feel better." Amy pulled her close and hugged her, kissing the top of her head. "I love you, Baby doll."

"I love you, too, Mommy."

Katy snuggled against Amy. They rocked in silence, listening to the cadence of the crickets. Amy rested her cheek on the top of Katy's head, staring out the window into the blackness.

Katy's tired voice broke the silence. "Mommy, can you sing to me?"

"Sure, Baby. What do you want me to sing?"

"A mace an' krace."

Amy stifled a laugh. "Okay, close your eyes." Amy cradled Katy close, softly singing Amazing Grace. Katy's breathing grew deeper and slower. Amy could tell she had fallen asleep before she'd reached the chorus.

Chapter Nineteen

The next morning, Andy called. Cindy, just a few months pregnant, was on bed rest. They wouldn't be able to make it for Thanksgiving. He knew how hard these last few months had been on Amy. Andy was anxious to see how Amy was making the adjustment. She always claimed to have things under control, and knowing how capable Amy was, she probably did. But he wanted to see for himself. And, he knew she could use the break a couple extra pair of hands could provide. He offered to come alone, but Amy knew Cindy needed him there.

Amy hung up and sat holding the phone, feeling drained and disappointed. There was always Dave's offer to spend Thanksgiving with his family. Dysfunctional though it may be, it would be fun to meet his mom and sisters. She could only imagine the stories they could regale her with. That is, if the offer was still good. He claimed he wanted to be friends, but after last night, she wasn't sure if she'd ever see or hear from him again.

She'd barely hung up before the phone rang again. Ten minutes later, Amy hung up, having made plans to send the kids to Tennessee to spend the holiday weekend with their grandparents. She had been invited, too, but she held out hope that Dave would call and make good on his earlier invitation. After what he'd said last night, she should wash her hands of him, but she couldn't. She'd always been told that actions speak louder than words. His words might be saying that they were just friends, but his actions were screaming something else.

True to his word, Dave called. Amy told him about her brother not being able to make it in and the kids going to Tennessee. She expected him to remind her of his offer to spend Thanksgiving with him and his family, but he didn't. He commented he was sorry about her brother, but that it sounded like the kids would have fun. Then, he changed the subject. Amy was crushed. This was the first Thanksgiving without Susie and Greg. Then Andy cancelled. Then she agreed to let the kids go to Tennessee. Now, with Dave reneging on his invitation, she was going to have to spend it alone — or working. Patsy asked for volunteers to work. She was too nice to force anyone to work on Thanksgiving, and Lynn was the only one who had offered to come in. Amy would let Patsy know she could work, too. She bit back the tears, thinking how juvenile this was. Dave's sudden coolness came about because someone had called her his girlfriend.

Amy sat in the dark, listening to Dave talk. If he noticed she was exceptionally quiet, he didn't mention it. She wondered if he would even notice if she sat the phone down and went to bed. It almost felt voyeuristic, as though she were reading his private diary. He talked about the court hearing earlier that day. He talked about Ginger, her drug problem and her attempt to thwart the drug testing. "She cut her hair so short, there wasn't enough to test. The results came back inconclusive."

"So what happens now," Amy asked, not really caring.

"I guess the Judge was smart enough to see through her scheme and ordered supervised visitation. If she wants to see Cathy, it has to be at her parents' house here in Savannah, and one of her parents has to be there the whole time. Dale threw her out, so she doesn't have the money to pay an attorney. Without an attorney, she's not in a position to bargain."

Amy didn't comment. She was sick of hearing about Ginger.

"She claims Dale threw her out because of me and the stress I'm putting on her with this drug thing, but Dale called me earlier. He told me she'd been acting strangely for a long time, but he didn't know why. He'd never known anyone on drugs, and Ginger is a master at hiding it. He said when he came home and she'd all but shaved her head, he knew she'd done it to screw up the drug testing. He begged her to get help, but she kept insisting she didn't have a problem. He told her to either get help or get out."

"Why did he call you?" Amy asked.

"I guess to let me know what was going on, and to let me know he was on my side. Good news, huh?" Dave said. "My wife's boyfriend is on my side."

Ex-wife, Amy thought. "Where is she staying?" She asked, hoping he wouldn't say he'd offered to let her stay at his condo.

"Dale gave her a little money, and she moved into a cheap hotel. I told her she could stay at my condo."

Amy felt like she'd been stabbed in the heart. "Do you think that was wise?"

"I had to, Amy. What was I supposed to do, let her live on the streets when her money runs out? What would I tell Cathy?"

"Does she have a job?"

"No."

"Does she have any money?"

"I'm paying for the condo, of course. She's got the income from our condo in Pensacola. The amount varies, but at the very least, it gives her grocery money." Dave and Ginger had retained joint ownership of their condo in

Pensacola, Florida. When together, they had used the condo two consecutive weeks in the summer and two non-consecutive weeks at various other times throughout the year, as well as other weeks when their schedule allowed and it wasn't rented to vacationers. In the divorce, they each got one week in the summer and one other week of their choosing. The rental income from the unit, minus expenses, was divided equally and paid to them quarterly.

"Did you at least put any stipulations on her staying there?"

"No."

"Don't you think you should?"

"Okay, Amy, you're apparently the expert. What should I have done?"

"I don't know — maybe pick a date and tell her before then she has to get a job, save some money and find a place of her own. Tell her if you find any drugs or drug paraphernalia, she's out."

"I can't throw her out on the street."

"If you don't set some ground rules, aren't you just enabling her?"

"She's my wife. I can't let her live on the streets like a homeless person."

The words cut through her. "She's not your wife, she's your ex-wife, and if she ends up on the streets, it's her own fault. Where are you going to stay when you go to Atlanta?" She was immediately sorry she had asked. She already knew the answer.

"I'll stay at the condo."

"Does Ginger know you plan on staying there?"

"I do own the place, and she knows I stay overnight in Atlanta on a fairly regular basis."

"What if she has a man over?"

"Amy, she's not going to be dating."

Was he beating around the bush trying to tell her something? "Are you guys getting back together?" She held her breath as she waited for the answer.

"No, but I think she knows she can't bring men home while she's living in my condo."

"Don't you think that's rather manipulative?"

"No."

"So you think she's just going to play house with you?"

"We're not going to be playing house. She doesn't have to sleep with me to stay."

Doesn't have to? Was that an option? Was he hoping she would? "That's not what I meant, but thanks for the visual. All I meant was that she may think you're giving her the condo for as long as she needs it. She may not know you plan on staying there, too." Amy rubbed her forehead. "Look, Dave, I don't want to argue. I'm just playing devil's advocate here. It doesn't sound like you've thought about how she's going to view the offer. Suppose she doesn't want to live with you, even temporarily. Are you prepared for that?"

He should have known Amy wouldn't understand. To keep from saying something he'd regret, he said nothing.

"What about all the things in your condo?"

"What about them."

"She's an addict with limited means of support. Your possessions could easily turn into drug money."

"I'm way ahead of you there. I moved anything of any real value to my storage unit in the basement. About the only thing left is furniture and some old televisions." Dave's voice softened. "Look, Amy, I know what Ginger is now, but that's not who she really is. She's good, and decent, and kind. Everyone has turned their back on her. If I abandon her, she'll never get help. She'll die alone in an alley or some flop house. If for no other reason, I owe it to Cathy to help Ginger any way I can. I've got to help her."

"I know you do," she said in resignation. If Amy harbored any doubt that Dave was still in love with Ginger, it was gone now. Amy knew Dave's heartfelt obligation to help Ginger went beyond his desire to spare Cathy. She listened to Dave talk, torturing both of them with his obsession to help a woman who didn't want his help.

Hours later, Dave was finally talked out. It was all Amy could do to muster up the energy to turn off the phone. Amy let the phone fall to the floor then fell asleep on the sofa.

Chapter Twenty

"Mommy," Katy screamed excitedly, "Santa came! Santa came!" Katy launched herself into the air, landing on top of Amy. "Get up, Mommy! Santa came!"

Sitting on the edge of the bed, Amy rubbed the sleep out of her eyes. The baby monitor on her nightstand told her Sammy was waking up, too. She put on her robe and slippers, and changed the baby's diaper while Katy bounced off the walls in unbridled excitement.

Katy was in heaven. Not only did she get to open her own mountain of gifts, but she got to open Sammy's, too. After everything was opened and the wrappings cleared away, Amy headed to the kitchen to fix Katy's favorite breakfast of cinnamon pancakes.

Amy alternated her eyes from the griddle to Sammy, on

his hands and knees, rocking back and forth, trying to will his body to move.

When the pancakes were done, Amy put Sammy in his highchair and called Katy to the table. Katy came skipping into the kitchen, holding a Barbie.

"Where did you get her?" Amy asked. The doll was obviously new, and it wasn't one Amy had bought.

"From Santa," Katy answered, laying the soon-to-be-naked doll on the table before climbing into her chair. "An' he brought me a book an' a car toy thingy for Sammy."

Santa? Amy knew Santa hadn't brought that doll. Had Jane or one of her girls put it under the tree without her knowing? "What kind of paper did Santa wrap it in?" Maybe that clue would shed light as to its origin.

"Santa paper silly," Katy answered, giggling.

Amy went to the family room and found wrapping paper on the floor. She picked it up, searching for a card. There were three cards in all; one for each of them, all signed by Dave. Where had Katy gotten them? Dave hadn't been over since before Thanksgiving. Among the discarded wrapping paper was Sammy's toy; a steering wheel with a working horn, a gear shift and colorful buttons that made a variety of noises. Tossed off to the side was the book Katy had mentioned. The Tale of Three Trees by Angela Elwell Hunt.

She picked up the book and went back to the kitchen. "Sweetie, where did Santa leave these presents?"

"In the rocker on the porch. I saw them when I looked out the window to see if Santa was still here. I wanted to see the reindeer, but they was already gone." With gooey hands, Katy pushed her tangled hair out of her face, smearing syrup everywhere. Seeing the book in Amy's hands, Katy added. "Read us the book, Mommy." Her mouth was so full of food Amy could barely understand her.

"I'll read it to you after we eat and clean up. And don't talk with food in your mouth."

"Sorry, Mommy," Katy said, her mouth still full of food. She put her hand in front of her mouth and giggled.

"You," she said, kissing Katy's forehead, "are the cutest little girl in the whole wide world — even if you are too sticky and talk with your mouth full."

Amy read the book to herself while the kids finished their breakfast. It was a short, sweet story that tugged at her heartstrings. She was blinking back tears by the time she finished. Katy will love this book, Amy thought. Katy loved any book that made Amy cry. One of Katy's favorite books was Love You Forever by Robert N. Munsch and Sheila McGraw. Every time Amy read that book, she got choked up at exactly the same place, and had to pause to gain enough control to continue reading. As Amy neared the page that caused the emotions to peak, Katy would quit looking at the illustrations and would look up at Amy, anticipating the water show that would soon begin. Amy would struggle to blink back tears, and Katy would giggle, causing Amy to laugh while she cried.

Amy walked into the family room, and laid the book on the coffee table, unsure how much of the emotion she was feeling was caused from the story and how much was due to the fact that Dave bought her the book. Amy hadn't seen him since the night of Mr. Anderson's party. Dave had called her the next night to talk about the outcome of the hearing, but he hadn't called since. She had talked to him a few times since, but it was on her initiative, not his. The painful truth hung like a neon sign over the silent phone. Dave didn't want her. Dave didn't love her. Her head told her she should write Dave off entirely, but her heart wouldn't let him go.

She felt like she had a heavy weight sitting on her chest, making each breath an effort. She opened the book, running her fingertips over the inscription inside, trying to feel him in the words. *Oh, Dave, I love you so much. Why can't you let Ginger go? Why can't you love me?*

Chapter Twenty-One

With the top of the convertible down, Dave pulled onto Interstate 16, headed towards Atlanta. Ginger had been living in his condo for about five months. Living by herself, her drug abuse was spiraling out of control. With no one to witness the drugs, there was no reason to hide it. Even though Dale had asked her to leave, he had tried to remain in her life. Much to Dave's chagrin, Dale visited her at Dave's condo, trying to make sure she ate and bathed. Dale had wanted to help her, but he finally gave up, washing his hands of her. Dave knew he was all she had left. He was the only thing standing between her and an overdose, dying alone in an alley. Dave cringed at the thought of his beautiful Ginger, lying on a cold slab at the morgue while the morticians searched missing person records for this unidentified Jane Doe. Ginger didn't deserve his devotion, but he couldn't help himself. Why couldn't he stop loving her?

Loving Ginger made no sense. He knew that, but he couldn't help how he felt. How do you make yourself stop loving someone? If he knew the answer to that, he would have stopped loving her and torturing himself with thoughts of her long ago. But he kept remembering the Ginger she used to be. He didn't love the Ginger she was right now, he loved the Ginger she had once been. With help, she could be that Ginger again. With luck, and perhaps divine intervention, the new, old Ginger could be his Ginger again.

It was almost exactly three years ago that Ginger had left. When would the pain end? Why couldn't he heal? He knew others who had been divorced, even under similar circumstances, and they'd been able to move on. Why couldn't he?

Hopefully, this would be his last trip to Atlanta to see Ginger in this condition. His hope was to convince her, once and for all, to check herself into rehab. She wouldn't be able to afford all of it on her income from the Florida condo, so he was prepared to offer to pay the difference, which meant a second mortgage on his house in Savannah.

Several people had tried to persuade Ginger to get the help she needed, but she had turned a deaf ear to them. Dave hoped he had found the thing no one else had thought of. It was apparent she would not get help for her herself. She wouldn't get help for her daughter's sake, either. She wouldn't get help for her family or anyone else who loved her. Dave planned to appeal to the one thing every woman held dear — her vanity.

Dave knew Ginger didn't look good, but he didn't realize just how bad she looked or how much she had aged in such a short time until he happened upon their old photo albums a few weeks before. There, by the light of a single bulb in the linen closet, he pulled the nearly forgotten box from the top shelf and sat on the floor, looking through the photographic evidence of their lives together. There were pictures of their wedding, with her unsuccessful attempt to hide her enormous belly. He looked at a picture of the young Ginger, her eyes shining with obvious pride and complete happiness at Cathy's birth. For a moment, Dave allowed himself to think of Ginger's second pregnancy. He soon forced himself to not let his mind wander to the baby forever lost to him.

The albums were full of pictures of the three of them, smiling leisurely on vacation or contentedly at home. There was no denying how beautiful Ginger was. Cathy had inherited her mother's perfect teeth and infectious smile. She had the same dark curly hair. Cathy, like Ginger, hated her curls, longing for poker straight tresses, but Dave loved their curls.

Dave removed several dozen photos of Ginger and her family throughout the years. These photos, along with a handful of others Cathy had taken of her since their divorce, and the one Dave planned to take upon arrival, were his last hope. She might not get help for the reasons everyone else thought important, but when she saw what the drugs were doing to her looks, surely that would sway her resolve. There would be no way to refute the evidence he was going to lay before her.

As he drove, his mind drifted back to this time last year. He'd been sitting in Centennial Park feeling sorry for himself, when he spied Amy and her friend Jenny. He stifled a sarcastic laugh. Jenny had been the one he was attracted to. How much different would things be if he had dated Jenny instead of Amy? He had been so attracted to Jenny, he had barely even noticed Amy. It wasn't until he saw her on River Street in Savannah that he was able to truly see her. Spending time with Amy had transformed his feelings toward her from casual to full fledged hunger.

Guilt ate at him whenever he thought of Amy. He turned the radio up, trying to drown out his thoughts. It didn't work.

Dave had known Amy was in love with him. He had also known she was under the impression that he loved her as well. She felt he had led her on, even used her, but he hadn't, not entirely anyway and certainly not intentionally. He did love her, just not the way she wanted him to love her. He knew she was upset over that stupid girlfriend comment at Mr. Anderson's party. Every time he thought about that night, he could almost hear a commentator saying *'The Girlfriend Incident, as it came to be known'*. The fact that her feelings of betrayal were justified only added to his shame.

He was at a loss over how to fix the mess he'd made of things with Amy. The only problem was, he couldn't be near her and keep his passion in check. The physical attraction between them was too strong. If he were to see her, he would make sexual overtures towards her. She would interpret his advances as affection, and they weren't. Not entirely anyway. His feelings for Amy were somewhere between love and lust. He might have deep feelings for Amy, but his heart belonged to Ginger.

Amy had called a number of times. Sometimes he took her call, sometimes he let it roll into voicemail. Hearing her voice made him weak with desire. Seeing her, or simply thinking of her, and he was consumed with a longing to make love to her. The safest way to deal with Amy, he found, was to minimize any contact with her. He knew she was feeling abandoned, but for the time being, that couldn't be helped. In time, Dave theorized, his physical desire for her would wane and they could go back to being the friends they were in the beginning.

Memories of Amy and Ginger fought for control of thoughts as he made the lonely drive to Atlanta.

───────────────

Dave opened the door to his condo and was assaulted

with a foul stench. It was a combination of a high school locker room and a latrine at camp. It was dark and eerily quiet. Once he got past the smell and the quiet, he wondered about the dark. One entire wall of the living room was floor to ceiling windows. The blinds, even when closed, filtered prying eyes, but not much light. Dave deposited his keys on a table in the foyer and made his way down the short hallway to the living room.

Blankets, nailed without care, were covering the windows. Angrily, he yanked the fabric down. Later he would care, but at the time, he didn't even hear the sound of fabric ripping. Light poured into the room. It took a few moments for his eyes to adjust. When his eyes could focus again, Dave surveyed the room and the piles of dirty laundry everywhere. His stomach rolled when he saw Ginger on the sofa.

Naked from the waist down, her pants were balled up on one ankle. What had she done? Forgotten to pull up her pants after she went to the bathroom? Disgusted with her, he made his way towards her. To his horror, he stepped on someone lying on the floor in front of the sofa. He looked down at what he had thought was a pile of clothes, only to realize it was a heavily tattooed man, his filthy pants pushed down around his equally dirty ankles. The sight made him feel physically sick. He fought back the nausea — and fury — knowing they had had sex, or at the very least, had tried to. He hoped it was the latter.

Resisting the urge to kick the man, Dave nudged him with his foot, yelling at him to get dressed and get out. As Dave yelled, more piles of what he had thought to be laundry began to move. Two other men and a woman sat up, dazed and confused.

Dave looked at Ginger in utter disbelief. The woman who held his heart captive all these years now repulsed him. "Get some clothes on," he said, choking back his despair. As Ginger dressed and the others scurried out like roaches exposed to the light, Dave turned his attention back to the windows, removing the rest of the blankets. This time, with much more care than the first. He turned around to see Ginger sitting on the sofa, now fully dressed.

He had gotten a good look at her 'friends' and was filled with sadness. They looked tired. And old. And dirty. He had never looked at Ginger that way, but that's how others saw her. To them, she looked just like the pathetic souls who had just stumbled out of his home. They were husbands and wives. Mothers and fathers. Brothers and sisters. They had parents and friends out there, wondering where they were. Wondering if they'd ever see them again. Wondering if they were alive or dead. Meth, in Dave's opinion, came from the devil himself.

"That was totally uncalled for."

He had a plan and it didn't involve arguing with her. He ignored her comment, and sat on the coffee table directly in front of her. "Are you hungry?"

"Not really."

Even at a distance of several feet, her breath was rancid.

What he wanted to ask, but didn't, was when was she last time she took a shower, or brushed her teeth. "When's the last time you ate."

She shrugged her shoulders.

"You need to eat."

"I need to sleep." She rubbed her face. Dave noted the dirt caked under her once perfectly manicured nails.

"Well, I need to eat and you're going with me. Last time I checked you were still human. You need to eat." He wasn't in the mood to negotiate. "Take a shower, brush your teeth and put on some makeup. Try to look your best."

Ginger rolled her eyes. "You've got to be kidding?"

"Hurry up. I'm hungry." Ginger didn't budge. "I'm going to hound you until you do it, so the sooner you clean up, the sooner we can eat, and the sooner you can come back and get some sleep."

"Fine," she said, standing up and stretching, "but I'm going to get up and walk out if you start talking about rehab."

When Ginger was finished getting ready, Dave took her picture with a Polaroid camera.

"What's that for?" Ginger asked, as Dave laid the photo on the dining room table.

As Ginger came closer, she noticed Dave had laid dozens of pictures on the table. She looked up at him questioningly. "What's this?"

She looked at the photos. Dave talked very little. He didn't have to — the pictures themselves spoke volumes. They were undeniable evidence of the toll the drugs had taken on her appearance. The once vibrant young mother now looked more like her own mother.

The look on Ginger's face told Dave his point was hitting home. She may not care how the drugs were ravaging her insides, but she still had enough vanity to care about what it was doing to the outside. Her eyes misted over as she looked at the photographs of herself just a few years ago. She picked up the Polaroid Dave had just taken. Staring at the image, she asked Dave "Is this really what I look like?"

He swallowed hard. "Yes."

Tears streamed down her face. Ginger slumped into a chair, cupping her free hand over her mouth, muffling her words. "Oh my God." Her eyes traveled up and down the rows of images.

Dave let her soak in the visual evidence of her steady decline. After that, it didn't take long to convince her she was out of control and incapable of stopping on her own. After agreeing to a rehab center near Savannah, Ginger packed up her meager belongings into a plastic grocery bag. She looked pitiful. Dave's heart broke for her.

"Where are the rest of your things?"

She shrugged her shoulders and shook her head. "I don't

know."

"Where's your suitcase?"

She shrugged her shoulders again.

"Wait here." Dave left the room, returning a few moments later with an old suitcase. "Here," he said, handing it to her, "use this."

Dave called ahead to confirm Ginger's arrival. The ride to the rehab center was the longest ride of Dave's life. Ginger cried softly, thumbing through the pictures she had retrieved from the table.

Dave sat on his deck, nursing a drink. He couldn't get the image of Ginger, looking like a whipped pup, out of his head. In the month Ginger had been at the rehab center, he had only been to see her once. He wasn't sure if he would go again. He was willing to help finance this latest attempt at sobriety because she was the mother of his child and because he had once loved her so much, but this would be his last gesture of goodwill. From here on out, it was up to her family, and friends if she still had any, to see her through whatever crisis her life brought.

Still digesting the fact that the Ginger he knew and loved was gone forever, a black cloud had settled over him. He had never mourned losing Ginger because he had never considered her truly lost. Now, after the vulgar display in his condo, he didn't ever want her back in his life. Even clean and sober, she would never be the same. For the first time since she left, he felt the profound loneliness of losing her. He still loved Ginger, but he was no longer in love with her.

He didn't want Ginger back. Not anymore. He just needed a friend. He needed someone to hold him. He needed Amy.

This last month, being the anniversary of the accident that claimed the lives of her sister and brother-in-law, would have been particularly hard for her. Had she made any friends in Savannah yet? Had there been anyone there to help her through this? Jenny, Dave knew, would have made sure Amy wasn't alone on the anniversary of the deaths.

Dave exhaled loudly and picked up the phone. With the courage that came from a couple of drinks, he dialed Amy's number.

Even before she looked at the caller ID, she knew who it was. Dave was the only one who ever called this late. Filled with apprehension, Amy answered the phone on the third ring.

"Hey, Stranger," she said, hoping he couldn't detect the nervousness she felt.

"Hi, Doll."

With those two words, her resolve flew out the window. Amy was once again under his spell.

Chapter Twenty-Two

Together again, Amy assumed Dave was finally ready for a relationship. The attraction had not diminished at all. If anything, it had grown stronger. When he made advances towards her, she told herself that Dave would honor the promise he made to her last fall. If he was treating her this way, it was because he wanted more than friendship. Likewise, when Amy didn't remind him of the boundaries she expected, he told himself they no longer existed. Both deluded themselves into believing the rules had changed.

One night, as they were making love, Amy whispered "I love you". She was answered by a passionate kiss. Afterwards, as she lay in his arms caressing his chest, she couldn't help but wonder — was the kiss intended to shut her up, or was it a physical response to her proclamation? Afraid of the answer, she didn't ask the question.

Dave ignored the warning signs telling him he was in too deep. It felt good to be with her. She was happy. He was happy. No one was being hurt. Drawing upon that reasoning, he began planning an adventure he'd fantasized of since childhood. Amy's birthday was only a couple months away. It would be a fabulous present for her.

———————

Dave thought back on his childhood, and how the seed of this adventure was planted all those years ago. Though he had grown up poor, there had been ample food in the house. Their diet may not have varied much, but they never had to go to bed hungry. His mother also saw to it that he and his sisters had nice clothes. Bought at a local discount store, they weren't the expensive designer clothes some of the other kids wore, but neither were they a banner of poverty.

Their basic necessities were taken care of, but niceties, such as color television and air conditioning, were luxuries they could only dream of. Without so much as a fan to stir the thick, humid air, it was impossible to stay inside during the summer. To beat the oppressive heat, Dave and his sisters spent as much time as possible at one of the local pools. One day, walking home from the pool, Tammy had to go to the bathroom. Not all stores allowed unsupervised children inside, so Dave looked around for a place that would let them use the restroom. Turning the corner, Dave spied a library in the middle of the block.

Dave pulled open the library's ornate wooden door. It was thick and heavy, heavier than any door Dave had ever opened. He could feel the cold air rush past as he leaned against the door to hold it open for his sisters. It felt wonderful.

The girls walked to the restroom, their sandals clicking on the marble floors, echoing off the walls. The librarian looked up. Dave watched her face for signs of disapproval. If she was upset that the children had entered, she didn't show it. Still, Dave knew children weren't supposed to be in a library. They'd leave as soon as the girls were done. He wished they could stay and enjoy the air conditioning for a while, but he knew the librarian would never allow that. She might be kind enough to let the girls use the bathroom, but she'd never let them loiter.

Dave waited for his sisters near the front desk, quietly reading the book titles on the closest shelf. The librarian, who Dave thought could quite possibly be the oldest woman in the world, glanced at him now and again. "If you're looking for the children's books, they're downstairs," she said softly, motioning towards a stairway at the opposite end of the room.

Children's books? They had children's books here? Other than the library at school, which only had books for kids, Dave had never been to a library. He thought the big libraries like this only had books for grown ups. The library was so quiet and somber. Dave wasn't sure if he was allowed to smile, so he hid his excitement when he answered. "Yes, ma'am. Thank you."

The librarian in the children's section was just as old, and just as wrinkled as the one by the entrance upstairs. She was also just as kind. Looking back, Dave could only assume the women were glad the kids were there reading, filling their minds with knowledge rather than running around the streets getting into mischief.

Dave spent countless hours of his childhood at the library, reading to his sisters in the indulgent comfort of air conditioning. As the years passed and the girls learned to read for themselves, Dave finally left the world of talking animals behind and was able to read the books that spoke to his heart.

Dave was drawn to the biographies of the strong, brave men who forged America from an unknown wilderness. He read everything he could about Abraham Lincoln. If a man born into such humble beginnings could become one of the greatest men to ever live, maybe Dave could, too. Abraham Lincoln gave Dave hope that he could rise above his circumstances and become a great man as well. A book on Frank Lloyd Wright piqued his interested in architecture, which would one day became his livelihood. He read everything he could on architecture. For someone interested in architecture, Savannah was heaven on earth. Homes in the historic district dated back to its origins in the 1700's.

How wonderful, he thought, to build something that lasted for centuries.

He devoured books on American wars, the Civil War being his favorite. Being from Georgia, he was morally obligated to root for the South, although he was quite sure the cause for which the South fought didn't directly affect his family. Given his current status in life, Dave figured his impoverished forefathers were probably not much better off than the slaves. He guessed the only thing his ancestors possessed that slaves didn't was their freedom.

But his favorite books, by far, were books on mariners, and pirates in particular. It didn't matter if the stories were real or not, he loved them all. Perhaps because his young life was so full of responsibility, the lure of freedom on the sea, and the riches of treasure buried along its shore were irresistible. As he grew older, Dave, his sisters, and their friends would ride bikes to nearby Tybee Island, the older kids toting the younger ones. They'd spend the day at the beach, romping in the water, building sand castles, and Dave's favorite — playing pirates and digging for buried treasure. No one dug harder, longer, deeper or faster than Dave.

If he found a treasure chest, he knew exactly what he'd do. He'd buy a boat and sail around the world and find even more buried treasure. He'd sail down to the Caribbean then up to the Carolina's and find Blackbeard's treasure. He'd sail up the Savannah River and find the gold buried along its murky shore by the looting marauders long ago. There was a time when you couldn't spit in Savannah without hitting a pirate. He knew there had to be treasures buried all up and down the river. The pirates would have buried their treasure along the shore, he knew, so that they could dig them back up without anyone in town seeing them. He knew they were there, he just had to find them. Countless summer afternoons were spent digging along the banks of the Savannah for these long lost treasures.

With the fortunes he dug up, after he was tired of sailing, he'd buy a mansion and a whole fleet of limousines. He'd hire a bunch of servants to do everything for him and his sisters. He wouldn't have to take care of anyone. And Dave, for the first time in his life, would have something other children took for granted — someone would be taking care of him.

Dave would stand on the shore, staring mournfully at the ocean, daydreaming of the day he'd be out there on his own boat. One day, he'd know the freedom of the sea.

Today, almost thirty years later, the ocean still beckoned to him.

———————

With all of Ginger's medical bills, Dave couldn't afford to by a boat right now. But if you were certified to sail one, they could be rented for as long you wanted. He'd found a thirty foot sloop moored in Georgetown, South Carolina. If

Amy could get away, he'd make the appropriate reservations, and they'd both have the adventure of a lifetime. He'd already mapped out their course and researched accommodations and restaurants along the way. And, since the sailboat didn't have a shower, he noted the harbors that had shower facilities for traveling boaters. He was hoping to sail to Blackbeard's old stomping grounds along the Outer Banks of North Carolina before returning to Georgetown. It was an ambitious trip, but it could be done. He really hoped Amy was able to go. He picked up the phone to call her.

"Can you take off the week of your birthday?"

"They'd probably let me off, but I don't get any paid vacation. I'm not sure if I can afford a week with no pay." She'd done a little substitute teaching, but to make ends meet, she had continued to work at the Seafood Station whenever she could. Now that it was summer and she wasn't teaching at all, she was working there full time, but she didn't have any benefits.

Knowing her precarious financial situation, Dave had anticipated that. "I thought you might say that, so I have an idea. For your birthday present, how about I give you a week's pay. You can —"

"Dave," Amy interrupted, "I can't let you do that."

"Hear me out before you say no, okay?"

"Okay, but I'm not going to change my mind."

Dave explained his lifelong dream of sailing up the

Intracoastal Waterway with a beautiful woman by his side. "Actually, as a kid, I always imagined I'd have a boat full of beautiful women. My own harem."

"I think you'd still take a harem if you thought you could get by with it."

Dave laughed. "Keep talking like that and this conversation will go downhill fast."

He talked of his dream of living on a boat and sailing around the world. While he no longer wanted to live on a boat or sail around the world, he did want to captain his own ship up and down the Intracoastal Waterway. He'd like to sail it from New England to the Gulf of Mexico, but such an excursion was the domain of the wealthy or the retired. He told her of the sailboat he had found. "I'd love for you to go with me." Dave felt like he had when he had been trying to convince her to go to Tybee with him this time last year.

"Dave, I —" She paused. He could hear her resolve weakening.

"Please? I really want to share this with you."

He heard her take a deep breath and release it slowly. "It's not just work. I'd have to find someone to watch the kids."

"I know."

"Let me think about it and get back with you on it. Okay?"

"Fair enough."

"And Dave."

"Yes?"

"If I can go, I'm not taking any money from you."

"It would be your birthday present."

"No, that's too much. The trip will be more than enough."

It was well past midnight by the time Amy went to bed. She lay awake, watching the numbers on the clock change. She was excited about a week alone with Dave, sailing up the coast. But it also seemed like a big step. She could take it, but could he? Every time she got close to him, he turned and ran. Would it happen again?

Dave had told her what happened in Atlanta. He appeared to be getting over Ginger — at least she didn't dominate their conversations anymore. From what Amy had gathered, he had only been to see Ginger one time. Dare she hope that there was now room in his heart for someone other than Ginger?

———————

Anxiously anticipating an entire week alone on the water with Dave, the next couple of months seemed to last forever. A few days before Amy and Dave were to set sail, Shirley and Roger drove down to Savannah. They stayed in Savannah overnight before heading back to their home in Tennessee, their grandchildren in tow.

Amy walked around the house, picking up toys, tiny socks, and the ever present naked Barbie as she went. It was completely quiet. It was a sad quiet. She wouldn't see the kids for ten days. She had never been away from them that long before. To little kids, ten days was a really long time.

She had invited Dave and Cathy over for dinner, but Dave politely declined. "I know Cathy would love you, but with all that's going on with her mom at the moment, I'm not sure how well she would deal with a woman in my life right now."

Amy said she understood, even if she didn't necessarily agree.

After three months of intensive therapy as an inpatient, Ginger had recently left the rehab center for a transition house. Like the halfway houses used by prisoners after being released from jail, the transition house was meant to ease the addict back to a normal life while still under the supervision of counselors. The only condition was that they get a job and stay sober. The hope was that they would assimilate themselves back into society, and with the help of the others in the house, learn to deal with the triggers that could cause a relapse.

While what Dave said made sense, it still stung. She had known Dave for over a year, and she had never met Cathy, his family or any of his friends. She'd met his co-workers last fall, the party with the girlfriend comment being the last function she had attended with him. He had been to several parties since they'd gotten back together, but she hadn't been invited. She tried not to get her feelings hurt over this slight, but she couldn't help it. Dave was a part of every facet of her life. It hurt to be so excluded from his.

Amy ate a light supper of salad and fruit, and then finished packing. Dave called just as she was getting into bed. The sound of his voice soothed her fears. Dave loved her, and they would soon be spending seven glorious days sailing, snorkeling, swimming, sunbathing, and making love along the Carolina shores.

Chapter Twenty-Three

Dave picked up Amy long before dawn. Two hours later, they were sitting at a restaurant overlooking the harbor in Georgetown, watching the sunrise. Dave told Amy of the things they'd see and the places they would pass. He was animated as he spoke, and Amy couldn't help but smile watching him. His enthusiasm was contagious, and Amy soon found herself as excited about what she would see as she was to simply spend time with him.

The next week went as quickly as the preceding months had gone slow. Days were spent sailing lazily up the coast, Dave at the helm, Amy lounging on the bench next to him or sunning on the foredeck.

Occasionally, Dave would find a safe spot to drop anchor and they'd go below deck for an afternoon tryst. Dinner was always seafood at a dockside restaurant along the waterway. While there, they'd always pick up something for lunch the following day. In the future, Amy would look back on food of that week and drool. At night, they would moor in the harbor and sleep on the boat, using the marina's shower facilities in the morning.

Evenings were spent sitting on deck, Amy often sitting between his legs, leaning against him, staring up at the countless stars. Dave would tell stories of his childhood. Sometimes Amy would laugh so hard she would cry. Some of the stories tugged at her heartstrings. Dave was romantic and sweet and attentive. It was the most peaceful, most relaxing week Amy had ever had.

The last day dawned warm and clear. The skies were as blue as the water. Amy woke at first light to Dave sitting beside her on the bed, a plate of fresh fruit, muffins and coffee sat on the table beside the bed.

She smiled and stretched, reaching over to caress his side.

"Good morning, Doll," he said, leaning down to kiss her forehead.

"Did you make me breakfast?"

"Nope, this is mine," Dave answered, trying to hide a smile. He popped an orange slice into his mouth. "Go get your own."

They stayed in bed a while longer, enjoying the food and each other, before getting dressed and going up on deck. After showering, Dave readied the boat for another day's sailing, and took his position behind the wheel. Amy lounged on a bench near him. The only sounds were the water lapping against the boat and the wind whipping against the sails. She closed her eyes as they got underway.

By sunset, they would be back in Georgetown, and the adventure would be over. What a glorious week this had been. She didn't want it to end. She'd miss this. She'd miss Dave. She'd miss falling asleep in his arms. She'd miss the feel of the boat and the sounds of the sea. She'd miss the sun heating her skin and the constant breeze that cooled her. Dave had been right. This was a week she would never forget.

She knew Dave was disappointed that they'd only made it as far as Beaufort, North Carolina. He was past the age of digging for buried treasure, but with so much of his youth spent fighting imaginary pirates, he had been excited at the thought of walking where the bigger-than-life villains had tread. Amy smiled thinking about how excited Dave became when he talked of pirates and buried treasures.

Dave looked over at Amy. She had no makeup on, but to Dave, she'd never looked prettier. Dave preferred her with no makeup, but, like all women, she hated the way she looked without it. Her body was toned and tanned — and his for the asking. The more he looked at her, the more he wanted her. If they didn't have to make it back to Georgetown this evening, he'd drop anchor and drag her down below.

"What are you smiling about?" Dave asked, as a small grin appeared on Amy's face.

Amy opened her eyes and the small grin turned into a full fledged smile. "I was just thinking about you, digging for gold doubloons or pieces of eight or whatever it was that pirates buried. Did you, per chance, think to bring a shovel?"

"Aye," he said, in his best pirate accent.

Amy laughed as she sat up. She watched Dave steer. The muscles rippled under his skin every time he moved. If she had custom ordered a man to her unique specifications, Dave would be the result. Tall. Intelligent. Witty. Strong. Romantic. Talented. He was her idea of the perfect man.

She moved to the seat behind Dave, wrapping her arms around him, laying her head against his back. He leaned back into her, stroking her arm with his fingertips.

"Mmmm," Amy said, barely above a whisper, "That feels good."

Dave squeezed her arm, a non-verbal reply.

"I love you." Amy involuntarily tensed. Had she said that out loud? She'd only meant to think it. Dave, again, squeezed her arm in response. She had said it out loud, and once again, he said nothing.

Amy's heart was beating wildly, and she was sure Dave could feel it pounding against his back. She was humiliated. If they'd been closer to shore, she might have considered jumping overboard and swimming to the beach, but land was no where in sight. She knew he had to be able to feel her heart pounding against his back, so she leaned away from him and began rubbing his shoulders.

Her mind was racing, trying to figure out a way to extricate herself from the situation and, perhaps, salvage her pride. Was it possible Dave couldn't say I love you? No, he was too much of a romantic. He was too articulate not to be able to say those words if he felt them. He was able to tell Amy anything. That only meant one thing — he didn't love her.

Tears threatened to spill down her cheeks. She needed a few minutes to compose herself. "Ready for a snack?" she asked. "I think we have some crab dip left, or some of that steamed shrimp. What sounds good?" She wasn't hungry. In fact, she felt like she might lose her breakfast, but it was the first thing that came to mind.

"Either one sounds pretty good. Surprise me."

"Okay," she said, releasing his shoulders. "Be back in a sec."

———————

Dave watched Amy disappear through the hatch. Once she was out of earshot, he let out a big sigh. That was awkward, he thought. He tried not to flinch when she'd said it. Had he? He knew she was in there feeling foolish, and who could blame her, but she didn't completely understand. He did love her, he just wasn't in love with her. But, if he actually said those words to her, she would think this relationship thing was something more than it was. They were just friends. Really great friends. She knew he cared about her. Couldn't she tell? Did he actually have to say those words for her to know how he felt?

It wasn't Ginger or her memory holding him back this time. It was fear. Fear that he might fall in love with another woman — only to fail her, too.

———————————

The rest of the trip was uneventful. If Dave was uncomfortable at her unanswered declaration of love, he didn't show it. He was the same sweet, attentive man he'd been the entire week.

They arrived in Georgetown at sunset. The harbor was a bustle of activity. Dave expertly pulled the boat into her slip. They both worked quickly in the waning sunlight, removing their things and cleaning the boat, trying to leave her as pristine as they had found her.

It was late by the time they reached their hotel. After a shower and a quick dinner, they fell into bed exhausted. Dave pulled Amy close. "Mmmm," he whispered. "You smell good." Moments later, he was asleep.

Amy lay in his arms, curled around him, listening to his rhythmic breathing. Aside from the children, she had never loved anyone so completely. In her eyes, he was just about perfect. Like everyone, Dave had his flaws, it's just that they were flaws she could live with. The flaws made him real. To Amy, he was as close to perfect as a man could be.

Did he love her? He certainly acted like it, but he'd never told her. Twice now she had professed her love for him and had been met with embarrassing silence. Last fall he had promised he wouldn't touch her like he loved her if he didn't, so he must love her, right? Why, then, didn't he say it? What if he were one of those men who couldn't say it? Could she live the rest of her life never hearing those words? Something inside Amy told her Dave Baldwin didn't fall in love often, but when he did, he would have no problem saying those words. That left only one option.

It was too painful to think about, yet she couldn't think of anything else. She lay in his arms, watching him sleep. It was hours before slumber finally overtook her.

Amy woke as light poured into the room. It was early, and she was still tired, but she knew she wouldn't be able to go back to sleep. She started to rise, only to be pulled back into bed.

"Where do you think you're going?"

Amy turned to see Dave, barely awake, smiling at her.

"I was going to make some coffee."

"I don't want coffee right now."

"You don't?"

"No," his smile turned mischievous. "I want you." As he made love to her, tender and slow, Amy fought back the urge to tell him she loved him.

Afterwards, he held her, his fingertips caressing her arm. She looked up at him. Something had changed. Anyone in the room with them wouldn't have been able to see the change. If asked, the closest she could come to describing it would be something akin to the twin phenomena, where one twin, so attuned to the other, instinctively knows what the other is feeling. She knew Dave almost as well as she knew herself, and something about him had definitely changed.

Nothing about Dave's demeanor gave anything away, but she could feel him slipping away. Not physically, but emotionally. He was transitioning from attentive lover to polite friend. It was a transition she would come to know well.

———————

It was impossible to convey the change that came over Dave each time he readied to leave. The change, imperceptible to anyone else, was blazingly obvious to Amy. The problem came when she tried to describe it. She couldn't. Even Jenny, normally sympathetic and understanding, couldn't make sense of her fears.

"Maybe you're just being paranoid, Aim. I mean, it doesn't sound like he's any different. Maybe you're reading too much into it. Do you think maybe you're just jumping to conclusions?"

"Yeah, I guess. Maybe. You're probably right," Amy

responded. But she wasn't imagining things. She couldn't explain it, but Dave did change. She could see it in his eyes. How do you explain the lack of intensity in someone's eyes? How do you explain a small inflection in the intonation of a voice? How do you explain a feeling no one else can see?

"You know," Jenny added, "If you think there really is something to be concerned about, you should talk to him about it. "

"Do you realize I've never met Cathy?"

"Yes, you have. You —" her voiced trailed off. "Haven't you?"

"Nope."

"But I remember you talking about all the things he'd invited you to so that you could."

"Something always came up. I never got to meet her."

"Do you think the excuses were fabricated?"

"No, not really, at least, I didn't at the time." Amy paused, running her fingers through her hair to pull it back from her face. "I still don't, but all that was last summer. The last time I said something about meeting Cathy, he said with everything going on with Ginger that Cathy had too much to deal with. He didn't think it was a good time."

"When was that?"

"Before we took the boat trip."

"That's been a while. Maybe things have settled down some by now. You could always invite them for dinner and see what he says. What could it hurt?"

What indeed.

———————

Amy tried to silence her fears and enjoy her time with Dave, but it was becoming increasingly more difficult. Each time she saw him, the pain of him pulling away from her was excruciating.

The strain she felt was manifesting itself physically. She had no appetite and had to force herself to eat. It was affecting her sleep, too. She had difficulty falling asleep and would wake several times throughout the night. Sammy had gone from crawling to running, and keeping up with him took more energy than she had. She'd fall into bed exhausted, begging for sleep to overtake her, only to find herself replaying her moments with Dave over and over in her head.

It wasn't that he simply withdrew after being physically satiated, because more often that not, their encounters weren't intimate. She had spent enough time with Dave, and knew him well enough to know that he wasn't emotionally distant, until it came time to leave. And it wasn't just work on his mind. It was something else. Could he still be in love with Ginger? Amy didn't think so, but there was definitely a shield around his heart.

She knew she would have to talk to Dave soon. She just had to get to the point that denying the truth hurt worse than accepting it. When she was with Dave, she felt like the most important person in the world. He made her feel special, desired, and loved — like nothing mattered more than her. Yet after he left, she couldn't help but wonder if she'd ever see him again. Wasn't love supposed to feel good when you were apart, too? Wasn't the best part of loving someone knowing they were thinking of you and looking forward to being with you just as much as you looked forward to being with them?

The only time Amy felt like she mattered to Dave was when she was with him. She wasn't a part of Dave's life. Amy's kids knew and loved Dave. Her coworkers knew him. Her friends and family knew him. He was a part of every aspect of her life — and she didn't even exist in his.

Chapter Twenty-Four

Dave came over with a bottle of champagne to celebrate Amy being chosen to take the place of a teacher leaving on maternity leave sometime in October. Until then, she'd continue to sub as needed and work at the Seafood Shack when asked. Rumor had it that this particular teacher wouldn't come back to work, and Amy would likely be asked to take over her class as their full-time, permanent teacher.

Dave followed Amy into the kitchen. She reached into the cabinet to retrieve the glasses, standing on her tip toes to reach the top shelf. Her shirt rode up in the back as she reached, revealing her smooth, tanned skin. She had a great shape; tiny waist, nice butt, shapely legs. Dave enjoyed looking at her. Amy set the glasses on the counter, knocking a toy car to the floor. When she bent to pick it up, he grabbed her hips and pulled her into him.

"Dave Baldwin, you're a naughty boy." She stood, turning around to face him.

"I can show you naughty," he said, scooping her into his arms and whisking her to the bedroom.

After depositing Amy onto the bed, Dave shut and locked the door. He took off his shirt, staring down at her. He could really fall for her if he let himself. But he couldn't. He knew he was playing with fire, but she was like some kind of drug he couldn't get enough of. He told himself over and over that he needed to tread lightly with her, but he always acted like an animal in her presence.

He pushed his thoughts aside, finished undressing then lay down beside her, pulling her close. As he kissed her, his hands expertly removed her clothing. He made love to her with an intensity that left them both breathless.

"Wow," Amy whispered, burrowing closer to him.

"Wow indeed," he echoed.

And then, as always, it happened. Before he even released her, she could feel him leaving. It wasn't long before he was reaching across her to gather his clothes. He put on his pants, and then sat with his back to her, shirtless, putting on his shoes and socks.

She reached over, lightly tickling his back with her fingernails. It was now or never. She had to know where she stood with him.

"Is everything okay?"

"Sure. Why do you ask?" He answered without turning around.

"Oh, I don't know. It just seems like every time you get ready to leave, I don't know, it's kind of like you're already gone."

"I have a lot on my mind."

She expected that answer. "I know, but it's more than that. It's like you're," she paused a moment. "It's like you're cleansing yourself of me or something."

Without turning around to reassure her, he reached for his shirt. "That doesn't even make sense."

She stopped tickling his back as he put his shirt on. He stood and faced her, buttoning his shirt. His expression betrayed his words — he knew what she was talking about. She reached deep inside and summoned the courage to continue, trying to sound light and cheerful. "How about you and Cathy coming over Friday for dinner?"

"I think she has something going on Friday night."

"What about Saturday?"

Dave sat beside her on the bed. He knew this conversation would take place someday, he just hadn't expected it tonight. "I don't think that's such a good idea right now."

"What isn't?"

"Bringing Cathy over to meet you."

"Why?" Amy asked, already knowing what he would say.

"There's too much going on with her mom right now." Dave explained that Ginger had left the transition house and was living with some 'low life piece of trash'.

Amy bit her tongue. Ginger was no different than that man. If that man was a low life piece of trash, then so was Ginger.

"Cathy hates him. I don't trust him. And I don't know how long she'll stay clean living with another addict. If he falls, he'll take her right down with him."

Poor helpless Ginger, Amy thought. Was anything ever her fault?

"And having dinner with me would be too traumatic for her?" She couldn't hide the sarcasm in her voice.

Dave sighed heavily. "I just don't think it's a good idea. I've never introduced her to anyone I've dated. If I brought her over here, she'd think we're," he stopped, unable to finish the sentence.

"What? Serious?"

He didn't answer.

"What are we then?"

Dave stared straight ahead, taking a deep breath before answering. "We're friends, Amy. Very good friends."

Friends? Good friends? Amy felt like she'd been slapped — again.

"For the record, I don't sleep with my friends. Apparently you do, so it begs the question — how many *friends* do you have?" Amy asked, enclosing the word *'friends'* in air quotes.

He shook his head back and forth. "Amy, I'm not sleeping with anyone else."

"Why not?"

He looked at her, his mouth pursed in irritation.

"Surely I'm not the only woman friend you have, and you obviously see nothing wrong with sleeping with your friends, so I can't help but wonder how many friends you have?"

He tried to hold her but she pulled away from him. She could feel tears stinging the corners of her eyes.

"If we're just friends, what have these last few months been? Buddies hanging out?"

"No. I mean, you are my friend. My best friend. I have fun with you. I like being with you."

"Most people call that dating."

"Amy, stop."

"Dave, I know I slept with you early in our relationship. Maybe you've gotten the wrong impression of me. It's not something I take lightly. I'm not promiscuous." Her voice grew softer.

"I know that, Amy, and I do care about you."

"But you don't love me."

It was statement, not a question, so he didn't answer.

"We've been together on and off for over a year. If you don't love me by now, you never will."

Dave didn't reply. He didn't know how to respond. It

was true. He would never love her. He would never love any woman again. He could never allow himself to be vulnerable like that again. Ever.

They were silent for a long time, both lost in their thoughts. Dave sat beside her on the bed, grasping for the words to salvage the situation. Amy lay on her back, staring at the ceiling, trying to find the courage to continue. Her soft voice finally pierced the silence, almost startling him.

"You broke your promise to me."

"What promise?"

"You promised not to touch me like you loved me if you didn't."

Dave was getting tired of this conversation. "You have a mouth, Amy. You could have said no."

"But you promised."

"That was last year." Dave stood up and tucked in his shirt. He needed to leave and let her calm down.

She sat up and looked at him, clutching the covers to her chest. "I didn't realize your promises had expiration dates."

He couldn't think of anything to say except, "I'm sorry. I didn't mean to mislead you."

Several minutes passed without anyone speaking.

"I need you, Amy. I need your friendship. Can we still be friends? You can set whatever boundaries you want. Okay? Can't we just be friends?" As Amy mulled the question in her head, he added, "Please?"

This was it — the moment of truth. She didn't know if she could go back to being just friends with Dave. She couldn't imagine the pain of having him in her life and not being able to touch him. But she also couldn't imagine him the pain of not having him in her life at all. "Does your word carry the same expiration date as your promises?"

He shook his head and kissed her forehead. "I'll call you," he said as he left the room.

Amy waited for the front door to open, then threw on a robe and went to the front window. She watched him get into his car and drive away. Now she knew the truth. It hurt, but she didn't have to wonder anymore. She felt like a huge weight had been lifted from her shoulders — and had settled on her heart.

Chapter Twenty-Five

All Dave could think about was the pickle he'd gotten himself into. He'd promised to just be friends with a woman he couldn't keep his hands off of. He'd always prided himself on his self-control. The first few years of his marriage, when he barely liked Ginger, much less loved her, he was able to contain his lust for other women. Though he'd had countless opportunities, he had never cheated on her. It was self-control to a promise, not love, that had kept him from straying. Where was that self-control in the presence of Amy?

There was only one way he was going to be able to keep his word — he could never allow himself to be alone with her. That meant no more lunches. More often than not, the kids were taking a nap or getting ready for one when he arrived for lunch. If the kids were awake, he'd be safe, but he could hardly ask her if the kids were up before accepting an invitation. It wouldn't take rocket scientist to figure out he was hiding behind the kids.

It also meant no more late night dates. Once again, if the kids were up, he'd be safe — or rather, she'd be safe. He would either visit before eight o'clock, when the kids went to bed, or he wouldn't go. No more running errands too close to Cathy's bedtime for her to tag along, and no more slipping out after she'd gone to sleep.

He still couldn't figure out the hold Amy had over him. She wasn't even his type. His type was tall, very tall, like Ginger. Amy couldn't be more than five feet four. His type possessed a vivacious personality, like Ginger, not the quiet, shy personality of Amy. And, Amy was too skinny. She had a fabulous shape, no doubt, and heads turned when she walked into a room, but he preferred a woman with a little more meat on her bones. He liked brown hair. Amy was a natural brunette, but she lightened it to a dark blonde. Ginger would try anything, while Amy was somewhat reserved. He didn't want Ginger back. He just wanted someone like her.

Amy was beautiful and sweet. She was kind and caring. She was funny, intelligent and forgiving. God knows she was forgiving. Too forgiving. How could she possibly forgive him after what he'd done to her, not once, not twice, but three times? How could she agree to be his friend after the way he'd hurt her? It was either a testament to her love or her stupidity — and Amy wasn't stupid. She loved him. She loved him a lot. And he'd used her.

No, he thought. He hadn't used her. He did care about her. The problem was that she wanted him to be in love with her. He wasn't, and he never would be. He couldn't help it if she wanted him to love her more. He couldn't help it if he treated her in a way that made her think he did. Should he treat her badly? What did she want from him?

The problem, as he saw it, was that she wanted this relationship to go someplace he wasn't ready to go, that he would never be ready to go. It's not like he'd ever made any promises about a future together. He had no doubt she would say yes if he called her up right now and asked her to marry him. If she had made assumptions about their future, it wasn't because of anything he'd said.

He would apologize for hurting her. He owed her that. He knew she was feeling used, but that wasn't his fault. If she got the wrong impression, or wanted more, that was her problem.

Dave knew he should just walk away and let her get on with her life, without him, but he couldn't. He needed her. She really was the best friend he'd ever had. Amy knew him better than anyone, including Kevin or Ginger. He'd told Amy secrets he'd never confided to anyone else — ever. She was so easy to talk to. And, she was just far enough removed from his life to have an objective opinion. She was level headed and logical. She helped him find solutions to the countless problems he laid in her lap.

She was always there for him. Her door was always open. She was never judgmental, even when she had a right to be. He had even cried in front of her — a lot. He could count the number of times on one hand that Ginger, or anyone else, had ever seen him cry. With anyone else, he was too much of a man to cry. With Amy, he wasn't afraid. He didn't have to worry she'd think he was weak. He could be himself with her and she accepted him completely. He'd never found that kind of unconditional love. He may not have used her, but if he was honest with himself, he had taken advantage of her.

Dave vacillated between rage and guilt, and the more he thought about her, the more he realized — he didn't deserve to be her friend.

———————

Cathy had volleyball practice until five-thirty. Dave figured he'd head over to the school around four-thirty and catch the last bit of practice, then take her out to eat. He checked his email one last time to make sure there wasn't anything he needed to take care of before he left.

There was an email from Amy. He paused a moment before opening it. He wasn't sure he wanted to read what she had to say. He sat down and clicked on the icon. It was a long, rambling email. He didn't have time to sit and read it, so he printed it. He'd read it while he waited for Cathy.

Walking into the gymnasium, he was assaulted with the familiar sounds and smells that brought back memories of his days in school, playing ball with a bunch of smelly, sweaty guys on a squeaky wooden floor. School gymnasiums seemed to smell the same, then and now.

He found a place on the bench away from the other parents. Cathy smiled and waved as soon as he sat down. He smiled and waved back. Cathy was beautiful. Like Ginger, she was tall and graceful. Unlike Ginger, she was a natural athlete. Her body was filling out now, and boys were already lining up at his door. He wanted his little girl back. He wasn't ready for her to become a woman. What kind of woman would she be with him leading the way? God knows he didn't know the first thing about them. She needed a mom. He was angry at Ginger. How could a mother abandon her beautiful little girl?

When Cathy took the bench, Dave turned his attention to the hastily folded paper in his pocket. Amy's email. He could only guess what it said. Reluctantly, he pulled the paper from his pocket, unfolded it slowly, and began reading.

Dave,

I've known for a long time that something is holding you back. I don't know what it is, but something is definitely stopping you from allowing me to get any closer to you. I put off saying anything to you because I was afraid of your response. I had to get to the point that the pain of pretending was greater than the pain of knowing. Last night, I crossed that threshold.

I believe you when you say you no longer love Ginger, but I don't think you're over her. I don't think you're over the pain she caused. I can't help but wonder if my presence in your life is allowing you to bypass the grieving process. If you don't grieve her loss, you'll never cleanse her from your heart, and there will never be room for me — or anyone else.

I would be lying if I said I wasn't hurt that you don't want Cathy to meet me. Last summer you seemed to want me to meet your friends and family, but now it seems as though you want to keep me hidden. I kept trying to figure out why. Do I embarrass you? I kept wondering if perhaps you now see something in me that you didn't see in the beginning. Something, for lack of a better word — bad. Now it all makes sense. Why risk letting them love me if you don't? After all, I'm only going to be in your life until you meet someone else, right?

I'm feeling very foolish right now. I feel foolish for allowing myself to fall so hard for someone who was obviously not ready to commit. I feel foolish for not listening to the voice inside that told me my heart was in danger. I feel foolish for professing my love, only to be met with utter silence. You must think I'm a complete idiot. You're not alone — I do, too.

I kept telling myself you never told me you loved me because you were afraid to admit it. I pretended to believe you did because I wanted it to be true. Now I can see that it wasn't true, and that I wasn't fooling anyone — not even myself. Deep down, I think I knew you didn't love me. I just wasn't willing to accept it.

If it sounds like I'm blaming you, I apologize. I'm not. I'm equally to blame. Like you said, and very eloquently I might add, I have a mouth. I could have spoken up. Instead, I chose to ignore all the warning signs because I wanted you so badly. Unfortunately, you can't build a relationship with someone who doesn't want one.

Now you say you want to be friends. All I can say is that I will try. I'm not sure if I can just be your friend. I don't think I can handle listening to you talk about other women, so please be considerate of what you confide in me.

Truthfully, Dave, I can't imagine just being your friend any more than I can imagine you not being in my life. I'll try to be your friend, but I can't make any promises. If you want to be friends, you need to respect the boundaries of friendship. And please don't make promises you can't keep.

Amy

Consumed with guilt, Dave pinched the bridge of his nose. *Dave Baldwin,* he thought, *what have you done?*

———————

Once again, communication between them was reduced to the occasional phone call, email, and instant message chat. Amy sent long messages, filled with stories of the kids or her classes at school, while Dave was more comfortable passing along the many jokes he received. The few times they had spoken on the phone, it was always Amy who called Dave. Hearing her voice, he knew, was enough to make him want her. He was trying very hard to keep his promise to her, and that meant keeping their contact as vanilla as possible.

The ringing woke Dave from his sleep. In a fog, he reached for his phone, trying to focus his eyes on the clock. It was after three in the morning. Who would be calling at this hour? Was it Ginger? Had she been arrested? Was she — he couldn't finish the thought. His heart was pounding. "Hello?"

"Dave, its Amy. I'm sorry to bother you at this hour, but have you been watching the weather?"

"Huh?"

"That hurricane? Floyd? They're saying it might hit Savannah."

"They are?" he said, yawning.

"Yes, and I don't know what to do."

"Amy, that thing is days away from hitting land."

"But what if it does hit here?" She was nearing hysteria.

"They haven't given evacuation orders, have they? Any warnings?"

"A tropical storm watch, but some of their projections show a direct hit on Savannah."

"A watch just mean there's a possibility. Do you know how many watches we get and barely even see a wave?"

"Well, I'm from Indiana. We don't have hurricanes in Indiana. I've never been through anything like this before. I guess I'm afraid of not getting out in time and putting the kids in danger."

"Amy, calm down. Look, if you're that worried, there's a section in the front of the phone book that tells you what you need to do. You're worrying yourself silly for nothing."

She laughed nervously. "You're probably right, but my worry switch is already turned on, and I don't know how to turn it off."

"You need to turn off the television and go to sleep. Even if it does hit Savannah, and it probably won't, it would be days before it hit. Get a good night's sleep and worry about what to do tomorrow. Or better yet, worry when they tell you to worry."

"Jenny said we could stay with her." She didn't sound as frantic now. "I think we'll leave in the morning, after I do whatever I need to do around here."

"I think you're jumping the gun, but go ahead if it will make you feel better. It would do you good to spend some time with Jenny."

"I do miss her."

Dave, now fully awake, put his pillow behind him and sat up, refraining from asking her the question that had sat on his lips since he'd first heard her voice. He forced himself not to ask her what she was wearing.

"Amy, what are you doing up at this hour?" He laughed a little as he said it.

She wanted to say I woke up thinking of you and couldn't get you out of my mind, then I saw the hurricane and got scared and needed to hear your voice. Instead, she said, "I woke up and couldn't go back to sleep, so I turned on the Weather Channel."

"Maybe you should have turned on one of those infomercials instead."

Amy laughed. It was good to hear her laugh.

"Hey," she said, "I'm sorry to call you in the middle of the night like this.

"A good night's sleep is vastly overrated."

"I know I'm being silly, but I've never been in a hurricane before, and I was just — scared. The size and power of this thing kind of freaks me out. Have you seen it? It's huge."

"If you need me to pick up some plywood or help you put it up or something, let me know," he said, hoping she wouldn't take him up on the offer.

"That won't be necessary. Greg installed hurricane shutters, but thanks anyway. I may need help with them, though. I'm not sure how they work." She paused a moment. "I'm sure I can figure it out, though. How hard can it be? And listen, I really am sorry for waking you."

"No problem. That's what friends are for."

Rub it in that we're just friends, she thought. "Goodnight, Dave. Sweet dreams."

"'Night, Amy."

———————

On September 14, 1999, Amy was safely in Atlanta when evacuations were ordered from Florida to the Carolinas. It was the largest peacetime evacuation ever, and it quickly turned into chaos.

Watching the traffic nightmares on television, Amy was glad she had fled when she did. Vehicles were crawling at a snails pace. Cars were breaking down and running out of gas, further snarling the congested thoroughfares. Emergency vehicles were trapped along with everyone else. Realizing the public would not be able to evacuate in time, authorities opened up the eastbound lanes of Interstate 16 to westbound traffic. Soon, the eastbound lanes were as congested as their westbound twin. Vehicles in those lanes, too, began to break down and had to be abandoned. Amy couldn't imagine traveling with two young children under those conditions.

She watched anxiously as the hurricane ravaged the Bahamas on the verge of a category five storm. Her heart fell when, as predicted, it turned north, heading straight towards Savannah. Famous for its moss draped avenues, Savannah would never be the same if it were hit by a storm as large and powerful as Floyd.

Even more than the damage to the city of Savannah, she worried about Greg and Susie's house. It was in her name now, but she still thought of it as theirs. Would it survive? She and the children had lost so much in the last year and a half. She didn't know if she could stand losing anything more. Greg had used the latest in hurricane resistant products and techniques when renovating the house, but it was surrounded by ancient, enormous trees. If any of them fell on the house, it would cause major damage.

Mercifully for Savannah, the storm took a more northerly path, skirting the coast. Savannah escaped relatively unscathed. The residents near Cape Fear in North Carolina, where Floyd made landfall as a category two storm, weren't so lucky. North Carolina, already soaked by recent storms and Hurricane Dennis only a few weeks before, was inundated with water. Amy's heart broke at the images of the North Carolina coast. The ground, saturated by rain and storm surge, began ripping open. Caskets floated down city streets alongside debris. The damage to homes and businesses was in the millions.

When the danger had passed, Amy hugged Jenny good-bye, and headed back to Savannah, praying her house had been spared.

The closer Amy got to the house, the bigger the knot in her stomach seemed to grow. She nearly cried with relief when she saw the house had made it through with no visible damage. The weeping willow tree Susie and Greg had planted near the end of the driveway, however, was lying on its side across the drive and front yard. Luckily, it hadn't hit the house or any other trees, but Amy was heartsick over losing it.

Susie had loved that tree. There were more trees than they needed on their lot, but she had insisted on planting a weeping willow near the creek's edge. Greg teased Susie endlessly about the tree, calling it a cry baby. Before long, the tree was always referred to by its unofficial nickname — Cry Baby.

The kids were sound asleep in their car seats as Amy pulled into the drive. Cry Baby was blocking the drive, but she pulled in as far as she could. She turned off the engine and left the door open while she inspected the tree. She touched its smooth bark. The branches that used to sway so gracefully in the breeze now lay in a tangled mess in the yard. Without warning, she started crying.

Get a hold of yourself, she thought. It's only a tree. It was just a tree, but losing it was like losing another piece of Susie.

Without Amy even having to ask, Jane and Earl soon came over with a chain saw, offering to cut the tree into firewood. Cry Baby would help warm the house this winter.

It almost seemed cannibalistic to burn her.

That night, Amy lowered herself into bed and turned off the light. Jenny had called earlier to see if there was any damage, but Dave hadn't called. She was sure he wouldn't endanger his daughter by ignoring a mandatory evacuation order. If he had evacuated, and she was certain he had, he would have headed to his condo in Atlanta. He'd been in the same city, and hadn't called to see how she was doing. He said he was her friend, but it didn't feel that way. She was always his friend, but he seemed to be her friend only when it was convenient.

She thought about calling him to make sure his house was okay, but talked herself out of it. If he wasn't concerned about her, why should she be concerned about him? And, if she were honest with herself, she didn't really care how his house fared. She knew his house was okay. If it weren't, he would have turned to her for comfort. Calling to check on his house was really just an excuse to hear his voice.

She was able to resist the urge to phone him for almost a week before she broke down and dialed his number. She told him about Cry Baby falling and getting cut up for firewood. She got so choked up she couldn't finish the sentence without crying. Dave laughed, but he understood the significance of the tree, and he empathized with her pain. He didn't mention it to Amy, but Ginger's prized azaleas, the showpiece of their yard, had suffered a similar fate. Like Amy, he, too, had mourned the loss of something cherished by someone he had loved so dearly.

The call was brief, as Dave had a meeting to go to, but he said he'd call as soon as he got a chance. After a week had gone by with nary a word, Amy surmised *'meeting'* was code for *'date'*. All she wanted to do was crawl into the corner, lick her wounds and try to heal. Amy decided she would quit trying to force herself on Dave and leave him alone. She only hoped he would show her the same courtesy.

Chapter Twenty-Six

Renovation of homes in the historic district of Savannah was booming. Anyone wishing to make visual changes to the exterior of their home had to obtain a Certificate of Appropriateness from the Savannah Historic District Board of Review. The Board met on the second Wednesday of each month. As the deadline for each meeting neared, Dave's clients grew more demanding. Though Hurricane Floyd merely sideswiped Savannah, there was some damage, though it was minimal. Nevertheless, homeowners used it as an excuse to make cosmetic changes to their property. Dave, being an expert in historical architecture, was overwhelmed with work. Pouring over plans and making changes up to sixteen hours a day was exhausting, but it kept his mind off of Amy — most of the time.

A few weeks after the hurricane, Dave was standing in a

client's yard, surveying the property as he waited for the homeowners to arrive. His eye kept wandering to an attractive redhead tending to her flowerbeds next door. She must have noticed the handsome stranger staring, for it was she who spoke first. "Glorious morning, isn't it?"

"Yes, it is."

"They're not home."

"Pardon?"

"Michael and Dawn. They aren't home."

"I have a meeting with them at nine o'clock. I came a bit early to look around."

"Oh," she said as she looked up, a surprised look on her face. "Are you a real estate agent? They aren't thinking of selling, are they?"

"No, quite the contrary. I'm an architect, and they're thinking of doing some renovations."

She flashed a satisfied smile. "Good. I'd hate to lose good neighbors."

"I was just admiring your garden. Did you do all this yourself?" Dave moved closer to the fence that divided the properties.

She looked towards Dave, flashing another dazzling smile. "Well, yes and no. I had a professional landscaper plant everything, but I take care of it." She stood up. She was tall and voluptuous, her long red hair was pulled back in a braid. As she took in the beauty of her yard, Dave admired her beauty. "I love working in the soil. If you think the front garden is nice, you should see the back. They did a masterful job. Would you like to see it?"

She spoke with a sweet, southern lilt so characteristic of the women of Savannah. Dave had a weakness for sweet, southern women.

"I'd love to," Dave said, walking to the sidewalk, then entering her yard through an ornate wrought iron gate."

"Are these original?" He said, running his hand along the graceful curves, admiring the craftsmanship.

"Mostly. I had to have parts of it repaired. There's a company up in Beaufort that specializes in this type of work. Isn't it amazing? You can't even tell which parts are old and which are new." She put her hand to her mouth. She removed her glove, extending her hand to Dave. "Where are my manners? I'm Andrea O'Neal."

Dave shook her hand, the delicate handshake he was accustomed to giving to just such a woman. "Dave Baldwin. It's nice to meet you."

"It's nice to make your acquaintance, Mr. Baldwin."

"Dave. Call me Dave." He released her hand, wondering if it was the temperature or the woman causing him to sweat.

"Then Dave it is. Please, Dave, follow me."

Andrea led Dave to the most amazing garden he had ever beheld. Like most yards in the historic district, it was small, but exquisitely manicured. Every available inch had been perfectly planned. Cobblestone paths cut a meandering

'X' in the yard. In the center, where they all intersected, was a three-tiered fountain. A bistro table and chairs sat on a small patio to one side, and a wrought iron love seat and chairs were arranged around an outdoor fireplace on the other. The wrought iron furniture mimicked the detail in the fence, barely visible through the ivy and flowering vines. Potted and hanging plants, as well as the ground beds, held a variety of flowers and greenery. "Andrea," Dave said, drinking it in, "this is incredible."

"Thank you. I was very pleased with how it turned out. I truly enjoy reading my paper and having my morning coffee here. I do wish I could sit and enjoy it more."

Dave heard a car door slam, wondering if his client had arrived. "I'd love to stay, but I think my clients just pulled up." He motioned towards the front.

"Oh, the Montgomery's?" She said, craning her neck to see around him. "Yes, I do believe that is their car."

He extended his hand again. "It was a pleasure to meet you. And thank you for sharing your beautiful garden with me."

She placed her hand in his. "The pleasure was all mine, Mr. Baldwin."

"Dave," he corrected.

"Of course. Dave. It was truly a pleasure to meet you. If you like, come back when you're done at the Montgomery's, and I'll give you the name of my landscaper."

"Thank you, Andrea. I'd like that."

She smiled a flirty smile and led him back to the front yard. He watched her hips sway as she walked and had to force himself not to let his mind wander. He rang the Montgomery's doorbell, watching Andrea from their porch. With any luck, he thought, he'd walk away with more than the number for her landscaper.

He'd been seeing Andrea for about six months now. The woman had no fear. She'd try anything. When she sang karaoke, which she seemed particularly fond of, her voice was off just enough that it made your teeth hurt. The woman could not sing, but that didn't stop her. She knew she couldn't sing, but everyone could tell she was having so much fun that the audience clapped like they were at a Garth Brooks concert. She'd even gotten a standing ovation once.

Andrea was fun, no doubt about it, but she was definitely high maintenance. He'd never had to work so hard to make someone happy. It was draining. He often thought about ending things with her. Every time he started to bring the subject up, she'd have one of her crazy ideas for some wild adventure, and he'd be sucked back in. She was wild and uninhibited, in life and in the bedroom. If the woman had one ounce of self-consciousness, he'd never seen evidence of it. Her enthusiasm for the unknown and the dangerous was exhilarating. He'd never met anyone like her.

Unlike Amy, Andrea began calling Dave on his home phone. It was unlisted to keep clients from calling all hours of the day and night with design changes. Dave gave the number to Andrea in case of an emergency, but told her to call him on his cell. Now, he wished he had never given it to her. In the beginning she called him on his cell, but that changed after the first month. He wouldn't have minded so much if he didn't know the reason why. She didn't tell him why, of course, but it wasn't difficult to ascertain her agenda.

At first she'd just left a message with Cathy to have Dave call her. It wasn't long before she was alluding to all the time she spent with Dave. Cathy, her curiosity piqued, began having longer and longer conversations with this mystery woman her father was seeing. One evening, after dinner, Dave retired to his office to work, leaving the door cracked to let Cathy know it was okay to interrupt. When it was closed, she knew he wasn't to be disturbed unless it was absolutely necessary. It didn't really matter if he left the door open or not, as his and Cathy's definition of absolutely necessary were completely different.

Dave heard the doorbell ring, then Cathy bounding down the stairs to answer. It wasn't long before he heard squeals of delight from Cathy and the muffled sound of another voice. He paused in his work. That voice — was it

Andrea? Curious, he made his way to the entry hall. His mouth fell open when he saw Cathy hold a pair of jeans to her lower half with one hand, and a shirt to her chest with the other. Shopping bags were cast aside haphazardly.

Andrea saw Dave walk in and smile that dazzling smile of hers. Cathy turned and saw him standing in the doorway.

"Daddy," she said smiling, "look what Andrea bought me. Isn't it awesome?"

"It's great," he said, trying hard to conceal his growing anger. "Why don't you go try it on?"

"Okay," she said, running up the steps two at a time. "Be down in a second."

Dave turned to Andrea, but before he had a chance to speak, Andrea began answering the questions he had yet to ask.

"I took the girls to the mall today and remembered Cathy told me she's been eyeing those jeans for months, so I picked them up for her." While Dave seethed, Andrea stood there smiling in mock innocence. 'The girls' were her two daughters, Tiffany and Heather, ages six and eight respectively.

Andrea's daughters were basically good kids, but prone to temper tantrums when they didn't get their way. They'd scream and cry and yell and pout. In return, Andrea would scream and cry and yell and pout right back. Dave never understood the exchange, because in the end, Andrea always gave in to the girls. Always. He pitied the men those girls would one day marry.

Gesturing wildly with his hands, but keeping his voice barely above a whisper, he asked. "What in the hell are you doing?"

"What?" she replied, producing a well practiced pout that had no effect on him. "Cathy said you've been working so much lately you haven't had time to take her to the mall. I thought I was doing you a favor picking them up for her."

Before Dave could respond, Cathy came back down the stairs. "They fit perfectly. Thank you." She threw her arms around Andrea and hugged her. Cathy turned to face her father, excitement shining on her face. "Do you like them? And look at this shirt. I love it."

"You look beautiful, Baby." He smiled at his daughter, who looked at him beaming. She did look pretty, but Andrea had no right to do this. He wasn't angry at Cathy. She was just an innocent pawn in Andrea's game of manipulation. He was, however, furious with Andrea.

"I've got to call Rachel." She raced back up the stairs, leaving Dave and Andrea in the foyer.

"You need to leave," he said through gritted teeth. "We'll talk about this later."

Andrea put one hand behind his neck and kissed him on the lips, a kiss he didn't return. She opened the door, then paused, seemingly oblivious to his rage. "Okay," she said, "are we still on for dinner tomorrow night? I could come over and cook for you and Cathy here. Cathy said she likes

—"

"No."

"No? No what?"

"You're not cooking dinner for us."

"Dave," she cooed, coming closer to him, fixing his collar and smoothing his shirt. "It's obvious that she doesn't mind you having a girlfriend."

He grabbed her wrist and removed her hand from him. Still holding her wrist, he reiterated, "No. Now you need to leave. I'll call you. And I won't be able to make dinner tomorrow. I have too much work to do."

He released her wrist and backed away. Apparently unfazed, she blew him a kiss and shut the door.

————————

How he allowed it to happen, he's wasn't sure. Perhaps it was Cathy's enthusiasm at having a woman to talk to. Perhaps it was a weakness for her feminine charms, but he allowed Andrea to ingratiate herself into his life. Cathy's initial enjoyment of having a woman to go to soon gave way to disillusionment. Andrea's overbearing personality soon soured her welcome.

Andrea's temper, once revealed, scared Cathy, and Tiffany and Heather's tantrums wore on everyone's nerves. It was obvious to both Dave and Cathy that Andrea was grooming them to become a family. Neither Dave nor Cathy had any intention of allowing that to happen. Cathy made it her mission in life to break them up. Her rude, snide comments about Andrea, and to Andrea, embarrassed him, even when he agreed with them.

Cathy constantly nagged Dave to dump Andrea, and Andrea constantly nagged Dave about getting his daughter under control. Dave and Andrea's arguments grew more frequent and more explosive. When Andrea became violent towards him, he walked away and never looked back.

Chapter Twenty-Seven

It had been a long time since Amy had spoken to Dave, by phone or instant message. She'd quit emailing him, too. He had answered her long emotional emails with short perfunctory notes, generally doing nothing more than acknowledging he'd received and read them.

As the weeks turned into months, the weight on her heart began to lift. She dated a few men, but none came even remotely close to being serious. Dave was out of her life, but not her heart. When her dates began to press for intimacy, visions and memories of Dave flooded into her head. It was crazy, but just thinking of being with someone else felt like she was betraying Dave. As thoughts of moving forward with each of these men began swirling in her mind, an email from Dave would appear in her inbox. Just seeing his name caused the fading ache to roar into a blinding pain all over again.

To Amy, though, the timing was more than uncanny. It was a sign that those relationships weren't right. With nothing more than a silly email to fuel her reasoning, she held out hope that Dave would find his way back to her. The men she dated never really had a chance

———————

Watering the flowers, Amy looked towards where Cry Baby had once stood tall and graceful and elegant. Though now filled with flowers, the spot still seemed empty. Lonely. Or maybe, she thought, I'm just projecting my own feelings on that silly patch of dirt.

She looked at the kids, playing on the porch. Katy, excited about starting kindergarten in the fall, was trying to play school with her little brother. Sammy, being a two-year-old boy, had a short attention span when it came to playing the grown up games his sister preferred. He tried to please his sister, but he kept getting out of his seat. Katy grew frustrated trying to contain his energy and called for recess. Sammy bolted from the chair and ran to his bucket and shovel sitting by the nearly dry creek. Katy soon joined him and school was forgotten.

With the flowers watered, Amy sat on the steps, watching them scoop dirt into the bucket. Amy often talked of their mother and father to them, showing them pictures and home movies, Katy enjoyed them, because she was the star, but Sammy was too young to see any value in them. Amy wasn't sure how many memories Katy still had of her parents, most likely precious few, and those would fade in time. Pictures and movies kept them alive for Katy, making her parents' memories Katy's memories as well. The pain of losing Susie and Greg had dulled, but it still cut pretty deep.

The ringing phone brought Amy out of her thoughts. Shaking off the memories, Amy grabbed the phone from the porch. "Hello?"

"Hi, Doll," Dave whispered. "Can I come over?"

———————————

After Dave left that evening, Amy sat down on the sofa, staring at the empty fireplace. She reached for her glass of wine, downing the last bit in the glass. Next, she reached for Dave's glass. She sipped the wine, feeling somehow closer to him knowing her lips were touching what his lips had touched.

Dave had been a perfect gentleman, but Amy had seen the look of desire in his eyes. It wouldn't have taken much on her part to seduce him, but that was a road she wasn't ready to go down again. Especially not after the bombshell he'd dropped on her.

He had shown up with a bottle of wine and a story Amy had been unprepared to hear. Amy listened to him drone on and on about Andrea, about how everything was great at first and then how she'd manipulated Cathy in an effort to incorporate herself into his life. It was over now, he had said, and he needed a friend to talk to.

Once he was done describing his life this past year, he asked Amy about herself, her love life, the kids, work — all the questions you'd expect a long lost friend to ask. When describing her love life, if you could call it that, Amy didn't go into quite as much detail as Dave had. She made sure to stress that her encounters with these men never became intimate. In her mind, it was important that he knew she'd been faithful to him. She couldn't tell if he cared or not.

Amy had been as supportive as she could. When he asked for a hug, she held him. They ended up lying together on the sofa, but that's as far as it went. It was agony to lie beside him. Sometimes when he talked, Amy would watch his mouth as he talked. Her mind would wander to what those lips were capable of doing to her. She had to force herself to look away in order to concentrate on his words — words that ripped open the lacerations in her heart that had finally begun to heal.

She held the now empty wine glass to her chest and closed her eyes. He had integrated Andrea into his life completely. Andrea, albeit through deceit, had accomplished everything Amy longed for. If Andrea hadn't been so neurotic, it would have worked, too.

Having had salve spread on his wounds, Amy figured Dave was probably at home, sleeping like a baby. Tears slipped down her cheeks. She curled up on the sofa, still gripping Dave's wine glass to her chest, and cried herself to sleep.

———————————

This time, Dave was the friend he'd promised to be. A few times, when Cathy was spending the night with friends, he'd spent the night with Amy, leaving early in the morning before the kids woke up. When his hands would wander, Amy would move them and he'd stop.

Amy was grateful he wasn't more persistent. It was all she could do to stop him once or twice. If it was torture for her, she knew it was double the torture for Dave. She appreciated his restraint, but sometimes she wanted him so badly, she wished he wasn't so gallant.

Dave never spoke of Andrea again, and he often asked about any potential men in her life. When she spoke about the men who asked her out, he encouraged her to go. She went, not out of desire to get to know these men, but to elicit a response from Dave. When it produced nothing but encouragement, she resigned herself to the fact that to Dave, she was just a friend, and that's all she would ever be.

Though she didn't want to, she turned her attention to Gene, a man she'd gone to dinner with a few times. He was the track coach at Savannah High School. Amy had met him last spring when he'd visited her school to help organize a track meet for the kids. He was kind and had a sharp wit. He was good looking, even more so than Dave.

She enjoyed the time she spent with Gene, but Amy still found herself looking for pieces of Dave in him.

Bolstered by his ability to sleep in the same bed with Amy and simply hold her, Dave gave himself permission to spend more time with her. Standing in her kitchen, watching her load the dishwasher, Dave kept recalling their conversation from last night. Gene had asked Amy to go to Hilton Head with him for the weekend. And Dave was green with envy. He was okay with Amy dating other men, as long as all they did was go to dinner or the movies. His stomach churned at the thought of her sleeping with one of them. And if she went to Hilton Head, he knew that would happen. Or at least what Gene expected to happen.

Amy closed the dishwasher, opened the refrigerator and offered Dave a beer. He accepted the drink, opening hers for her.

"So, are you going to go?"

"Go where?"

"To Hilton Head. Have you given him an answer yet?"

"Oh," she took a drink, then looked at the bottle, picking at the label. "I talked to Shirley, and she said they'd love to have the kids for the weekend, but I don't know. I don't think I've known him long enough to go away with him like that." She wanted Dave to tell her not to go. She wanted Dave to tell her he loved her and couldn't stand the thought of her in another man's arms, but she knew that wasn't going to happen.

"Have you kissed him yet?"

Amy looked up at him, taken aback by the question. He was leaning against the counter, only a few feet away from her, looking at her with a look she recognized very well. Her heart started racing.

"Of course," she laughed nervously. "But that's all, not that he hasn't tried —"

"Does he kiss you like this?" Dave said, setting his beer on the counter. He took a step towards her, wrapping her in a passionate embrace, pinning her against the counter. He leaned down and kissed her. His kiss was hard and demanding. Instinctively, she put her arms around him and kissed him back.

He pulled back slightly, breathing hard. One hand slipped to her breast. She closed her eyes, stifling a moan. "Does he make you feel like this?" He kissed her again.

Her head was spinning. After he left, she couldn't have told you if she walked to the bedroom or if he had carried her.

She didn't go to Hilton Head with Gene.

Chapter Twenty-Eight

Just before Christmas, Amy found herself having the same conversation with Dave that she had had the year before. It was like watching a rerun. He wasn't in love with her. They were just friends.

As a confused Amy tried to heal her perpetually broken heart, Dave's calls went from sporadic to non-existent.

Then came September 11, 2001. Dave was watching the news when the second plane hit the tower. If Susie hadn't died, it could have been Amy on one of those planes. She hadn't worked for that airline, but who's to say she would still work for the same carrier? Dave watched coverage of the third plane hitting the Pentagon, the flight downed in a remote Pennsylvania field, then the sickening images of the towers collapsing.

Did Amy know anyone on those planes? She must be

terrified. He called her at home, then hung up as he realized she was at school. He called her on her cell phone, hoping he might get lucky and she'd be able to answer. He got her voice mail and left an emotional message for her to call him. He'd been seeing Linda for the past few months, but it wasn't serious. Just the thought of losing Amy like that, of her being gone forever, made him want her desperately. Leaving Linda hurt and confused, he rushed back to Amy's open arms.

A few months later, he and Amy were having the same old, tired conversation. He didn't love her. They were just friends.

Amy was devastated. How many times did he have to tell her he didn't love her before she got the message? How many times was she going to hand him her heart, only to watch him throw it away? Unlike several of the women he'd tried to bring into his life, with disastrous results, Amy had yet to meet his daughter or his family. Yet he had the audacity to come crying to her when these liaisons failed, expecting her to help him glue the pieces of his heart back together. And she always did.

What was wrong with her? What was wrong with him? Why did she keep allowing him to do this to her?

He may not know, she reasoned, exactly what he was doing to her. After all, he didn't love her, and he likely had no idea as to the depth of her love for him. An old saying came to mind: hurt me once, shame on you; hurt me twice shame on me. Dave's actions were wrong, of that she had no doubt, but he wasn't doing anything to her that she didn't allow him to do.

———————————

Amy busied herself putting away groceries. As she put the fruit in a bowl, she looked at the green apples and smiled, remembering all the times she had gotten sick eating green apples from the tree in the backyard where she had grown up. The tree was perfect for climbing, and it was a popular gathering spot for all the neighborhood kids. They'd climb up, find a seat where a branch forked, and talk for hours. Amy couldn't remember any particular conversation, but she did know they'd solved many of the world's problems while sitting among those leaves.

When the apples began appearing, Amy's mother warned them not to eat them. "You can't eat green apples. They'll give you a stomachache."

To Amy and the other kids, this made no sense at all. Not understanding the difference between the green apples from the grocery and unripe, green apples on a tree, they ate to their hearts' content. It wasn't long before they were all feeling queasy. Their mother was sympathetic, but reminded them, "I warned you not to eat them. I'm sorry you don't feel good, but let this be a lesson to you."

Unfortunately, they didn't learn the lesson easily. Once the memory of the stomachache faded, they were right back in that tree, eating more green apples. They had tried to eat just one apple, but the apples were small, and one tiny apple only whet their appetite for more. Amy wasn't sure how many years they spent eating those apples and getting sick before they heeded their mother's advice.

That's what Dave is, Amy thought. He was the forbidden fruit that beckoned her to indulge, the temptation she couldn't resist. She couldn't eat just one green apple, nor could she be satisfied with only a small piece of Dave. It only made her want more. Yes, she thought, Dave was a green apple, and she couldn't allow herself even one bite.

She sat down at the computer and penned what she hoped would be the last letter she would send him. She would say good-bye. And let him know how much loving him had cost her.

––––––––––––

Dave knew it was just his imagination, but the papers in his pocket felt like they were burning his skin. He'd been carrying them around for months. Aside from a brief apology, hastily typed in the middle of the night, he hadn't tried to contact her. He was trying to leave her alone, but he missed her. He needed to sever the ties to her forever, but he didn't know how.

Though they were very close, Dave rarely talked to his sister Paula about his love life. Out of sheer desperation, he'd called her and asked her to meet him for dinner.

Hearing the pain in his voice, she quickly agreed, asking what was wrong. He told her it was a long story, but he'd tell her everything at dinner.

Paula walked into the restaurant, one Dave had chosen for its award-winning wine selection. To tell Paula the whole sordid story, he was going to need wine, and a lot of it.

Over dinner, Dave told her the saga of Amy. Paula interrupted occasionally to ask a question to clarify the facts, then went back to listening as Dave talked, picking at his food. Paula noted the pain in his voice as Dave described his final encounter with Amy.

"She sent me a couple of emails in the days that followed."

The waiter stopped to remove their plates. Seeing Dave's barely touched, he started to leave it, but Dave stopped him and told him he was done. As an afterthought, he ordered a bottle of wine.

Paula waited until the waiter was out of earshot. "What'd they say?"

Without answering, he reached into his coat pocket and retrieved the dog-eared documents. He opened one slowly, pressing open the creases. Dave laid the paper on the table in front of her.

Nodding toward the paper, Dave said, "That's the first one."

Dave,

To be with you, I pay a price. The price exacted from my soul grows exponentially each time I am in your arms, each time your lips cover me with kisses, each time your hands sear my flesh with their fiery touch.

To feed the hunger of your desire, I must sacrifice a piece of my own sustenance, leaving my already famished heart starving for more. Each time you leave my arms, my soul is crying out for a morsel of hope that what you feast on satiates more than just your desire.

Each time you pull me close, I am naively trusting, drawn into your spell by the intensity of your passion, responding instinctively to the sweet song of seduction your body sings to mine. I hold my heart out as you expertly maneuver around it, touching it only to keep it from touching your own. Its mournful cries go unheeded as you pacify it with the urgency of passion.

I feel your heart pounding violently against my chest, its rhythmic cadence beating in my ears. Your mouth covers mine, devouring the words that sit on my lips. I fall prey to you, your will becoming mine. The inferno ignited within me burns without restraint, yearning to be extinguished.

I feel your desire. I taste your sweat. I smell your magnetic fragrance. Separate, our appetites are monstrous. Together, they are ravenous, almost cannibalistic — feeding off each other in an impassioned frenzy.

As I lay beneath you, aching for more, I sense your

eminent departure. Even as you hold me, the abyss widens. The armor is put on slowly, piece by piece, until I'm left in the haunting embrace of your image.

You grant me the audience of your soul, yet you will not permit me to touch it. You implore me to embrace your heart, yet you will not allow me to hold it. You fill my heart with a melody, yet deny that I should sing it.

Barely conscious, I struggle to maintain composure as I watch your shadow retreat into the darkness, back into a world where I don't belong.

Yes, my gallant warrior, to be with you — I pay a price. Amy

Paula read it once, then once again. She laid the paper on the table. "Wow."

"Yeah," Dave said. "Wow."

"What did you say to her?"

"What could I say? I apologized. I told her I was sorry, that I hadn't meant to hurt her. The same things I've told her every other time I ripped her heart out."

"What did she say?" Paula asked, her voice dry and scratchy, the way it always got when she was trying not to cry. She reached for her glass, emptying the contents with one large gulp. Dave refilled her glass, then opened the next email, once again smoothing the creases flat with tender reverence.

Paula took the paper, once again noting the pain in

Dave's eyes.

Dave,

Letting go of you, of everything I thought we were and would be, will be one of the hardest things I've ever had to endure. In a life filled with loss, losing you has been one of the most painful. Perhaps that's because when I think you're gone from me forever, you reappear — only to ultimately have to lose you all over again. At least Susie only died once.

The cuts in my heart are so deep, I'm not sure if they'll ever heal. Right now, my heart is so fragile, I'm afraid to take a deep breath, for fear it will shatter completely.

The line between lust and love seems to blur, and I'm too weak to stop myself from the force of your passion. I've proven over and over again that I don't possess the strength to resist you, that I'm powerless against your hunger.

The journey you led me on has lasted years, and its left me exactly where I started. I haven't moved and nothing has changed. It's like being lost in the woods and walking in circles. At some point, you've got to realize the foolishness of your actions and take a new path.

I've been deluding myself for years that I could just be your friend. I've been lying to myself, pretending that whatever bone you threw me would be enough. But it was never enough and I can't do this to myself anymore.

If I can't be to you what you are to me, and it's obvious I never will, then I can't have you in my life. I love you too much to just be your friend. I love you too much to simply be your lover and confidant. I can't be your soft place to land in between heartaches. I can no longer be your refuge in a storm.

I love you, Dave, and a part of me always will, but I've got to get on with my life. I need to heal, and I can't do that if you keep rushing back in, ripping off the bandages and reopening the wounds.

If you ever cared for me at all, if you have even one shred of love for me, if you have any compassion and human decency in you, you'll leave me alone — forever. Please.

Amy

Paula looked up as the waiter arrived with another bottle of wine. Dave reached for her glass, but she put her hand over it. "No thanks. I can't drink anymore. I have to drive."

She watched Dave pour another glass and knew he would soon be in no condition to drive. "When we leave, I'm driving you home."

Dave nodded his acceptance.

Why had he asked her here? What did he want her to do? "Do you want me to help you get her back?"

He shook his head.

"Do you want to know what you should say to her?"

He shook his head again.

"I don't understand. You said you needed some advice."

His eyes moist with tears, he looked up at Paula. "I need to know what to do to get her out of my life forever. I can't keep doing this to her."

————————

T-ball practice started in forty five minutes. Amy set the sandwiches on the table and called the kids to dinner. While they ate their sandwiches, Amy sliced celery and carrots. She poured ranch dressing into small bowls, then set it on the table for them. They abandoned their sandwiches and began devouring the vegetables. They loved ranch dressing and would eat nearly anything drenched in it.

"You guys keep eating," she said, "and I'll go get your clothes ready for you."

Amy was rummaging through the kids' drawers when the phone rang. She ran to her bedroom to answer it, not bothering to look at the caller ID.

"Hello?"

"Hi."

Amy was glad the bed was behind her, as her legs suddenly didn't seem to be able to hold her weight.

"Hi," she said, not knowing what else to say. Dave. Why was he calling her? She couldn't go through this again.

After a few minutes of pleasantries, Amy remembered the kids. She checked on them — they were still eating, so she returned to her bedroom.

"Um, Dave, I'm in kind of a hurry. I have to get the kids to baseball practice."

"Okay, I just called to tell you some news."

"News?" News, she suspected, she didn't wanted to hear.

"Good news, actually." He paused a moment. "I'm getting married."

"You are? That's great," she lied. The color drained from Amy's face. Married? How could he be getting married? Less than eight months ago, Dave was lying in her bed making love to her. She felt sick to her stomach. "Tell me about her. How'd you meet?"

He told her about meeting her when he and Cathy rented a boat in Charleston, South Carolina. "She's great, and Cathy loves her."

Amy felt dizzy. The nausea rising in her stomach threatened to spill over. "That's great, Dave. I'm happy for you. I hope you're very happy together. "

"Thanks. We will be."

"Hey, Dave, I hate to cut you short here, but I really need to get the kids to practice."

"Okay, I just wanted to let you know the good news."

"I'm glad you did," she lied again. "I hope everything works out."

"It will. Good-bye, Amy."

"Good-bye, Dave." With the phone still in her hand,

Amy ran into the bathroom and threw up.

Later that night, she called Jenny. Amy was crying so hard, Jenny was barely able to understand her.

"Hey, how about you come to Atlanta this weekend?" Jenny offered. "The pool is open and the water's fine." Jenny, now married to a wealthy investment banker, had put the finishing touches on her new in-ground pool that spring. "Ronnie has to go out of town and the kids will be with their dad. It'll just be me and the dogs."

"Thanks, but the kids have games this weekend. I think I'll just hang around here."

"Well, then," Jenny said, "leave the mints on the pillow in the guest room. I'll be there around nine o'clock Friday."

Dave hung up the phone, feeling a mixture of relief and regret. She had seemed genuinely happy for him. Was she or was it just an act? Amy had always thought he was this great and wonderful man. If only he were half the man she thought he was.

He knew one thing for sure; he would never do to another woman what he had done to Amy.

Chapter Twenty-Nine

Amy pulled up in front of the house. Katy jumped out of the van and ran towards the house to change. Now ten years old, she no longer let Amy dress her in cute, frilly dresses for church. Katy wasn't a baby anymore. In a few years, she will be wearing a bra. A bra! Amy wasn't ready to let the kids grow up yet, but they kept growing despite her attempts to hold back time.

"Sammy, can you bring the paper in please?"

He smiled and ran towards the mailbox.

After lunch on the patio, the kids ran off to play with the kids who had moved in across the street. "Make sure to look both ways," Amy said.

Amy couldn't see, since Katy's back was to her, but she was sure she had rolled her eyes. "Yes, Mother. We won't make a mess, and if we do, we'll help clean it up. We won't ask for —"

"Okay, I get the message. Go. Have fun." With that the kids ran across the street and disappeared behind the house.

Amy settled into the rocker on the porch to read the paper. She glanced at the names and ages in the obituary section. She sat upright and looked again. Ginger was dead?

———————————

Amy felt bad lying to Jane, but she couldn't risk being seen in her own car. She'd listened to stories of Ginger for years. She felt like she knew her, even if they had never met. Ginger's grave wasn't too far from Susie's. Amy got to the cemetery long before the funeral procession arrived. She parked close enough to see what was going on, but far enough away to keep from being seen. This far away, and in Jane's truck, her presence would appear as nothing more than a stranger visiting a loved one's grave.

Her stomach was in knots as the cars started rolling in. The hearse pulled in, followed by twin limousines. Dave emerged from the second one, turning to help a tall blonde from the car. That must be her, Amy thought. Dave's wife.

Amy felt exposed. She knew she should leave, but she felt riveted to her spot. Dave had honored her request and left her alone. What had she hoped to accomplish by coming here, spying on their grief? But she knew why. She wanted to see the woman who now held his heart. She wanted to see the woman who had everything she ever wanted.

Amy lost sight of Dave and his wife as they were swallowed up by the crowd of mourners. Later, when most of the cars had already left, Amy watched Dave pick flowers from the various bouquets that would be laid upon Ginger's grave. Then he looked right at her.

Amy froze, filled with panic. How would she explain being here? Her face flushed with embarrassment. As Dave walked towards the truck, she reached for the key. She stopped when he veered to his right and walked directly to Susie and Greg's burial plot. Amy watched as he divided the flowers and gently filled the vases beside their graves. He bent down, took out a handkerchief and wiped debris off the tombstone. His head was bowed, as though in prayer, but Amy could tell he was crying. Why was Dave crying at Susie's grave? Maybe, she thought, he now understood the immense loss that Amy had been living with all these years. Maybe he finally understood the gaping hole left in your heart when someone you love is gone forever.

Chapter Thirty

As usual, Dave was invited to spend Memorial Day Weekend with Kevin and his family at the house on Tybee Island. Cathy, newly graduated from college, joined him, along with her fiancé. Everyone at the house was part of a couple, Dave being the sole exception.

Needing a break from the world of twos, he jogged down the beach at the water's edge, wondering how his life had gotten so off track. He was now forty-eight years old, though most guessed him much younger, despite the gray at his temples. Tall, handsome, and athletic, he was still considered quite a catch. Even after all these years, he had no problem catching the ladies' eyes. So why was he alone? He wasn't supposed to be alone at this stage in the game. He was supposed to be planning his early retirement with the woman who was going to be beside him the rest of his life.

The air was warm, and the cloudless sky was a brilliant blue. The sound of the surf pounding against the shore mingled with laughter and the sounds of children calling out to their parents to watch. Little kids dotted the beach, their concentration intense as they filled brightly colored pails with wet sand, then dumped them upside down. Their faces were shining with pride at their accomplishment. To the untrained eye, it looked like a pile of wet sand in the shape of a bucket, but to the skilled eye of a child, it was the Taj Mahal or Cinderella's castle.

"No. Stop. Don't." Each word was punctuated with familiar laughter. It sounded like Amy's laugh. Dave's head snapped up at the sound — and there she was. Amy. A man, a very strong, tanned man, had his arms wrapped around Amy's still tiny waist, and was carrying her towards the water. She was squirming to get away, helpless against his muscled bulk. Her hair was shorter, just barely past her shoulders, and no longer blonde. She looked even better as a brunette. Dave stopped and watched as the man effortlessly carried her into the ocean and went under water with her.

Amy surfaced laughing, splashed water at him, then threw her arms around his neck and kissed him. He carried her back out of the water, setting her safely on the sand. She took off running as soon as her feet hit the ground, laughing as she looked back at the man chasing her. She wasn't watching where she was running and ran right into Dave's arms.

Her smile immediately disappeared. It was replaced with — what? Dave couldn't place the emotion. It wasn't fear. It wasn't shock. It was almost — sadness.

"Dave," Amy said, barely above a whisper.

The man caught up with Amy and slipped his arm around her, pulling her close. She leaned into him, putting her hand on his stomach. Her hand looked so small resting on his rippled abs. Dave immediately didn't like him.

"Hey, sorry man," the man said to Dave, "this little filly gets completely out of control sometimes." He laughed, squeezing her so tight she squealed.

Dave wasn't impressed. Little filly? Who used words like little filly?

"Nick," Amy said, looking up at the man, "this is Dave Baldwin." She removed her hand from Nick's stomach and gestured towards Dave. "Dave, this is Nick Taylor, my fiancé."

Fiancé? He had to stop himself from recoiling at the word. Dave forced a smile and tried to act as though he hadn't been kicked in the gut. He extended his hand to Nick. Nick gave no indication he recognized the name as someone Amy used to date. The name *Dave Baldwin* apparently didn't mean anything to Nick. Amy hadn't mentioned him? "Congratulations," Dave said, shaking Nick's hand, "You've got quite a lady here."

Nick smiled down at Amy with obvious adoration,

squeezing her tighter. "That's an understatement. Hey," he said to Amy, "I'm starving. What do you say I round everyone up for lunch?"

"Sounds good," Amy said.

"Dave," Nick said, reaching out to shake his hand again, "It was nice to meet you." Nick kissed Amy on the forehead, and swatted her bottom before hurrying away.

Amy's eyes followed Nick as he ran down the beach and into the surf to retrieve the kids.

"Fiancé, huh?" Dave said, trying to mask his pain. "When's the big day?"

"Next year. Next spring." She looked up at Dave, her eyes still filled with the emotion he couldn't quite name. "Well, it was good to see you, Dave. Take care." Amy turned to walk away.

"Amy, why don't you all come to the beach house for lunch? Everyone is there and there's always more than enough to share."

She turned around to face him. "I appreciate the offer, but I don't think that's a good idea." She turned again and walked away.

He could feel her slipping away. He was desperate to keep her from leaving. "Cathy's here."

Ah, she thought, the Cathy carrot. He was trying to bait the hook and tempt her to have lunch with him. She turned around to face him, closing her eyes for a moment, then looked directly into his. "I really wouldn't be comfortable, and I'm sure your wife wouldn't appreciate you inviting your old girlfriend to lunch. Oh, wait. I forgot — I wasn't your girlfriend, was I? I was just a special friend you had sex with."

As Dave watched her walk away, he thought she was even more beautiful than he remembered. She had probably aged, but he didn't see it. In his mind, she looked exactly as she had the day they met. He watched Amy reach for Nick's hand, feeling like a hot poker had been stabbed through his heart. He couldn't believe how grown up the kids looked. Katy, very much a young lady, was taller than Amy now. Sammy, strong and tall for his age, didn't have much to go to pass Amy up, either.

Amy let go of Nick's hand to bend down and pick up a shell. Katy grabbed Nick's now vacant hand. Dave's heart sunk lower as he watched them walk away. One of Nick's hands held Katy's, his other was casually draped over Sammy's shoulder. That could have been me, Dave thought, and I threw it away.

Nearly nauseous with grief, Dave sat down on the sand, elbows on his knees. He pinched the bridge of his nose to ward off the tears

Chapter Thirty-One

Amy stepped into the shower and closed her eyes, letting the warm water pour over her. She couldn't get Dave out of her head. Why did he keep doing this to her? Every time Amy met someone she might have a future with, Dave came charging back into her life. He looked good. Older, but good. The grey at his temples hadn't been there before, and she'd seen a few grey hairs on his chest. Faint lines were forming around his eyes, but he'd still looked great.

Why was it that men aged so much better than women? She was under no illusion that she'd ever been any great beauty, but whatever beauty she had once possessed was beginning to fade. At forty-two, she told herself, it was all downhill from here. She was still thin, and her stomach was pretty flat, but time was beginning to take its toll. She didn't like what she saw when she looked in the mirror anymore.

Nick kept telling her how beautiful she was, claiming she looked just fine to him. But Amy had eyes, and a mirror, and she knew he was just being kind.

She grabbed the shampoo and lathered up her hair, reliving the scene on the beach earlier. Had Dave been able to detect the fact that part of her still loved him? Had Nick? No, she told herself, Dave might have picked up on something, but Nick wouldn't have. And why should he suspect anything? Amy did love Nick. She showed him, and told him, how much she loved him every single day. Nick was the first man Amy had let into the recesses of her heart since Dave. Nick was a wonderful man. Good looking, strong and powerful. A fireman. A hero. He would never have the kind of money Dave had, but that didn't matter. Amy loved him and trusted him. Unlike Dave, Nick enjoyed being in love with Amy.

Since meeting Dave, Amy compared every man she met to him. Until Nick, they had all come up lacking. Amy finished her shower hoping Dave Baldwin didn't come riding his white horse back into her life in an attempt to destroy what she had finally built.

Katy and Sam, now fourteen and eleven, were still asleep. Gone were the days when they rose with the sun, and for that, Amy was grateful. The smell of coffee, set to brew automatically at eight o'clock, called out to Amy from the kitchen. Out of habit, she turned on her laptop to check her email.

There it was — an email from Dave. Amy's heart started beating faster. Damn him. She knew she should just delete it, but she wanted to know what it said. She didn't have to respond. He would never know if she read it or not. Amy poured a cup of coffee with a generous shot of French vanilla cream, grabbed her laptop and headed to the patio.

She sat there, staring at the screen until it changed to the screen saver. She watched the photographs change every twenty seconds. Pictures of the kids and their lives together. Pictures of their last vacation with Nick. There were no fancy vacations with Nick, but they were fun. They had hiked, biked and swam. They went whitewater rafting. They had camped all over the state, staying up late roasting marshmallows and telling ghost stories. A Georgia native, Nick seemed to know every ghost story ever told about the lost souls wandering the South for centuries. And, sensitive to Amy's desire to keep their relationship G-rated in front of the kids, Nick insisted that Amy and Katy sleep in one tent, he and Sam in another.

Having put it off as long as she could, Amy opened the email. It didn't matter what Dave said. It didn't matter if she still had feelings for him, she couldn't trust him. And, he was married. Amy wondered what his wife would think of his actions.

Amy,

It was good to see you again. I've been thinking of you a lot lately. I've missed you. I could really use a friend right now. I'd like to get together sometime and catch up. I'll give you a call.

Dave

P.S. You looked great ;)

Too bad, she thought as she pushed delete key, then emptied the email from her trash. Dave was obviously having marriage problems, but he would just have to find someone else's shoulder to cry on this time.

————————

Dave signed on to the instant messaging program, hoping Amy would eventually sign on as well. She hadn't responded to any of his emails and didn't answer the phone when he called. He knew he should just leave her alone as she had asked, but he had to win her back somehow, and soon. Once she married, she would be off limits forever. He had just about nodded off when he heard the familiar tone indicating someone had signed on. Anxiously he looked at the screen. It was Amy. Nervously, he began typing.

MrVandelay: hi doll

Amy stared at her screen. The conflict raging within

her was enormous. She wanted to talk to him as badly as she wanted him to leave her alone.

>MrVandelay: I need to talk to you
>
>LadyBird67: talk to your wife
>
>MrVandelay: I'm not married
>
>LadyBird67: I'm sorry things didn't work out
>
>LadyBird67: I don't think this is a good idea
>
>MrVandelay: what
>
>LadyBird67: us talking
>
>MrVandelay: we're just a couple of old friends catching up
>
>LadyBird67: no we're not
>
>LadyBird67: we're not just old friends
>
>MrVandelay: can I call you? I need to talk to you.
>
>LadyBird67: no
>
>MrVandelay: is he there
>
>LadyBird67: goodnight

As Amy signed off, she was sure she could feel a new fissure beginning to form on her badly fractured heart.

———————————

Running on the beach was a luxury Amy never tired of. Being born and raised in the Midwest, the ocean had a magical lure, beckoning her to its shores. She enjoyed the solitude of the beach early in the morning, before the crowds of tourists hit. When the kids were little, Amy had loaded them in the all-terrain stroller and pushed them along the beach as she ran. The kids had loved it, and the added weight had given her a good workout.

Lately, all Amy could think about was Dave. She needed to run, to be alone and think. A part of her still loved Dave, and always would, but she wasn't in love with him anymore. She loved Nick. She feared that somehow, despite her efforts to the contrary, Dave was going to find a way to screw up her life. Again.

————————

Dave was careful not to overwhelm Amy with his attempts to talk to her. He limited himself to one phone call and a couple of emails every week, none of which were answered or acknowledged. She hadn't been signing on to the instant messaging, so that avenue was closed to him. He knew if he could just get her alone, if she would just listen to him, she wouldn't be able to say no. She still loved him — he could see it in her eyes. He just needed to convince her to act on it.

The sun had yet to come up when Dave reached for the phone. A groggy Katy answered the phone. He asked for Amy, biting his lip as he waited. Would she come to the phone? Katy got back on and said she was gone, that she'd probably gone to Tybee to run. Dave thanked her and headed towards the beach.

Pulling into the parking lot by the pier on Tybee Island, Dave saw Amy's van. Good, he thought, he hadn't missed her. Standing on the pier, he saw her in the distance, running in his direction, obviously on her way back. His heart skipped a beat when he saw her veer towards the pier. He moved back from the railing, turning his back to her to keep from being spotted. He had no doubt she would turn around and run back down the beach if she knew he was there.

He watched her walk towards the bathrooms. He followed, staying far enough behind to conceal the fact that he was following her. When the bathroom door closed, he looked around for the best place to confront her. He sat down at the nearest table, making sure to face the bathroom door. He took out his Blackberry and pretended to be checking messages.

It seemed like an eternity before he heard the door open again. He looked up, pretending to be surprised. "Amy."

His shock might have been fabricated, but Amy's was real. "Dave. What are you doing here?"

"I have to meet a client just up the beach in a bit. I thought I'd enjoy the ocean for a while first."

She had nothing to say to him. She turned to leave.

"Amy, why won't you talk to me?"

She stopped, putting a hand on her hip as she turned. "That might just be the dumbest thing you've ever said."

"I just want to talk with you."

Amy moved closer, visibly shaking. "No, you don't want to talk with me. You want to talk to me. You want me to listen to the details of your divorce and tell you how stupid she was to let you go. You want me to build you up and make you feel like a man again so that you can go off to your next conquest. You found out I'm happy and you can't stand it. You don't want me Dave, and you never have, so why does it bother you so bad when someone else does?"

"I do want you, Amy, that's what I've been trying to tell you. I've been trying to tell you how much I love you and how stupid I was to ever —"

She held up her hand to cut him off. "Don't you dare come back into my life proclaiming your love for me. You don't love me, you just can't stand it that someone else does. You want me sitting at home alone, available for you every time you need someone to put you back together. Well, Humpty Dumpty, I suggest you find all the kings' horses and all the kings' men, and if they can't help you, then, neither can I. You're on your own."

"I'm sorry I hurt you. I was stupid. I was confused. My head was so messed up back then. Please give me another chance. I'll spend the rest of my life proving to you how much I love you and how sorry I am for all I've put you through."

"No, Dave. I'm in love with Nick. I'm marrying Nick. There's nothing you can do to change my mind. Nothing. So

please, just do us both a favor and leave me alone. Please."
Without giving him time to answer, she turned around and
jogged off.

Nick let himself in and heard the shower running. He
was rummaging around the kitchen for a snack to go along
with his beer when the phone rang. He picked it up, but
before he could say hello, he heard Amy's voice.

"Hello?"

Nick started to hang up the phone, then stopped when
he heard Dave's voice.

"Amy, please don't hang up."

"You have to quit calling me."

"I can't. I mean, I know I should, but I need to talk to
you. Seeing you this morning only reminded me of how
badly I want you. I love you. When can I see you again?"

"No, Dave, I told you. It's over. We don't have anything
to talk about."

"I love you, Amy. You can't tell me you don't love me,
too. I saw it in your eyes."

"The only thing I had in my eyes was sand. I love Nick.
I'm marrying Nick."

"I know what I saw, Amy. I know you still love me."

"How is it you couldn't tell I was in love with you
before, but now you can? And do you know what? My love
for you was never the question. I was the one begging for a

scrap from your table, a scrap I might add, you only threw if you thought I might be slipping away. It doesn't matter if I love you or not. It's over. We're over."

"Amy, please. Tell me you still love me. Tell me I'm not too late."

"Good-bye, Dave."

———————

Without bothering to turn on the lights, Nick sat down on the sofa in the family room, waiting for Amy to finish her shower. Amy walked in wearing nothing but a towel and screamed when she saw the shadow of a man move.

Nick quickly turned on the light. "It's me, Baby. It's me." He rushed towards her to hold her.

"What are you doing sitting here in the dark? You scared me to death."

Remembering the phone conversation he'd overhead, he released her. Had she been with that man this morning? His thoughts were all over the place. He was having a hard time concentrating. "I was just sitting here thinking. I got here while you were in the shower."

She put her arms around him, and tip-toed to kiss him. "Why didn't you join me?"

"You know what, Babe? My brother called, and Dad's doing worse. Would you mind if we didn't go out tonight?"

"Not at all. Let me get dressed, and I'll whip up some dinner real quick. We can watch a movie or something."

"I don't think I'd be much company tonight. I think I'll just go home, think some things over."

Amy stepped back. She'd never seen Nick like this. His father had been diagnosed with lung cancer three months ago. They'd given him two to three years to live. Had something changed? Had he taken a turn for the worse?

"Is everything okay? How bad is your dad?"

"Pretty bad. I just need to be alone." As bad as he didn't want to know, he had to know what was going on with Amy and this Dave guy. He paused at the door.

"Amy, is that Dave guy still calling you?"

"Some."

"Are you still in love with him?"

"I love you. Where is this coming from? What's wrong?"

"What did you do this morning?"

"I went running on the beach. Why?"

"Alone?"

"Yes. Nick, what's going on?"

"Nothing. Never mind. I'll call you tomorrow." He kissed her, not on the lips, but on the cheek.

She went about her evening, trying not to jump to conclusions. Nick's behavior was completely out of character. She didn't know how, but she knew that Dave Baldwin had to be behind this.

Chapter Thirty-Two

Dave walked out of his office, fishing his keys out of his pocket as he walked towards his car. He looked up and recognized Nick, leaning against a shiny red truck, parked next to Dave's car.

Nick's arms were crossed against his chest. He watched Dave approach. Dave sat his briefcase in the backseat of his open convertible, keeping his eye on Nick.

"Dave," Nick said, when Dave got closer, "got a minute?" He walked up to Dave and shook his hand.

"Sure, what's on your mind?" Had Amy put him up to this? Dave was a big guy, and strong, but Nick was bigger —and stronger. As he hoped this would be a friendly encounter, Dave tried not to think about his Amy making love to the man standing before him.

"Wanna talk here, in front of all your coworkers, or

would you rather grab a beer?"

"I don't have a lot of time. Mind telling me what this is about?"

"Amy," Nick said, his expressionless gaze never wandering from Dave's face. "Don't worry, I'm not the violent type. I just need a few answers. I'm not leading you to an ambush. You pick the place. If you can't meet now, just tell me when and where."

May as well get it over with, Dave thought. He mentioned a bar on River Street, within walking distance.

Nick nodded. "Good enough. I'll see you there in a few minutes. I know you're in a hurry. This shouldn't take long." Nick shook Dave's hand again and started walking towards the bar. Dave, too, would walk over, but not with Nick. Dave waited until Nick was out of sight, transferred his briefcase to the trunk and headed to the bar.

After the bright sunshine, it took a moment for Dave's eyes to acclimate to the dim light in bar. Nick was sitting at a table near the back when Dave walked in. Dave walked towards him, dreading whatever was to come. His initial fear that this would become physical had waned. Nick seemed in control, but that could quickly change.

Dave got a beer at the bar before making his way to Nick, sitting across the table from him.

Nick leaned towards Dave, turning his bottle of beer in circles with his thumb and middle finger. Dave waited for Nick to speak.

"What's going on with you and Amy?"

That wasn't the question he'd expected. He expected Nick to ask why he continued to contact her when she gave him no reason to believe she was interested. He expected Nick to tell him to leave them alone.

"I don't understand."

"It's a simple question. What's going on with you and Amy?"

"Nothing." Dave searched his face for signs of impending violence and saw none.

"Do you deny seeing her yesterday?"

"Yesterday?"

"Yes, yesterday morning. Did she meet you somewhere?"

"No. I saw her, but she didn't meet me. I called her house early in the morning. Katy answered the phone and told me she'd gone running on Tybee. I drove out there in the hopes of catching her, to talk to her."

"And?" Nick prodded.

"And," Dave continued, "To borrow your phrase, I ambushed her. When she came out of the bathroom on the pier, she didn't know I was there. Hell, if she'd known I was there, she'd never have come out of the bathroom. She'd probably still be in there."

Nick didn't respond. He appeared to be thinking over Dave's answer and his next question. Dave saw the pain on Nick's face and knew he was the cause of it. He'd been in

Nick's position before and it sickened him that he was on the other side of the table, having this conversation.

"Look, Nick. Amy hasn't done anything wrong. She hasn't given me any encouragement whatsoever. I —"

"So why do you keep bothering her? Why don't you leave her alone?"

"I don't know," Dave answered. "Stupidity. Hope. Desperation. I love her. I want her back. I figured as long as she was still single, as long as she wasn't married, maybe there was a chance I could convince her to give me one more chance."

Nick remained silent a moment, then stood, offering his hand to Dave. Dave stood and shook his hand. That's it? That's all he's going to ask?

"Thanks. I appreciate your honesty." Looking defeated, Nick started to walk away.

"Nick," Dave said, as Nick turned around to face him. "You don't have anything to worry about. She made it pretty clear she doesn't love me."

Nick looked him directly in the eye. "I wouldn't be so sure."

Dave watched Nick walk out into the blinding sunlight, wondering what Nick meant.

———————

Amy parked near the pier on Tybee Island. Nick had called, asking her to meet him here. She was apprehensive.

Why hadn't he just picked her up? What was wrong? He'd been distant ever since he left her house a few nights ago, and Amy couldn't figure out why. She took off her sandals and carried them as she walked onto the sand. The sun would be setting soon. Nick loved watching the sunset. Is that why he'd asked her here? Was everything okay now?

"Hey, Hero," she said, coming up behind him. She wanted to rush into his arms, but she was waiting for a sign that he wanted her to.

He turned, opening his arms, which she promptly fell into. She breathed a sigh of relief. Everything was okay. He held her for a long time. Amy didn't want him to ever let go.

He pulled back and looked at her. "Wanna take a walk?"

She smiled and nodded. He took her hand, and they headed down the beach, walking just out of reach of the water. Something was on his mind. She could see the vein in his temple working, meaning he was thinking, working up to something, but what?

Several minutes passed before he spoke. "We need to talk."

Amy's heart fell. She'd never had a good conversation that started out with we need to talk. "About what?"

More silence, then finally. "I went to see Dave Baldwin earlier today."

"What? Why?" Amy let go of his hand and swung

around in front of him, blocking his way. She struggled for an intelligent question, but could only come up with, "Why?"

Nick saw a large piece of driftwood near the dunes. "Let's go sit down, okay?" Amy followed, sitting beside him, waiting for the answer to her question. What did Dave say that obviously upset Nick so much?

Looking down while he played with the sand with his feet, Nick began. "You know the other night, when you came out of the shower, and I was sitting in the dark?"

Amy nodded.

"I'd been there for a while. I guess I got there just as you were getting ready to get in the shower. I was in the kitchen getting a beer when the phone rang. I picked it up just as you answered."

Amy's head was spinning, trying to replay the conversation in her head. What had they said that upset him so much?

"He said something about meeting you that morning, and you said something about you couldn't see him anymore." His voice grew soft. He looked over at her, meeting her gaze. "I thought you were having an affair with him."

Looking back, she could see how it could have sounded that way. "I ran into him on the pier. I saw him when I came out of the bathroom. I didn't know he was there. If I had known I wouldn't have gone running at all."

"I know that now," he said, looking at his feet again. "But that's not how it sounded at the time."

"So everything's okay now? Between us, I mean?"

He turned and looked at her. "Do you still love him?"

"What? Nick, I love you. You know I love you. How can you even ask me that?"

Nick let out a small laugh, more a snort actually. He closed his eyes and shook his head.

"You don't believe me?"

"I believe you."

"Then what? What's wrong?"

"Do you realize you never say no to that question?"

"What question?"

"If you love him."

"I don't understand."

Nick drew a deep breath. "Dave asked you, more than once I believe, if you still loved him. You never said no, you just kept telling him you loved me."

"But I do love you."

"I know you do. But you've never denied loving him." Emotion choked his voice as he struggled to finish. "I think you're still in love with him."

Amy threw her arms around him. "No, Nick. You're wrong. I don't love him. I love you." When Nick didn't return her embrace, she feared she had lost him. "Nick, I love you. You believe me, don't you?"

For the next hour, Amy listened to Nick's plan for his

life, a life that no longer included her. After his parents retired, they moved to his father's hometown of Atmore, Alabama, a small farming community just north of Mobile, near the Florida border. Not long after, Nick's brother, Steve, had left the Savannah Fire Department, joining his parents in Alabama. Steve divided his time between helping his father on the farm and working for the fire department in Mobile to the south.

Nick's father was dying of cancer. He didn't have the two to three years the doctors had originally projected. It was more likely less than a year. Steve wanted Nick to move to Alabama, to spend time with their father. The Mobile Fire Department was hiring, and with Nick's exemplary record in Savannah, Steve assured Nick he would have no problem getting the job.

Amy was still trying to absorb what Nick was saying.

"I've decided I need to be with my dad right now. I can't miss what little time I have left with my father. I'm turning in my resignation tomorrow."

Amy was suddenly cold and could barely work up enough spit to pry her tongue from the roof of her mouth. "What about us?"

Another long silence stretched before them.

"I don't know, Amy."

There was no stopping the tears that began to flow down her cheeks. "Don't you love me anymore?"

"Amy," he said, grabbing her close. "I'll love you 'til the

day I die, but I've got to go to my family right now. And you," he paused, choking back the tears, "you've got to decide who you love. Me or —" He couldn't bring himself to say Dave's name. "Me or him."

"I've already made my decision," Amy cried indignantly. "I choose you. There was never a choice to make. I love you Nick. I don't love him."

"I wish I could believe you," Nick said. Even though it was now dark, Amy saw the moisture on his cheeks. It was the only time she'd ever seen Nick cry.

———————

Dave walked out of his office, fishing his keys out of his pocket as he walked towards his car. He looked up and saw Amy, leaning against her van, parked next to Dave's car.

Déjà vu, he thought. Even from across the parking lot, he could see the rage seething in her.

She walked to meet him. "We need to talk. Do you have any bottled water in there?" She motioned towards the office building.

"Yes."

"Grab a couple and meet me in Johnson Square."

Without waiting for a response, she turned around and walked away.

He left his briefcase in his office, grabbed a couple bottles of water and hurried to Johnson Square. First Nick, now Amy. He had a feeling Amy wouldn't be nearly as cordial as Nick had been.

Dave handed Amy a bottle of water, then sat at the far end of the bench. The last time he'd sat on a bench in this Square — and if memory served him correctly, this very bench, he'd ended up married. He wasn't sure if it was a good or bad omen that he happened to be in this same exact spot with Amy.

He glanced sideways at her. She was breathing hard, clearly angry. Like he had with Nick, he gave her time to collect her thoughts.

Amy purposely didn't look at Dave. She didn't want to remember him. She didn't want to remember them together. She didn't want to think about anything except the fact that he had waltzed into her life and ripped it apart yet again. She took a long drink of water, then recapped the bottle.

"Exactly what did you say to Nick?"

Dave looked at her. When he saw she wasn't looking at him, he stared at the fountain.

"He thought we were having an affair. I told him you haven't given me one ounce of encouragement. I told him he didn't have anything to worry about, that you loved him, not me."

That much, she already knew. "Anything else?"

"Not really. It was a pretty brief conversation."

A pretty brief conversation that destroyed my life, she thought. She took another drink of water.

"You treat me like I'm a damn boomerang," Amy said. "Like you can throw me away and I'll come back to your outstretched hand."

It was the first time Dave had ever heard her curse.

"I'm not a toy you can just play with until you get tired of it. You rip my heart out time and time again, then toss out some cursory apology like that makes everything okay, but it doesn't. And there's something even more important you're not considering. It's not just me you hurt when you sashayed in and out of my life. You hurt Katy and Sam, too. Have you ever once thought of what you did to them?"

Dave hung his head, ashamed of himself. He hadn't.

"It's not just me who was owed an apology. The kids deserved one, too."

"Amy, I —"

"How long have you been divorced? I'm guessing since right before you barged back into my life."

"Actually," he paused to take a drink of water, "I never got married."

"What happened?"

This was a conversation he knew he'd have to have with her, but he'd hoped he wouldn't have to have it today. "Nothing happened. I wasn't getting married."

She turned to look at him, confused. "Then why did you tell me you were?"

"To keep from hurting you anymore."

"What?"

"I knew if I told you I was getting married, that you'd leave me alone, that —"

"That I'd leave you alone?"

"That's not what I meant. Amy, at that time, you wanted more than I could give you. I was an emotional wreck. I knew if I was around you, I'd keep crossing that line. I'd keep hurting you. I couldn't be around you and not want you. I was too attracted to you to keep my hands off of you. I knew if I told you I was getting married, you wouldn't to try to contact me. And," he exhaled loudly, "I knew I wouldn't be able to come back into your life."

She stared at him, her mouth hanging open. She closed her eyes and shook her head momentarily. "Let me get this straight. You lied to me, telling me you were getting married, because you knew I would respect the sanctity of your marriage because you didn't have the integrity not to keep using me?"

"I didn't mean it the way you're making it sound."

"Exactly how, then, did you mean it?"

"I just wanted to burn the bridge. I didn't want to be able to cross it and hurt you anymore."

"That's a very clinical way to say it." Amy was shaking with fury. She finished her water, depositing the empty bottle into a nearby trash can. She walked back to the bench where Dave sat and stood directly in front of him. "You told me you were getting married to burn the bridge, huh?"

He didn't answer.

"Congratulations. You succeeded. Consider it burned."
She turned and walked away.

He called after her, knowing she wouldn't turn around.

Chapter Thirty-Three

Paula knew what a meeting with Dave at A-Vida's meant. He was going drink too much while bemoaning yet another crisis in his love life. Honestly, she thought, for a man who had every other aspect of his life together, his love life was sure a disaster.

Dave was waiting for her, along with a bottle of wine.

"A whole bottle already, huh?"

"Oh yeah," he said, pouring her a glass.

"Who is it this time?"

"Amy."

"You must like Amys. This is what, your third Amy?" Paula laughed.

"Actually, it's the first Amy."

Paula, getting ready to take a drink, quickly sat down her glass. "Oh no, Dave. You didn't hurt that poor woman again did you?"

"Yes and no," he answered. He then proceeded to tell her about running into her on Tybee Island over Memorial Day weekend, and of his attempts to talk to Amy, culminating in their confrontation a few days earlier in Johnson Square. He talked all through dinner and ordered another bottle of wine.

As always, Paula listened intently. Finally talked out, Dave sat back, awaiting her advice, but Paula remained mute.

"So?"

"So — what?" Paula asked.

"What do I do?"

"You can't be serious."

"Never more so," he replied.

"You walk all over this woman, how many times? You come to me years ago wanting to know how to get rid of her forever — because you don't have the self-control not to use her — and now you want me to tell you how to win her back?"

"As implausible as that sounds, yes."

"You're an idiot, do you know that?"

"Yup," he answered. "I've known that for a long time."

"So have I."

"But you love me anyway, right Sis?" He had three sisters, but Paula was the only one he ever called Sis.

"Yes, I love you, but I have to. Amy doesn't. And unless

she's as dumb as you are, she'll run screaming into traffic if she sees you heading her way."

"So, are you going to help me?"

Paula put her elbows on the table, a social no-no she often scolded her kids for. She laid her chin on her folded hands and answered. "Yes, big brother. I will help you. It may not be the kind of help you want, but I can help you. I always thought you got off on the rescue, that you'd find a woman who needed a super hero to come in and make right her life, but I was wrong."

Dave rolled his eyes.

"If you're not going to listen with an open mind," Paula said, "I'm done talking."

"Sorry, point taken. I'm all ears." Dave said.

"Yeah, I noticed that. I always thought you'd grow into those puppies, but they still look huge."

"Ha, ha." Dave said. "Very funny."

"Seriously, I know what you've been doing wrong all these years." When Dave didn't respond, she continued. "You keep looking for someone you don't even like." She smiled; pleased with herself, as though she'd just given him the answer to all his problems

"That's where you're wrong, because from where I sit, all I ever seem to find are women I don't like."

"I mean, smart-alec, that you're looking for a Ginger clone and another Ginger is not what will make you happy."

Dave was taken aback. "Of course she made me happy. I loved her. You're way off, Sis."

"I know you loved her, Dave, but if she hadn't gotten pregnant with Cathy, you never would have married her."

Dave opened his mouth to protest, but Paula continued. "But just because you loved her doesn't mean she's the kind of woman you're looking for."

"Okay, Dr. Freud, since you seem to have all the answers, enlighten me."

"It would be my pleasure." She poured them both another glass of wine. "You're looking for someone to save."

"I thought you said I didn't enjoy the rescue. How's that fit into your theory?"

"Oh, I didn't mean to imply that you don't get off on the rescue, you do. My point is, you think you failed as a husband or a man or whatever because you couldn't save Ginger, but you know what? You didn't fail Ginger. She failed herself. You know as well as I do that you can't change other people.

"It's like you need to validate yourself by saving someone. You couldn't save Ginger, so you unconsciously pick women with problems so that you can save them, as if in saving them, you can somehow redeem yourself. But there's nothing to redeem, Dave. Ginger brought her troubles on herself. You kept trying to help her long after most everyone else had given up on her."

Dave looked visibly defeated. He opened his mouth several times to speak, but in the end, he just stared at his wine glass and said nothing.

Paula reached across the table and laid her hand of Dave's arm. "Look, Dave, I don't mean to beat you up or belittle what you had with Ginger. I know you loved her. But if you're honest with yourself, finding another Ginger won't make you happy. Rescuing someone else won't take the pain away. You won't be happy, and no one will make you happy, until you forgive yourself for whatever it is you think you've done."

Paula leaned back in her chair and watched as Dave digested her words.

After several minutes, Dave finally found his voice. "You might be right, but it's easier said than done."

Paula's voice softened. "Describe the perfect woman."

"Well, I guess she'd be funny and sweet and beautiful. She'd be sentimental and forgiving. She wouldn't be materialistic. She'd prefer dandelions and wild daisies to expensive flowers. She'd find me witty and handsome and charming and …"

Paula laughed. "So your perfect woman is a little addle-brained?" she teased.

"Yeah," Dave laughed. "I guess she'd have to be."

Paula looked across the table at her brother. "Seriously, Dave, do you realize you just described Amy, not Ginger?"

"I know. I already knew Amy was perfect for me. I

came to you to find out how to get her back."

"Davy," she said reverting back to his childhood nickname, "I don't think I can help you with this one. I don't think anyone can. I doubt there's anything you can do to get back into her good graces. You worked hard to burn that bridge. It sounds like you may very well have succeeded. You ran away from her love all those years. You pushed her away time and time again. It sounds to me like you pushed her away too far to ever be able to pull her back."

He swirled the wine in his glass, watching the light play off the liquid. "I know, but I've got to try."

Paula stared at her brother. She hated seeing him in so much pain. "I know what eats at you about Ginger."

"You do?" Dave looked at his sister. Did she know? Had Ginger told her?

"Yes, I do." She leaned forward in her chair. "You wonder what would have happened if she hadn't lost that baby. You wonder if she'd been able to carry that baby to term then maybe she wouldn't have —"

Dave cut her off with a cynical laugh. "No, Sis, nothing could be further from the truth."

———————————

"Dave Baldwin, as I live and breathe." Jenny said, in that sweet, Southern voice that made every red blooded man weak in the knees. "I've been expecting your call."

"I didn't know who else to turn to. You've got to help

me, Jenny."

"Actually, Dave, my allegiance is to Amy."

"I know, but I'm begging you, Jenny. Please help me win her back." Dave could hear her breathing into the phone. "Please?"

"Do you realize," she finally said, "that you have effectively ruined every relationship Amy has had since that fateful day on River Street?"

"I don't know what you mean."

"Do you realize that Nick is the first man Amy allowed into her life since you left?"

He swallowed hard. "I didn't know that."

"Well, now you do. And, now, you're the reason Nick left."

Dave's mind reeled at the revelation. "What?"

"She didn't tell you?"

"No."

"I guess I shouldn't have said anything, then."

"It's a little late now. Why did he leave her?"

"I guess it doesn't matter now. He thinks she's still in love with you."

For the first time in a long time, Dave felt a glimmer of hope. "Is she?"

"Does it matter?"

"Yes. I have to know if I have a chance with her, however small."

"Haven't you hurt her enough?"

"I swear to you, Jenny, I'll never hurt her again. I just need another chance to prove it to her."

"If you love her as much as you say you do, you'll forget about her."

"I can't forget about her."

"Then let her forget about you." With that, Jenny hung up.

Dave held the phone in his hand until it started beeping, signaling the phone was off the hook. He dropped the phone in its cradle, leaned back and closed his eyes. No one was on his side. Not that he'd expected anyone to be, but he had hoped he could find an ally in his fight to win Amy back.

That was quite a bombshell Jenny had dropped. Nick had left Amy. When? It had only been a few days since Nick had come to see him. What made Nick think Amy still loved him? More importantly — did she?

The more he thought about Amy and all he had put her through, the more he realized Jenny was right. He needed to leave Amy alone and let her forget about him. As forgiving as she was, it was hard to believe she could forgive him for driving away the man she loved.

He did love her. He loved her enough to let her go.

Chapter Thirty-Four

Driving in silence, Dave drove towards Bonaventure Cemetery. Bonaventure, meaning *'good fortune'* in Italian, Bonaventure Cemetery, sits high on the bluffs overlooking the Willington River, just south and east of Savannah. Dave remembered something an old Savannahian had told him — *'It is believed that to be buried in Bonaventure is almost better than being alive anywhere else'.*

Now a resting place for thousands, Bonaventure had once been home to a wealthy plantation owner, Josiah Tattnall, Jr. The grand home burned to the ground during a party in 1800. When servants alerted their host that the home was hopelessly on fire, he instructed them to carry the tables, chairs, and food outside to the front lawn, where the guests continued the festivities by the light of the burning mansion.

One unknown guest made a toast — *'May the joy of this party never end'*. Everyone raised their glasses and drank to the toast, then smashed their crystal goblets against a nearby live oak. It is said that on calm nights, particularly in autumn, the sound of silverware clanking against plates, muffled laughter, and the sound of crystal breaking can still be heard.

Having stopped for a bouquet of bright spring flowers on his way, he arrived at the cemetery shortly before they closed. The guard stopped him, telling Dave the gates would be closing in thirty minutes. Dave thanked him, telling him he wouldn't be long, and headed inside., leaving his window down to enjoy a rare summer breeze.

Carefully navigating the narrow dirt roads that meander through the graveyard, with graves dating back to 1846, he knew all too well how easy it was get lost among those winding dirt paths.

As he picked his way through the narrow roads, he glanced out the window. Long before Bonaventure became a tourist attraction, he'd spent countless childhood hours here playing hide and go seek among the intricately carved, towering tombstones. He always wanted to play at night, but his sisters were too afraid. His sisters' fears also kept him from being able to come back at night in the autumn to witness the ghostly party he'd heard so much about.

Carloads of tourists drove slowly up and down the lanes, lingering near the graves of some of the more famous residents. Dave ignored them. The tourists, keeping their sightseeing to the front of the graveyard, rarely, if ever, ventured into the newer, less picturesque sections in the back. For that, he was grateful. He didn't want any witnesses to what he had to do. He was on a mission to say good-bye.

Dirt and grass clippings had been flung onto Ginger's tombstone, filling in some of the letters deeply engraved in the thick granite. His normal routine was to wipe the stone clean of debris, but he didn't this time. He simply stared at the stone, chewing on his bottom lip.

"Ginger," he began, "I owe you an apology. I didn't always love you like I should have. I'll go to my grave believing you would never be where you are if I had loved you better. You wouldn't have become addicted to drugs if I had taken better care of you after the accident. You wouldn't have run off with Dale. You wouldn't have moved to Atlanta or started doing meth.

"It might not have felt like it, Ginger, but I did love you. I loved you the best I knew how. I'm not sure I'll ever be able forgive myself for what happened to you.

"I've done a lot of soul searching. All these years I've been beating myself up, blaming myself for everything, drinking in the blame and soaking it up like a martyr. I made a lot of mistakes, but I loved you and I was faithful to you. I honored our vows. Nothing would have made me happier than to grow old with you by my side.

"I have been so lonely and felt so lost all these years without you. I threw away every chance I had at love because it felt like I was betraying you. Betraying your memory. Betraying us.

"I came here today to tell you I forgive you. I forgive you for leaving, for the drugs, and for all the hurtful things you said and did. I can forgive you the drugs and the infidelity. I can even forgive you for abandoning Cathy, but there's one thing I don't think I can forgive you for."

He was crying now, angrily pointing his finger at her grave. "But you killed our baby. You let me hold you night after night while you cried yourself to sleep. You let me think you were crying because you had a miscarriage, but you were crying because you had an abortion." He spit the words at her. "It's bad enough that you did it, but it's despicable that you told me. You had no right to tell me. There was no reason to tell me. How could you do that to me? You knew how much I wanted another child. You told me just to hurt me. It was nothing more than pouring salt in a wound — and it was just cruel. Maybe you told me so that I'd hate you, so that losing you wouldn't hurt so bad. But I didn't hate you, Ginger. I hated myself."

He stared off into the distance, his breaths coming in ragged gasps before slowly calming down.

"No, Ginger, I take that back. I forgive you for that, too. I forgive you, and I hope before you died, that you were able to forgive me, too.

"I came here to tell you good-bye. I won't be coming back. I hope you find the peace in death that so eluded you in life."

Having purged himself of the guilt he'd so carefully cultivated over the years, he wiped his face and got back into his car. It was over. Ginger was gone.

He drove the short distance to Susie and Greg's graves, grabbing the flowers before he got out. Dave pulled the nearly dead flowers from the vases, then divided the flowers evenly before placing them into the urns. After wiping the headstone clean, he got in his car and drove off. Having finally forgiven Ginger, Dave felt lighter. More importantly, he had forgiven himself.

For the first time in his life, he was truly free.

Chapter Thirty-Five

Saturday dawned bright and clear. It promised to be a perfect fall day, crisp without being cold. He was going to see Amy today with the hope of building her porch with the brick she'd purchased years ago. She had bought those bricks for Susie and Greg over a decade ago. He recalled it had been a Christmas present, bought with the intention of replacing the wooden porch Greg built when they first bought the property. Dave was going to offer build the porch for Amy. He didn't know how she'd react. He didn't know what he'd do if she refused, since he'd already bought everything he needed to complete the job. He could always take it back, but he hoped he wouldn't have to.

He had noticed a while back that the bricks were no longer in the driveway. At first he thought she'd gotten rid of them, and was a bit miffed that she hadn't sold them to him, and then he noticed them stacked next to the garage.

Dave rang her doorbell. The door was open and he could hear music playing softly from somewhere inside. "Just a minute," Amy yelled. Dave stood back, waiting for her to come to the door.

The look on Amy's face when she saw Dave broke his heart. She stopped as soon as she recognized him, crossing her arms defiantly. "You're a little early. I haven't started dating anyone yet. There's no relationship to ruin. Check back in a couple of months."

"I came to ask you if I can build your porch."

"I already have a porch, but thanks anyway." She turned to leave.

"Don't, Amy. Look, you have every right to hate me." She had stopped walking, but kept her back towards him. "I didn't come here to try to convince you to give me another chance. I don't deserve one. I know that. I just want to do something to show you I'm sorry. I want to build the brick porch for you, like Susie and Greg always imagined."

She turned to face him, but kept her distance. "I appreciate the offer, but no thanks. Susie and Greg don't much care about the porch anymore."

"No strings attached. I know how much you've always wanted the brick porch and I want to do it for you. I'll work during the day, while you're at school. You won't have to see me. I'll be gone by the time you get home. I promise." She didn't answer. Was she contemplating saying yes? "No strings attached, Amy. I'll build the porch, and you'll never see me. You'll never have to see me. Okay?"

She stared at him, considering his offer. "Okay, but on one condition."

"Sure," he said. "Anything."

"If I so much as see the taillights of your truck as you're pulling away, you pay someone to finish the porch for you."

"Okay," he agreed.

"I mean it."

"I know. I'll start Monday."

She didn't answer. She just turned around and disappeared into the kitchen.

Dave had vastly overrated his masonry skills. It took him almost two weeks to do what a skilled brick layer could have accomplished in a just a few days, but he was finally done. He had to admit, the porch turned out beautifully. He'd been shy several bricks, so used some from the sidewalk. His architectural firm had an inventory of old cobblestones. He purchased enough of them to fill in the missing bricks from the walkway. It had taken some rearranging of the bricks to incorporate the cobblestones evenly throughout, and it had turned out better than he had expected.

Jane had taken to stopping over every day, bringing a snack or cold drink, or both. He could tell by the look in her eyes that she sympathized with his plight. After praising his work, she had patted his hand. "I'm going to miss you."

"I'm going to miss your cookies," Dave said, laughing.

"Give her time, Dave. Don't push. She may never let you back, but she does love you."

Her unsolicited hope surprised him.

"Don't look at me that way. I know what's going on. I may be old, but I know love when I see it. Just give her time. And pray."

With that, Jane made her way to the bridge. She waved without looking back.

Dave wished he could see the look on Amy's face when she saw it, but he honored his word to her. He cleaned up the yard, replanting the vegetation in front of the porch and was gone only minutes before she pulled into the drive.

Amy got out of the van, staring at Dave's handiwork. The porch looked like it had been there a hundred years. He'd replaced the small square columns with more substantial round ones. His note had said they fit the architecture better. He was right.

She walked onto the porch, running her hand over the rails and the columns. Dave had touched every inch of this wood. She laid her forehead against the column, closed her eyes and cried.

Chapter Thirty-Six

A few days before Halloween, Amy came home to find the kids in the kitchen, surrounded by pumpkins. Pumpkin guts filled the sink. The kids sat on stools at the island, each carving designs into the hollowed shells.

"Where'd you get the pumpkins?" Amy asked.

The kids looked up at her, then at each other. "We thought you bought them," Katy said.

"No, it wasn't me." Amy sat her bags on the counter. "Maybe Jane brought them over."

Amy asked Jane about it the next morning. "No," she replied, "it wasn't me. Maybe you have a secret admirer," she said winking, leaving out the fact that she had helped Dave carry them onto the porch.

Amy laughed. "More likely I was visited by the Great Pumpkin."

"What about your boyfriend? Maybe he brought them."

"He's not my boyfriend, but that must be it."

Amy excused herself, and drove to work. She'd only gone out with James a couple of times. It was possible he'd brought the pumpkins by, but she doubted it. Later that day, he confirmed that no, he was not the benefactor of the pumpkin crop bequeathed to her.

A few weeks later, Amy pulled out of the drive and looked at all the leaves in the yard. She and the kids would have to get outside this weekend and rake them before it got too cold. She'd left them on the ground one winter and it killed the grass in the spring. She hated raking leaves. So did the kids. If doing things you didn't like to do gave you character, as Jenny so loved to claim, Amy surmised she must be quite the character.

When Amy returned home that evening, the yard was clean. Did the kids do this, she wondered happily? "Katy? Sam?" she called out as she entered the house. They looked up from their homework on the family room floor. "Did you guys rake the leaves? How'd you get done so quickly?"

"We work fast," Sam said, smiling.

Katy popped him on the head with her pencil. "Sam."

"Hey," he said, pushing her off her pillow.

Katy laughed at her brother. "We didn't do it, Mom. There was a yard service out there when we got off the bus. We thought you hired them."

"No. I can't afford a lawn service."

"Think they got the wrong house?" Sam asked.

"Probably," Amy answered. She was pleased at the mistake, but figured someone was likely to get in a lot trouble over this.

———————

A week before Thanksgiving, a frozen turkey was sitting in the rocker on the porch, complete with a big red bow and dressed in a tiny pilgrim outfit.

Amy laughed, assuming that was the kid's idea of a turkey with dressing.

As the weather grew colder, Amy eyed the dwindling pile of firewood stacked between the trees by the creek. They'd need more soon. Maybe Earl would be kind enough to let her borrow his truck to pick up a load. Before she had a chance to ask, the pile grew to overflowing.

Jane feigned ignorance of its appearance. Once again, she failed to offer the fact that it had taken Earl and Dave and more than an hour to unload all the wood.

On Christmas morning, Amy awoke to excited squeals. Kids, it seemed, were perpetually four years old on Christmas Day. The kids came bounding into her room, jumping on her bed to wake her, just like they had when they'd been little.

"It's awesome, Mom," Katy beamed.

"It is pretty cool." Sam agreed.

"What is?" Amy asked, stretching lazily as the kids

cuddled beside her. Sammy lay on top of the covers, while Katy had burrowed beneath the thick down comforter.

"The trees." they both exclaimed.

Amy laughed. "The trees? Did we get an ice storm or something?"

"Huh?" they said in unison. The kids, having grown up in Savannah, had never seen an ice storm.

"Surely it didn't snow," she said, adding, "Did it?"

"Nope," Katy said laughing, snuggling closer to Amy. "Mmmm. You're warm."

"Okay, I give. I'm out of guesses."

"You're funny," Katy said, giving her a kiss on the cheek.

Amy had no idea what the kids were talking about. She looked towards the window, but her view was obscured by the lace panels. "Let me up," she said, extricating herself from beneath blankets and kids. "I want to see what you're talking about."

Amy walked to the window, grabbing her robe and wrapping it around her. The sidewalk and driveway were lined with small Christmas trees, their twinkling lights barely visible in the morning sun. She pressed her face to the glass to try to see closer to the house, but a shrub was blocking her view. She slipped on some socks, then made her way to the porch. The kids followed, all smiles.

Wow was right, she thought.

On the corner of the house, where the porch wrapped

around to the kitchen, was a huge Christmas tree, decorated in white lights and red ornaments. A huge red bow perched at the top where a star would normally be, its ribbons cascading down the tree. Under the tree were presents wrapped in shiny gold paper.

Amy checked the packages. There were presents for all three of them — from Santa. She stood and looked at the yard. Dozens of small trees lined the drive and walk, one every couple of feet.

"How did you do all this without us hearing?" Katy asked, throwing her arms around Amy. "I'm going to get the camera." With that, she disappeared inside.

That night, sitting by the fire, Amy's thoughts drifted to Dave as she absent-mindedly played with Katy's hair. She knew he was behind the tree caper, and the other small gifts left on the porch over the last several months. Like before, Jane had feigned ignorance, but Amy didn't need anyone to confirm her suspicions. She knew Dave was responsible, and she couldn't decide if she should be angry or flattered.

The presents Dave had placed under the tree on the porch weren't extravagant, but they had been thoughtful. For Katy, there was a small bottle of perfume and some costume jewelry that thrilled her to no end. For Sam, the labels read *'Sammy'*, there was a small bottle of cologne appropriate for an eleven year old boy, collectible Hot Wheel cars and a vintage car model set to put together. He, too, was thrilled. Amy's packages contained cinnamon candles, her favorite, and a small replica of every lighthouse they had passed on the long ago boat trip she'd taken with Dave on the Intracoastal Waterway.

While he was no longer trying to contact her, he wasn't completely honoring his word of leaving her alone. It was a sweet gesture, but she couldn't let herself get caught in his web again.

The gifts continued in the ensuing months. In January, there was a basket of cocoa mix, marshmallows and stoneware mugs. The next week, a tiny snowman, no more than eight inches tall, was waving at her from the ledge outside her window one morning. Where had Dave found snow — in Savannah? She took a picture of it, then carefully picked it up. Amy put it in an old metal cash box she'd found in the garage, and put it in the freezer.

February brought chocolates and a single red rose in a hand-blown glass vase. In March, Amy was the recipient of a big stew pot that looked like the pot at the end of the rainbow, filled with frozen stew meat, vegetables and seasonings. She laughed when she cooked it. After adding the seasoning, it turned green.

April's surprise brought Amy to her knees. Driving home from work, she was thinking of all the things she needed to do. She pulled onto her street and her heart leaped. Was she seeing things?

Amy stopped in the road just before the drive. There, where Cry Baby had sat before Hurricane Floyd blew her down was a new weeping willow tree. She wasn't as tall as Cry Baby had been, but the new tree was a very large tree nonetheless. She pulled into the drive, then walked to the tree. Was she dreaming? Was it really here? She touched the tree, its graceful limbs floated around her, as if welcoming her home. Tears slipped down her cheeks. "Thank you, Dave," she said aloud.

———————

Amy visited Susie and Greg's graves regularly, though not as often as she had in the first few years. Each time she came, she brought something for them. She always brought photographs of the kids, their school pictures, photos taken at their sporting events, or just hanging out. She often brought some of their school work to let Susie and Greg know she was mindful of the kid's education. When the kids were little, she'd take pictures the kids had painstakingly drawn and colored. In the early years, Susie and Greg were stick people with wings, hovering in the sky. As they grew older, the stick people with wings became ethereal angels, always keeping watch over them.

Amy would leave the items in a gallon size plastic bag under a rock on their grave. When the bag could hold no more, Amy would take the bag home, replacing it with a new one.

Stopping in front of their gravesite, Amy noted the presence of fresh flowers, just beginning to wilt. Who was leaving them? She'd once mentioned the flowers to Greg's brothers, but neither they nor their wives knew anything about them. Jane claimed no knowledge of them, either. It could be one of Susie's friends. If anything happened to Jenny, Amy would make sure Jenny's grave always had flowers, and she was sure Jenny would do the same for her. Susie had had friends, but Amy couldn't think of one who would bring flowers to her grave so faithfully.

Amy kept remembering Dave leaving flowers on Susie and Greg's graves after Ginger's funeral. Could Dave be leaving them? No, that was preposterous. Dave wasn't leaving the flowers. Why would he bring flowers to Susie and Greg and not Ginger?

Amy never left the cemetery without driving by Ginger's grave. There had been flowers on her grave for a while after she died, but now it was always barren. Amy couldn't help but feeling sorry for her. Was she already forgotten by her family?

Chapter Thirty-Seven

The teachers' lounge was nearly empty when Amy made her way in. A few of the younger teachers were gathered at one of the tables, eating and talking. Amy sat at a different table, choking down a sandwich while she graded spelling tests. She should have done them last night. She was always sorry when she procrastinated like this. Now, instead of a leisurely lunch, she had to gulp down a sandwich while grading papers.

Amy was trying to block out the others' conversation, but it was impossible.

"He'll be playing there all week."

"I heard he's pretty cute."

"He is — and single."

"He's probably gay."

"Not from what I've heard." The women laughed.

Amy glanced over at the young teachers, one of them holding some kind of flyer. A new band must be in town, Amy thought.

"I used to go to The Mulberry Inn when he filled in for their regular piano player. He's mighty fine."

That got Amy's attention. Kevin's mother was often called to provide a name for a replacement piano player for The Mulberry Inn's daily tea time. Dave was usually her first choice.

Amy walked over to their table. "Can I see that?" she asked, motioning to the flyer.

"Sure."

From the flyer, the handsome face of Dave Baldwin smiled up at her. Amy skimmed over the type. 'Trained under the world renowned Linda Caldwell'. Amy recognized the name as Kevin's mother. She skipped further down the page 'Playing this week only 7pm-11pm at Savannah's newest hot spot — The Coastal Empire Piano Bar'. Amy had heard about the place, but she'd never gone.

Amy checked herself in the mirror one final time. She'd chosen a pair of dark jeans and a long sleeved navy shirt. The bar would be dark and she wanted to be nothing more than a shadow. Amy had no intention of letting Dave see her. She'd slip in, sit near the back for a few songs, then slip out unnoticed. If he saw her, she planned on leaving immediately, so what did it matter what she looked like? It didn't, she told herself. Still, she checked her hair and makeup one more time before she left.

Driving to the bar, she talked herself into and out of going to see him a million times. This was crazy, she told herself. What did she hope to accomplish? She didn't want to talk to him. She just wanted to see him, to hear his voice. He'd never even know she was there.

Amy walked in with a group of women, hoping to blend into the crowd. She found an empty table in the back and blew out the candle on the table. In the semi-darkness of the bar, and this far away, she was sure Dave wouldn't be able to recognize her. She sat sideways to him, watching him from the corner of her eye. He was playing a Billy Joel tune when she arrived. He was good. His fingers flew over the keys as he sang. He had a strong clear voice. She'd always loved his voice.

She stayed longer than she'd intended, and she was growing nervous. She was pressing her luck to be here this long and not be noticed. As she stood to leave, she heard him announce his next selection.

"This next song is an original, and it's my first time playing it in public. It's about a man who let the woman of his dreams slip right through his fingers. I hope you enjoy it. It's called Amy."

Hearing her name, Amy sat back down. Like everyone else, she was soon mesmerized by the low, mournful sound filling the room. She turned and looked at Dave. He was looking down at his hands as he played. She forced herself not to think of his hands. When he raised his head to sing, Amy started to turn away. She didn't want him to see her, but his eyes were closed, so she allowed herself to stare openly.

You were the shoulder that I cried on
My one and only fan
When I needed a place to fall
You were a soft, warm place to land

You're everything I've ever dreamed of
Everything I'll ever need
You were the food that sustained me
The very air I breathe

I can't get you out of my head
My friend, my love, my Amy
I die a little every day
And only your love can save me
Save me, Amy, save me
Come back to me and save me

You haunt me —

His voice cracked with emotion. He stopped singing, for

a moment, but his fingers never quit dancing on the keys. He swallowed hard and continued.

> *You haunt me in my dreams at night*
> *Your memory fills my day*
> *I had everything in the palm of my hand*
> *And I threw it all away*

> *I wish that I had one more chance*
> *To prove my love to you*
> *You're all I ever wanted*
> *And I was once all you wanted, too*

> *I can't get you out of my head*
> *My friend, my love, my Amy*
> *I die a little every day*
> *And only your love can save me*
> *Save me, Amy, save me*
> *Come back to me and save me*
> *Save me, Amy, save me*
> *Come back to me and save me*

Amy fought back the tears. She couldn't let him back into her life. He only wanted her because he couldn't have her. If she gave in to him, he'd only end up breaking her heart. She couldn't go through that again. She had to leave before she did something foolish, like throwing herself at him in front of all these people.

She needed a tissue. She headed for the bathroom to blow her nose, planning to leave through a side exit and not have to see Dave again before she left. Two women were at the mirror in the bathroom, touching up lipstick and combing their hair. Amy reached between them and grabbed a tissue.

They were younger than Amy, and, Amy noted, they were prettier, too. They were chatting about the handsome piano player. The woman on the right turned and introduced herself to Amy. "I'm Kelly, and this is Joanne."

Distracted, Amy shook her hand, forgetting to introduce herself.

"And what did you say your name was?" Kelly asked.

"Amy. My name is Amy."

"Cool," Kelly said, "just like that song."

"Yeah," Amy said, "just like that song."

Scolding herself for being so brazen, Amy returned to the bar every night, always sitting in the farthest, darkest corner. Dave played a mixture of pop hits, classical and a few of his own songs. When Dave asked for requests, Amy was surprised when several people in the crowd yelled "Amy".

Oh God, Amy thought, I can't bear to hear that song again. But no matter how hard she tried, she couldn't force herself to move. Night after night, Amy listened to Dave sing his song to her, his voice cracking with emotion at some point every single time. It was torture, and yet she couldn't pull herself away.

Saturday was his final night. The place was packed, and all the tables were full. Amy stood along the far wall, behind Dave. She couldn't see his face, but she didn't need to.

She'd only been there a few minutes when he announced he was taking a break. Fear instantly gripped her. She was caught. There was no way out without him seeing her. She turned away from him, stealing glances at him as he walked across the room.

Women vied for his attention as he made his way to the bar. He stopped and chatted briefly with them before moving on. At the bar, the bartender handed him a bottle of water. He leaned back against the bar, taking a long drink.

A tall, curvaceous blonde in a low-cut, tight-fitting dress that left little to the imagination sidled up next to him, engaging him in conversation. He smiled at her, obviously enjoying the attention. The woman laid her hand on his arm and leaned in to be heard over the loud track music piped through the speakers. He threw his head back and laughed. She leaned in to say something else, pointing to a table across the room. He nodded and followed. Looking at the beautiful creature leading Dave across the room, Amy felt old and frumpy. And exposed. She made her way to the bathroom, hiding out until he resumed playing again. When she was alone in the bathroom, she looked at herself in the mirror. "Well, Amy," she said aloud to herself, "what now?"

She didn't know what she was going to do until she actually did it.

———————

Dave didn't leave the bar until close to midnight. He walked towards his car. It had been a beautiful day and he'd left the top down. He slowed his gait when he saw someone sitting in the passenger seat. Oh, please, he thought, don't let it be that blonde.

As he came closer, he could tell this woman wasn't blonde. It looked like — Amy. Was it Amy? His heart quickened. He forced himself not to run. Amy heard the approaching footsteps crunching on the gravel and looked over at him. It was Amy.

He looked at her, not sure if he could believe his eyes. Was Amy really sitting in his car? She didn't speak. Dave didn't either. He didn't know what to say. He was afraid he'd say the wrong thing and she'd walk away again. He opened the door and sat down beside her.

"Hi," he said. Hi was safe, right?

"Hi."

Her voice was like cold water on a hot day. He wanted to ask her what she was doing here, but he figured he'd find out soon enough. So he sat, waiting for her to speak again.

"You were good in there," she said. "They liked you."

"They're drunk," he said, shrugging off the comment.

She laughed. "Yeah, they are."

He laughed, too.

"I guess you're wondering what I'm doing here," she said.

"It crossed my mind," he answered. He had a feeling that the less he said the better.

"I am, too."

When nothing else was forthcoming, Dave asked her, "How long have you been here?"

"I was inside a little while. I came out here when you went on break."

"Really?" He hadn't seen her. "Where were you sitting?"

"Behind you, along the wall."

"I wrote a song for you."

"I know. I heard it. It was beautiful."

"I meant every word of it. I'm lost without you. I love you, Amy. I need you."

Tears stung her eyes. "How can I trust you, Dave? How can I believe this won't be like all the other times? Do you have any idea how badly you hurt me?"

"Yes," was all he could manage to choke out. He turned to face her, taking her closest hand in both of his. "And I'm sorry, Amy. I am so sorry. I was a fool. Let me back into your heart, and I'll spend the rest of my life proving that my love is real. I'll never hurt you again."

He leaned in to kiss her, and she kissed him back.

Chapter Thirty-Eight

June 2010

With much trepidation, Amy allowed Dave back into her life. To her elated surprise, Dave was true to his word. He treated her as though the world revolved around her. And as far as Dave was concerned, it did. His world anyway.

Since their reconciliation, Dave called Amy every day, just to hear her voice. He called to reassure himself that Amy was really back, that he wasn't just dreaming. On workdays, Amy's alarm clock went off at six o'clock. Exactly three minutes later, the phone would ring, and she'd hear his sexy voice whispering to her. "Hi, Doll. What are you wearing?"

The truth being quite dull, a t-shirt and shorts or

sweatpants, she gave elaborate descriptions of sleepwear she didn't even own. Sometimes she teasingly said she was wearing nothing or described sexy lingerie. Most times, she had more colorful answers.

It was Monday morning, the last week of school. The alarm clock had gone off. Amy stretched lazily, awaiting Dave's call.

The phone rang right on cue. "Hi, Doll. What are you wearing?"

She leaned back into her pillows. "Oh, it's this frilly little number I like to wear when I'm feeling particularly sexy."

"Oh, really?"

"Uh-huh. I'm wearing my grandmother's old flannel nightgown. It's a stunning brown paisley, so in vogue during Depression-era America. I've got humongous wooden buttons from my naval to my chin. It's quite an amazing creation."

Dave laughed.

"But I was feeling naughty," Amy continued, "so I unbuttoned the top button, revealing my Adam's apple, and rolled my support stockings down below my knees."

"Women don't have Adam's Apples."

"Hmmm," Amy laughed, "Maybe it's not Grandma's then. I must have grabbed Grandpa's nightshirt by mistake."

Amy didn't realize it, but Dave would find her sexy in anything — including that hideous garment she'd just described.

———————

"Hi, Doll."

"Hey, Handsome," Amy said yawning. Did she oversleep? She bolted upright to look at the time. It was just after two o'clock in the morning. Wait, she thought, school was out for the summer. She didn't have to get up at all! Settling back down, she stretched lazily and closed her eyes. "What are you doing up at this hour?"

"I'm hungry."

"You are, huh? What are you hungry for?" Amy expected him to say he was hungry for her.

"A seafood omelet."

"Yuk. That sounds disgusting," Amy laughed.

"It does, but it's really good."

"Well, I hope you aren't expecting me to fix it for you. I don't think I have the ingredients or the stomach to make one of those for you!"

"No, I didn't want you to fix it for me. There's only one place I know of to get one. It's a little restaurant near the beach on St. Simon's Island."

"And?" She asked, knowing he had more to say.

"And I want to go get one. I want to watch the sunrise over the ocean, then go have a seafood omelet. And I want you to go with me."

"Okay," she said, "what time?"

"Now."

"Now?"

"Why not now?"

"Because it's two o'clock in the morning, that's why not."

"Good. That gives us plenty of time for the drive and a nice walk on the beach to find the perfect spot to watch the sunrise."

"Okay," she said. "Give me a half hour to shower and get dressed."

"Just go as you are."

"I'm in my pajamas."

"Speaking of pajamas, what are you wearing?"

Amy laughed. "Seriously, give me a half hour."

"I'll be there in ten minutes."

"I'll be in the shower in ten minutes, and no, you can't join me. The kids are here."

"Just throw some water on your face and brush your hair."

"No shower? No makeup?"

"I've seen you without makeup."

"Okay, but if they throw us out of the restaurant, you know why."

Amy threw on some clothes, washed her face, and brushed her teeth and hair. She put on some eyeliner and mascara, despite Dave's makeup ban. She scribbled a quick note for the kids telling them where she'd gone and taped it to the front of the television, where she was sure they'd see it.

By four o'clock in the morning, Amy and Dave were walking on the beach on St. Simon's Island, an hour and a half south of Savannah, near Brunswick. Amy had seen a man farther up on the beach when they first arrived, but he was gone now. The beach was completely deserted. They walked up the beach a while before Dave found just the right spot to watch the day unfold. Amy sat between Dave's legs, leaning against him.

"I love the beach." Dave said. Amy listened as Dave talked, reminiscing of his childhood days spent playing on the beach with his sisters and their friends.

"What's that?" Dave said, looking towards the water.

"What?"

"There's something sticking out of the sand."

Amy became animated. She sat up and looked at him, excitement gleaming in her eyes. "It's probably one of those big whelk shells. I've always wanted to find one." In all her days of walking the beach looking for a prize shell, she'd never found anything bigger than her hand. Amy started to rise to get it.

"Stay where you are my lady," he said, "I'll get it for you."

Amy watched Dave dig the shell out of the sand. "Is it broken?" she yelled.

"No. And it's not a shell." he said, jogging back.

"What is it?"

He held up his find. "It's a bottle, and there's something in it." He turned, tilting it towards the moon.

Amy walked up beside him, trying to peer into the tinted bottle. "Probably sand. Or seaweed."

"No. I think it's a note."

Dave pried off the cork, trying to poke a finger in the bottle. "My finger's too big. I can't get it out."

"Let me try." Her small fingers easily retrieved the document. "I wonder how long it's been here. It's romantic, isn't it? Who do you think wrote it? Where do you think it came from?" Her eyes twinkled with the mystery of romance.

"Well, there's one way to find out," Dave said, motioning towards the note.

She uncurled the document carefully. It was handwritten, but she couldn't make out any of the words. She held the paper in front of her, moving it around, trying to catch enough moonlight to read it.

"Here," Dave said, producing a flashlight.

"You're quite the Boy Scout, aren't you Mr. Baldwin."

He held up three fingers in a mock pledge. "I do my best, ma'am."

Dave held the flashlight for her and she began to read aloud.

Amy,

When I saw you on the beach that day —

It was addressed to her, in Dave's handwriting. She looked up at him. "You? You wrote this? You did this?" She looked to where they had found it buried, then back to Dave. "How?"

Dave didn't answer. He just nodded toward the paper, prompting her to continue. He would later tell her the man they saw up on the beach was Kevin, lying in wait to bury the bottle for them to find.

When I saw you on the beach that day, when you fell into my arms, I realized I was holding everything I've ever wanted. If I had had my way, I would never have let you go, but you weren't mine to hold. Releasing you was the hardest thing I've ever had to do.

Losing you made me realize what I had put you through all those years. I always held you just tight enough that you couldn't break free, but loose enough that you never felt safe. And it was cruel. Hounded by demons I couldn't exorcise, I danced around your love. It was like walking to the edge of a precipice, seeing how far I could go without falling. I always managed to save myself, and it shames me to admit that I never even attempted to save you.

I don't know how you ever found it in your heart to forgive me. I grieve for all the years I stole from you, and I will always regret that I can never give them back, but if you'll let me, I will spend the rest of my life earning the chance you've given me.

I love you, Dave

Tears blurred her vision. Amy's gaze traveled from the paper to Dave, then back again.

Dave knelt before her, on one knee, taking her hands. Amy could see his eyes were misted over. "Amy, I love you with all my heart. I will never take for granted the chance you've given me. I want to fall asleep holding you every night, and I want to wake up next to you every morning. I love you so much." Tears slipped down his cheeks as he slipped a ring on her finger. "Amy, will you marry me?"

Chapter Thirty-Nine

Dave stared out the window, watching the hummingbirds vie for a spot at the feeder outside his office window. Jenny had come down from Atlanta Wednesday evening to help Amy with the last minute details of the party. The two women were supposed to call in between errands to meet him for lunch.

Tomorrow was the day in which the last piece of the puzzle would be put in place, and Dave's life would be absolutely perfect. He tapped a pencil on his desk absentmindedly, feeling utterly at peace. Dave was excited. Excited to have lunch with Amy, and excited about tomorrow.

He'd waited for about six months after he and Amy married before broaching the subject with her, and he was thrilled when she had readily agreed. Katy and Sam agreed just as quickly, as did Cathy.

Tomorrow, at three thirty in the afternoon, Judge Wendell would preside over the final ceremony making Katy and Sam legally his children. Out of respect for Greg, he told the kids that he didn't expect them to change their last name. Out of love for Dave, Katy and Sam decided to add his name to theirs. Katy Elizabeth Hampton would become Katy Elizabeth Baldwin Hampton. Likewise, Sam would become Samuel Gregory Baldwin Hampton. No hyphen, Sam said. Now fourteen, Sam jokingly said he didn't want anyone to think he'd gotten married and had taken his wife's name.

Dave had known the kids since they were tiny. Sam was but an infant, and Katy had only been three years old. He'd watched them grow over the years, and he could honestly say he loved them as much as he loved Cathy. The many times he and Amy had broken up, Dave had missed the kids as much as he'd missed Amy, and he wondered why it had never occurred to him that the kids would miss him, too. After Friday, they would truly be his. It would feel good to say *'my kids'* and have it be really, legally true.

The phone rang. Dave picked up on the first ring. Amy said she and Jenny were almost done, telling him they would meet him for lunch in about a half hour. They were going to run by the bank to pick up Dave's grandmother's ring and his grandfather's pocket watch. To many, it would seem overkill to put nearly worthless items in a safe deposit box, but Dave, coming from a family with few traditions and even fewer ties from one generation to the next, held the heirlooms dear. Though he hadn't been close to his grandparents, he had wanted something to remember them by after they died. The inexpensive trinkets, albeit small, were the only link he had to his past. He was going to present them to Katy and Sammy at the party tomorrow night. Neither the ring nor the watch were worth much, except for sentimental value, but it was the only thing he had to pass along to them. Everything of any real value had long ago been given to Cathy. He wanted Katy and Sam to have something to hold in their hands that proved they were now part of his family, something they could one day pass on to their own children.

"Want me to order for you?" he asked. He wrote down their orders, then headed out the door, whistling as he went.

———————

Patsy kept coming by the table to see Amy. Spying Dave still alone, she stopped to talk. "Well, holler when they get here." Amy hadn't worked at the restaurant in years, except on rare occasions when Patsy was in a real pinch, and she was anxious to see her old friend again.

Dave kept checking his watch. Amy had called over an hour ago. They should have been here long before now. His imagination was starting the get the better of him, and he was beginning to worry, particularly since neither of them were answering their cell phones.

The next time Patsy came by, Dave asked for their orders. He'd take them to go.

The kids came home from school not long after Dave returned home. He sat and talked with them for a few minutes. They asked if he knew what time their mom would be back. One of Amy's errands was to pick up Katy's new dress, and she was antsy to try it on again. Dave told them she was still out running errands, but that they had to pick up Andy, Cindy, and their kids at the airport, so he was sure she'd be home soon.

Dave walked into his office and shut the door. They had added on this office soon after they were married. He loved this room. Aside from the bedroom he shared with Amy, this was his favorite room in the house.

Two walls were lined with thick, walnut, floor to ceiling shelves. One wall held photographs, diplomas and awards, and the other was all windows, with a French door leading to the back yard. No frilly throw pillows, and absolutely nothing pastel. The windows had wide wooden blinds, not delicate lace panels like nearly every other room in the house. It was his refuge. It was wood and leather and masculine.

Despite Amy's pleading, he wouldn't even consider a valance above the windows. "Nope," he had said, hands on his hips in mock defiance, "If I let you womenfolk put up a valance, the next thing I know, I'll come in and my computer will be sitting on a doily."

────────────

He tried Amy and Jenny's cell phones one more time. No Answer. Dave turned his attention to his work, getting little done.

Dave checked his watch: four-fifteen. It was time to leave for the airport. Amy hadn't seen Andy and his family since Christmas, and she had been counting the days until they arrived. Amy was notoriously punctual, and she would never be this late without calling. He knew something was terribly wrong.

Dave called Ron, Jenny's husband. "Have you heard from Jenny today?"

"She called this morning. Why? What's up? She out of money already?" Ron laughed.

"They called around one and said they were going to the bank, then they were supposed to meet me for lunch, but they never showed up. I can't reach them on their cell phones, either."

Dave could tell Ron was thinking, debating on what to do. "Think I need to come down?" Concern crept into his voice.

Dave sighed. "It's probably nothing."

"Probably," Ron said, "but I'll drive myself crazy with possibilities if I stay here. I'm leaving now. Call me if you hear anything."

"Likewise," Dave said.

Dave patted his pocket, checking for his keys. He grabbed some money from his wallet and handed it to Katy as he left. "I've got to pick up Andy at the airport. Order yourselves a pizza."

They were obviously pleased with the idea. Dave often wondered how much pizza they could consume before they grew tired of it. He suspected quite a bit.

"I've got my phone on me. Call me if you need me. I shouldn't be long."

"Hey, have you heard from Mom?" Katy asked, not worried, but curious.

"No, Baby, I haven't." He willed himself to stay calm.

"She's not answering her phone."

"I know. She probably turned the ringer off and forgot to turn it back on."

Dave backed out of the drive, then turned on the radio, afraid to be alone with his thoughts. A song finished and the news jockey read a list of teasers for the upcoming newscast. "Up next, more on the hostage standoff at the First National Bank of Savannah on Abercorn."

"Oh, God, no," he thought. He called the kids, trying to keep the fear from rising in his voice. "I'm stuck in traffic and won't be able to pick up Andy. If he calls, tell him to take a cab to the hotel. Give him my cell number and have him call me when he gets there."

He maneuvered to the left, made an illegal u-turn and

headed back towards town.

———————————

Police had cordoned off a three block radius around the bank. Dave parked as close as he could get, then got out and ran the rest of the way. A uniformed officer stood guard on the other side of the yellow police tape, making sure the gathering curiosity seekers didn't breach the outer perimeter.

Dave approached the policeman. "Officer, I need to talk to someone. I think my wife and her friend are in there." He could barely get the words out. He felt like he was suffocating.

"Okay," the officer said, lifting the tape for Dave to walk under. He talked into his radio, notifying someone of another relative on the scene. "Someone will be right over to get you."

Dave nodded, rooted to the spot, waiting for the promised escort. A moment later another police officer approached him. "Are you the relative?"

Dave nodded again.

"Come with me."

They took down Amy and Jenny's names, descriptions and contact information, as well as his and Ron's.

"Don't worry Mr. Baldwin. We're going to get your wife out safe." He sounded so sure of himself, like Dave's father had when he was a small child afraid of monsters in the dark. Dave found comfort in his assurances, but the gnawing in the pit of his stomach continued.

Dave looked around at the other people gathered together. All family members of those thought to be inside. The crowd grew as more people came to the realization that their loved one may be inside, and shrank when they were found elsewhere, safe and sound. Dave longed to be one of the lucky ones smiling as they were led back to the other side of the yellow tape, where they were simply spectators and had no real stake in the outcome.

No one knew for certain how many hostages there were. Some people had heard eighteen. Some said they'd heard as many as twenty-three. No one knew how many gunmen were involved, though it was thought to be two. Some said there had been gunshots fired. Everything at this point was just speculation and gossip.

Dave called Ron, who finished the drive to Savannah in record time, arriving not too long after Andy. Upon hearing the news, Andy had taken a cab to join Dave, sending Cindy and their kids to Dave's house to wait with Katy and Sam.

Please God, Dave prayed continually, *please don't take her from me now.*

Chapter Forty

Dave looked up and down the street. Police cars were stationed at every intersection. Policemen shielded themselves behind their cars, guns drawn. Fire trucks, rescue squads, and S.W.A.T. vehicles were everywhere, but what really made Dave's blood run cold was the row of ambulances lined up as far as the eye could see.

Someone brought coffee and water for the family members. Dave drank the coffee, hoping it was the caffeine making him shake. As time wore on, they were told they could leave, that they would be contacted if something broke. Chances are, the policeman said, nothing would be resolved until the morning. They were urged to go home and try to get some rest. Dave, Ron, and Andy, as well as most of the others gathered there stayed exactly where they were.

It was close to midnight when Dave noticed something happening. Policemen from the inner perimeter were running towards the bank, followed by medical workers pushing gurneys. Lots of them. Did they need that many? Dave prayed it was just a precaution.

The exhausted group of relatives, sitting in small groups on the hard concrete, jumped to their feet at the same time. Frightened cries rose among them. Everyone wondered aloud what was happening. The policemen in the outer perimeter stayed put, keeping everyone at bay.

Gurneys started coming back, most of them empty. The crowd scanned the occupied gurneys, praying they didn't recognize anyone. He didn't see Amy or Jenny. Was that good? Did they take the injured and leave the dead? It was a question Dave would have to wonder about, because he knew he'd never be able to ask.

"Jenny!" Ron shouted. "There's Jenny!" The three men didn't ask if they could go to her, they just went. No one stopped them.

Jenny was covered in blood. Dave sucked in his breath. How bad was she hurt? And where was Amy? He looked around, but didn't see Amy anywhere.

Ron rushed to her, searching her for wounds.

"I'm okay." she said, "It's just my arm." They looked at her arm, strapped to a board with blood-soaked gauze.

If it was just her arm, where did all the blood come from? "Where's Amy?" Dave asked.

"They took her already."

"Took her? Took her where?" *Who took her? The police? The paramedics? She hadn't been on any of the stretchers. Did that mean she was okay?*

"I don't know where she is." Jenny said crying. "They wouldn't let me go with her."

One of the paramedics working on Jenny offered, "They took the more seriously wounded out the other side."

"The other side?" But he thought Amy was safe. Wasn't that what Jenny meant?

"Can I go with her?" Ron asked as they loaded Jenny into the back of an ambulance. "I'm her husband." When they nodded, he dashed inside and they shut the doors.

Dave turned to the paramedic standing beside him. "How do I find out where my wife is?"

"If she's injured, they've taken her to St. Joe's. If not, the police have them isolated, getting their statements. They'll release them to you when they're done."

"How do I find out —".

"Sir," he said, "I need to leave, but someone will be over soon with a list of names. I hope things turn out well for you." The paramedic knew enough not to give Dave any false hope. And also he knew the lady in his ambulance had a critically injured friend.

He had to know. "Were there any fatalities?"

"I don't know," the paramedic lied, then hopped in the ambulance and drove off.

The next half hour was complete chaos. Finally, a police officer came over with a clipboard and a list of names. "If you hear your loved one's name called, come with me." Dave waited. He never called Amy Baldwin. "The rest of you, your loved ones have been taken to St. Joe's. Wait here and someone will take you there."

Dave looked at Andy, both knowing what the other was thinking. They weren't waiting around for another half an hour — or more. They took off towards Dave's car.

———————

Fighting their way through the media, they entered the crowded waiting room and registered with the receptionist. Dave looked around the room. Those who weren't crying were staring vacantly into space, expressionless. Andy had called Cindy on the way to the hospital. She met them at the hospital with Katy and Sam, as well as her and Andy's kids, Mike and Lucy. All four teenagers were eerily silent.

A short time later, Ron walked through the double doors, pushing Jenny in a wheelchair, wearing a hospital gown. Her arm was in a sling. No longer covered in blood, she looked better, and Dave was grateful.

Ron pushed Jenny up to Dave. Jenny smiled weakly up at him. Her eyes full of tears, she reached out, taking one of Dave's hands. "Have you heard anything about Amy?"

"Not really, just that they're working on her. They said they'll let us know something soon."

"How are you?" Andy asked.

"I'm okay. A bullet hit my arm, but I'm fine."

"Jenny," Dave asked softly, "how bad is Amy?"

Jenny looked up at Dave and began to cry.

When she was able to speak again, Jenny gave all the details of their ordeal.

———————————

The bank had been crowded when she and Amy arrived. While they waited to be let into the safe deposit room, they watched a young mother trying to corral her boisterous little boy. The child broke away and ran down the hall leading to the inner offices.

It was at that moment that the gunmen burst in. Two of them, Jenny said. They ordered everyone to the ground and told the tellers to put their hands in the air. One of tellers, they now knew, had been fast enough to set off the alarm unnoticed. One of the gunmen herded the bank employees into the room with the customers, demanding everyone move to one side. The other gunman disarmed the security guard, handcuffing him to a table. They demanded all purses and cell phones be tossed into the center of the room. One stood guard, screaming at everyone not to move. The other stuffed money into a bag.

They were tall, bulky men. They wore masks, obscuring their faces. All Jenny could see was that they were white.

The little boy came back around the hallway, screaming

for his mommy. Amy and Jenny, huddled together on the floor, knew what was going to happen and were powerless to stop it. The young mother rushed towards her son, calling out his name.

"I said, nobody move." The gunman opened fire with an automatic weapon. A stray bullet hit Jenny's arm, just deep enough to knick the bone, before passing through Amy's chest. The force of the bullet knocked them both over. Pandemonium broke out. Everyone was screaming, scrambling to get out of the way. "I said, nobody move," the gunman yelled again. Terrified, everyone stopped where they were.

"Amy," Jenny cried in horror as a dark red stain spread over Amy's right shoulder. "Oh, my God, Amy." Jenny knew she had to stop the bleeding. She leaned Amy up against her, pressing Amy's shoulder against her own chest. She wadded up the bottom of Amy's shirt and pressed it into the front of Amy's wound.

Jenny said Amy was conscious most of the time, but remarkably, Amy said she wasn't in any pain.

As the standoff continued, cell phones started ringing, startling the frayed nerves of their captors. To silence the phones, the gunmen took turns smashing the phones beneath their boots or the butts of their guns.

At first, Jenny said, Amy had been optimistic that they would get out alive. As time wore on, she began to confess that she didn't think she'd make it. Jenny tried to reassure

Amy that her wound wasn't that bad, but Amy knew better.

Amy asked Jenny to tell Dave and the kids how much she loved them. Again, Jenny tried to quiet her, telling her she was going to be okay. As time went on, though, Jenny knew it was important to let Amy talk. She couldn't let herself believe Amy wouldn't make it, but it seemed to calm Amy to talk.

"Tell Katy and Sam that I couldn't have loved them more if I had given birth to them. Make sure they know that. Tell them I love them and will always watch over them. Tell the kids I'm proud of them. Tell them Susie and Greg would be proud of them, too. Ask them to take care of Dave for me."

"They know you love them, Amy, and they know you're proud of them. Please don't talk like this. You're going to be okay."

Amy ignored Jenny's plea. "Tell Dave how much I love him and how happy he made me."

"You can tell him yourself when we get out of here."

"Jenny?"

"What Amy?

"I love you."

"I love you, too."

"I don't know what I'd have done without you. You're the best friend anyone could ever have."

"So are you," Jenny said, unable to hold back the tears.

"Thank you for always being there for me."

"I still will be. When we get out of here, I'll always be there for you. You're going to be okay. This will all be over and everything will be okay."

"Okay," Amy said, growing weaker.

Amy would lie quietly for a while, then speak in a soft whisper. "Tell Katy to use one of my cocktail bags for the party, not to use that ratty old purse she carries to school."

As time wore on, Amy's thoughts grew more random. "Tell Dave I haven't changed the oil in the van for almost 5,000 miles. He kept telling me to have it changed, and I meant to, but I never did."

Jenny noticed the bleeding had slowed, but wasn't sure it that was because the pressure she put on the wound was stopping the flow, or if Amy was running out of blood. She prayed Amy could hold on long enough for help to arrive.

"Jenny?"

"I'm here."

"Make them promise to water my flowers. Nobody ever waters them. I love my flowers."

"I know you do."

"Promise me you won't forget to tell them. I don't know why they never water them. Make them promise."

"I promise."

"Make sure they know how much I love them all."

"I will."

It wasn't long before Jenny felt Amy go limp. She still had a pulse, but Jenny knew Amy had lost a lot of blood.

And hope was fading.

As the night wore on, hospital personnel would appear and call out the name of someone injured. Every time the door would open, everyone would look up expectantly, hoping for news of their loved one. As each name was called, nervous family members would be led through the double doors.

"Amy Baldwin?" a voice cried out.

Dave stood up on shaky legs. "I'm her husband," Dave said. His mouth was so dry he could barely swallow.

"Come with me." Everyone moved to follow Dave. "Are you all together?"

"Yes," someone said.

"Okay, this way please."

All Dave remembered hearing was *"Mr. Baldwin, we're sorry."*

Chapter Forty-One

Everyone followed Dave home from the hospital. They were worried about him. After asking the doctor a myriad of questions, he hadn't said another word. Due to a mixture of pain pills, grief, and exhaustion, Jenny had gone right to bed. Dave sat on the sofa, sandwiched between Katy and Sam. In time, Katy laid her head in Dave's lap and fell asleep. Sam fell asleep sitting up. After Mike and Lucy fell asleep on the floor, Cindy, Ron, and Andy got them up and led them to bed. Cindy curled up in a chair and was soon asleep, too.

Dave, Ron, and Andy sat, staring into space, not saying a word.

In the morning, as news reports aired, the house began to fill up with friends and family. Newscasters were reporting two dead, Amy and the young mother. Seven more were injured, three seriously. One, they said, would never walk again.

Jane urged Dave to sleep. Dave walked back to his bedroom, willing himself to walk into the room he had shared with Amy. He lay down on the bed, but sleep wouldn't come. He could smell Amy on her pillow. He grabbed the pillow and held it tight, burying his face in it, drinking in her scent. His thoughts alternated between overwhelming grief at losing Amy, and maniacal rage towards her killers. He fantasized about killing them with his bare hands.

They would never walk freely in society again, of that Dave was sure. Even one of Amy's third grade students could successfully prosecute this case. But they were alive. Even if they got the death penalty, they'd be alive for years. They'd eat and sleep and play cards, and do whatever else murderers did in prison. Dave would likely be an old man before their punishment was carried out. Those monsters would live all those years while Amy lay cold and dead in the ground.

Dave heard a soft knock. He heard the door open, then felt the weight of someone sitting on the bed.

"Is there anything I can do, Dave?" Paula asked.

Not unless you can bring Amy back to life, he thought. She was just trying to help, but he was tired of people offering to help. There was nothing anyone could do.

"No," he answered, his voice sounded hoarse.

"Have you slept any?"

"No. I need to, though. We've got to leave for the courthouse around three."

Paula lay down beside him, holding him close. "I'm sure we can postpone it."

"I don't want to. Andy said he and Cindy would take the kids if I wanted. I told him no. I promised Amy I'd take care of her kids. I want to adopt them. I love those kids." He broke down crying, great wracking sobs that shook the bed. Dave's grief burst open and everyone in the house broke down at the heart-wrenching moans emanating from his bedroom.

———————————

"Daddy," Cathy said, gently shaking Dave awake.

How long had it been since she had called him Daddy? Hearing it, it made him realize how badly he'd missed being Daddy instead of Dad. His eyes felt like they had weights sitting on them. He willed himself to open them. "What time is it?" Dave didn't want to get up. He wanted to go back to sleep and never wake up.

"It's two o'clock. You need to get up and get in the shower if we're going to be at the courthouse on time." Cathy put her hand on her fathers arm. "Judge Wendell called. He said under the circumstances, if we want to postpone, he'd understand. He said to call when you woke up, and they can set it for another day."

Dave looked at Cathy. "How does he know our circumstances?"

"I don't know, but it's all over the news. We can do this another day, Daddy. Everyone will understand."

He met Cathy's gaze. "No, we have to do it today. Do you know how many times I broke my promises to Amy? When she took me back, I gave her my word I would never break another promise to her. And I never have.

"When I signed the adoption papers three months ago, I was giving her my promise that I would adopt those kids. I was promising I would love them and take care of them for the rest of my life. I can't go back on my word.

"And those poor kids," Dave said through tears, "They deserve to have a living parent. I can give them that today, just like Amy and I planned."

"Okay, Daddy."

"I'm getting up," Dave said, swinging his legs over the edge of the bed. "I need something to wear. Can you pick me out a suit? Amy was going to —" he couldn't finish the sentence. One of Amy's errands had been to pick up his and Sam's suits from the dry cleaners. The suits were either in her van or at the dry cleaners. He had lots of suits to choose from, even if it wasn't the one Amy wanted him to wear. It didn't matter what he wore, what mattered was that he honored his word to her.

"We've got your suit, Daddy. Kevin and I picked up Amy's van a few hours ago. It was hanging in the back."

"Can you call the restaurant? Tell them to cancel the party. Just have them send me the bill. And call the bakery, too. If they haven't delivered the cakes already, have them donate them to a daycare or nursing home or something." Amy had ordered a pink *'It's a Girl!'* and a blue *'It's a Boy!'* cake to be delivered to the restaurant. Dave hated to cancel all her carefully made plans, but no one felt like celebrating, least of all him. "I'm sure there are others we need to call, but I don't know who they are. Amy had a list around here somewhere."

"I'll take care of it."

Dave kissed her forehead and walked into the bathroom.

———————————

Five days later, Amy was laid to rest next to Susie in beautiful Bonaventure Cemetery. All of Dave's children were by his side, Cathy, Katy and Sam.

After the funeral, Dave sat on the back patio, looking at Amy's flowers. How often did he need to water them, he wondered?

Jenny came out and sat beside him. Her voice quivered as she spoke. "You know, Dave, when Amy told me y'all were back together, I thought she'd lost her ever lovin' mind. I just knew you'd hurt her again, but you proved me wrong. Amy was happier these last couple years than she'd ever been in her life. She loved you, Dave, and she knew how much you loved her.

"This may not be the fairy tale ending everyone dreams of, but she died happy. Towards the end, I think she knew she wasn't going to make it out alive, and I truly believe she died at peace. She died knowing Katy and Sam would be taken care of, and I'm sure that comforted her final thoughts." Jenny broke down crying.

"Thank you," Dave said, hugging Jenny, his voice filled with grief.

When Jenny calmed down, Dave let go of her and continued. "And thank you for being there for her. Thank you for always being there for her. You were a good friend to her, Jenny. Not everyone is lucky enough to find a friend like you."

Jenny smiled weakly, playing with the tissues in her hand.

"I need to water her flowers," Dave said.

"Want me to help you?"

"I appreciate the offer, but I want to do it."

They sat in silence, side by side, watching honey bees fly from blossom to blossom.

Without warning, the sky opened up, and it poured. Jenny ran inside, but Dave stayed where he was. There was no thunder or lightening, just rain. The shower lasted just long enough to give everything a good drink. Dave looked up to the heavens, towards Amy. She had promised to watch over them, and if that were possible, he knew she would. He would never tell anyone, but he felt sure Amy had just watered the flowers for him.

Dave stood on the porch, remembering the agony he was in when he built this for her. He wished he had been able to see her face when she had seen it for the first time.

He grabbed the hose and began watering the flowers. As promised, he and the kids watered them faithfully every day. Katy was watering the ones in the backyard, while Sam watered the plants inside. When Katy finished, she came out front. She leaned against the railing, watching Dave.

Dave looked at Katy. She looked a lot like the pictures he had seen of Susie, but he saw a lot of Amy in her as well. She had Amy's mannerisms and pleasant disposition. Amy had done a good job with these kids. He would, too. He would finish raising them to be the kind of man and woman Amy — and Susie and Greg — would be proud of.

"Are we going to the cemetery today?"

He nodded. "Just as soon as we finish watering her flowers."

"I'll go get Sam."

As if on cue, Sam walked onto the porch, hands in his pockets. He shrugged his shoulders and said "The inside plants are watered. I'm ready."

"Did you get the one in our bathroom?" That poor plant always seemed to get overlooked.

He nodded and said "Yup."

———————————

The kids placed flowers on Amy, Susie and Greg's graves, then stood silently, each lost in their own thoughts.

When the media had heard of their situation, they seized the story, describing Dave in almost superhuman terms. Everyone, it seemed, proclaimed him as some kind of hero, as though he were a selfless, grieving widower rescuing two lonely orphans. He knew the reporters were only doing their job, but it made him angry that they sensationalized all the pain these kids had gone through for the sake of ratings.

If they only knew, Dave thought. If it weren't for these two kids, he would never be able to will himself to get out of bed. As they walked back to the car, Dave draped his arms across their shoulders.

Dave knew what everyone was saying, but he knew the truth. He wasn't saving these kids — they were saving him.

About the Author

In addition to writing, Jackie Coleman is a technology professional with a large corporation in Evansville, Indiana, where she lives with her three children.

Her mother, Esther, was a voracious reader, instilling in her children the love of reading at an early age. Jackie considers this to be the greatest gift a parent can give a child. Growing up, the library was a constant fixture in Jackie's life. She has fond memories of her frequent trips to her local library with her mother and sisters.

For more information about Jackie and her books, please visit www.jackiecoleman.com. Follow her on twitter, @coleman_jackie, and on Facebook, Jackie Coleman – Author.

www.ingramcontent.com/pod-product-compliance
Lightning Source LLC
Chambersburg PA
CBHW060143260626
47160CB00001B/101